ROGUE TROOPER

CRUCIBLE

The two snipers looked at each other.

"How many?" asked Venner, shocked at the sound of his own voice. It had been the first time in over a week he had heard it and it sounded almost unfamiliar to him, especially when talking in the harsh, guttural language of the enemy.

"Twelve hundred and fifty-three," answered the Nort sniper, unable to keep the betraying hint of pride out of his voice, even at a time like this.

"Not bad," grunted Venner. The Nort nodded in acknowledgement, as one equal to another. Then Venner shot him almost casually through the heart. The man deserved respect, and a quicker, cleaner death than the one he had been facing.

"But nowhere near good enough," Venner added.

More 2000 AD action from Black Flame

Judge Dredd

#1: DREDD vs DEATH
Gordon Rennie

#2: BAD MOON RISING
David Bishop

#3: BLACK ATLANTIC
Simon Jowett & Peter J Evans

#4: ECLIPSE
James Swallow

ABC Warriors

#1: THE MEDUSA WAR
Pat Mills & Alan Mitchell

Strontium Dog

#1: BAD TIMING
Rebecca Levene

Durham Red

#1: THE UNQUIET GRAVE
Peter J Evans

Rogue Trooper created by Gerry Finley-Day
and Dave Gibbons.

ROGUE TROOPER

CRUCIBLE

GORDON RENNIE

BLACK FLAME

A Black Flame Publication
www.blackflame.com

First published in 2004 by BL Publishing, Games Workshop Ltd.,
Willow Road, Nottingham NG7 2WS, UK.

Distributed in the US by Simon & Schuster, 1230 Avenue of the
Americas, New York, NY 10020, USA.

10 9 8 7 6 5 4 3 2 1

Cover illustration by Dylan Teague.

ISBN 1 84416 111 0

A CIP record for this book is available from the British Library.

Printed in the UK by Bookmarque, Surrey, UK.

THE LEGEND OF THE ROGUE TROOPER

Nu Earth is a hellish, nightmare planet ravaged by war. The planet's atmosphere is devoid of life, poisoned by repeated chemical attacks and deadly to inhale. But the planet is close to a vital wormhole in space, a fact which has dragged its two rival factions – the Norts and the Southers – into a never-ending war. Now Nu Earth is a toxic, hell-blasted rock, where millions of soldiers in bio-suits wage bloody battles and die in their millions. Nu Earth is too important to lose. Not an inch of ground can be lost!

Here is where the legend of Rogue Trooper was born. Created by Souther forces, Rogue Trooper is the sole surviving example of the Genetic Infantrymen: a regiment of soldiers grown in vats and bio-engineered to be the perfect killing machine. Complete with protective blue skin and the ability to breathe the venomous atmosphere, the Genetic Infantrymen became renowned figures on both sides of the conflict. Moreover, the mind and soul of the GI could be downloaded onto a silicon chip in case of a mortal wound on the battlefield. Once downloaded, the dog-chip could then be slotted into special equipment and preserved until the soldier could grace a newly grown body.

Betrayed by a general in their own high command, almost the entire regiment of GIs were wiped out in the Quartz Zone Massacre.

The sole survivor managed to save just three chips from his former comrades and slot them into his gun, helmet and backpack. Now he is a loner, with just the disembodied personalities of his comrades for company, roaming the chemical wasteland in search of revenge: the Rogue Trooper.

"And when he gets to Heaven,
To Saint Peter he will tell,
I fought and died on Nu Earth, sir,
so I've served my time in Hell."

– So-called "Nu Earth Epitaph", author anon.
Found written on the grave marker of an unknown
Souther soldier, Nu Earth Battle Sector.

"I SAY TO YOU NOW THAT I WILL NOT REST AS LONG AS ONE ENEMY SOLDIER REMAINS ALIVE WITHIN THE RUINS OF NORD-STADT, AS LONG AS THE FOOTPRINTS OF ONE INVADER REMAIN PRESSED INTO ITS SACRED, BLOOD-SOAKED SOIL, AS LONG AS ONE COWARDLY SOUTHER RAT REMAINS HIDING THERE IN THE RUBBLE OF WHAT WAS ONCE A PROUD MONUMENT TO THE ACHIEVEMENTS AND GLORIES OF WE, THE NORDLAND RACE.

NORDSTADT IS OURS, JUST AS NU EARTH AND THE GALAXY BEYOND ARE OURS, AND WE ARE PREPARED TO TOLERATE EVERY SET-BACK, WE ARE PREPARED TO PAY THE PRICE OF EVERY SACRIFICE NECESSARY ON THE ROAD TO FINAL VICTORY; VICTORY IN NORDSTADT, ON NU EARTH, AND ON EVERY OTHER WORLD IN THE GALAXY WHERE OUR ENEMIES ARE GATHERED AGAINST US. LET THEM RAZE OUR CITIES TO THE GROUND, LET THEM HIDE AND BURROW LIKE ANIMALS AMONGST THEIR RUINS. WE WILL FIND THEM AND ROOT THEM OUT. WE WILL DESTROY THEM UTTERLY, AND UPON THEIR SCATTERED BONES WE WILL BUILD THE FOUNDATIONS OF NEW CITIES, CITIES GREATER AND MORE MAGNIFICENT THAN ANYTHING THEY WILL HAVE SEEN BEFORE.

LET OUR VOICE BE HEARD ALL ACROSS THE STARS, ON EVERY WORLD WHERE OUR ENEMIES STILL THRIVE. GATHER YOUR ARMIES, I TELL THEM NOW. RAISE UP YET MORE GENERATIONS OF YOUR BRIGHTEST AND STRONGEST. PUT WEAPONS IN THEIR HANDS AND SEND THEM OUT TO FACE US. NU EARTH WILL BE THEIR MASS GRAVE, AND THE NEW AND REBUILT NORDSTADT, CLEANSED OF THE PRESENCE OF THE ENEMY INVADER, WILL BE THE TOMBSTONE WE SHALL ERECT TO SHOW THE PLACE WHERE THEIR ASHES LIE."

Supreme War Marshal Vladimir Zell, addressing the seventy-fourth Concordat of the Sekretariat of the People's Deputies of the Greater Nordland Territories, on the twentieth anniversary of the commencement of hostilities on Nu Earth against the Confederacy of the Southern Cross Republics.

PART ONE
COMMS-SIGNALS

ONE

The secret of the art of killing, Venner knew, was patience. He was a very patient man, perhaps almost superhumanly so, and so it was no surprise to him at all that he was equally gifted when it came to the business of taking the lives of others.

His target was a hidden enemy listening post in the no-man's-land wildness between the two front lines. Those front lines were immense, stretching out for thousands of miles in both directions; jagged twin ranks of defence bunkers, trench works, missile silos, launch bases, gun batteries, fortified emplacements and siege bastions that spanned the entire breadth of a continent, marking out the borders of a huge battlefield that had remained mainly static for almost the last twenty years. Millions of lives had been expended by both sides on just this one continent-wide battlefield, with little or no gain for either party.

They had poisoned the air with their chemical weapons. They had blighted the very ground they died trying to control, leaving it completely sterile and barren as the toxins and pathogens they used against each other seeped down into the earth. Whole tracts of land, hundreds of kilometres wide, the so-called "hotspots", had been rendered completely uninhabitable by the unbridled use of nuclear weapons in various earlier stages of the conflict. Cities had been vaporised, forests and farmland burned to ash, deserts, plains and prairies transformed into endless frozen seas of fused glass by the heat of the nuclear fire. The radiation level in such places was high enough to cook the flesh from a man's bones, even inside the supposed protection of an armoured chem-suit.

This was just one campaign, just one battlefield on a world that had been transformed into one huge scene of battle carnage. This was Nu Earth, which both sides in the war needed to capture for themselves, even if it meant laying to waste the entire planet in the process. This was Nu Earth, where the killing never stopped.

Venner was stalking no-man's-land, destroying the line of enemy listening posts secreted there amongst the smashed debris of innumerable past battles and failed assaults. The work was child's play. He had identified and destroyed four of the facilities in the last week, travelling west along an eighty-kilometre stretch of the front, amusing himself along the way by picking off several small reconnaissance patrols of foot soldiers, not really caring which side they might have belonged to.

He had expected the enemy, as slow-witted as they were, to have reacted to the continuing loss of their listening posts by the time he found the fourth one on his list. Disappointingly, they had not, and all he had found waiting for him there, in the ruins of a bombed-out bunker that had probably changed hands dozens of times in the course of the last twenty years, were a few listless, incompetent sentries guarding the handful of technicians who operated the listening post's electronic eavesdropping equipment. He had dealt with them all ruthlessly and dispassionately, and they had all died even before they were fully aware that he was there amongst them.

After that, feeling irritated and even somewhat slighted by the enemy's slowness in reacting to his now clearly-signalled presence out here in no-man's-land, he had set the demolition charges to destroy the listening post and its equipment before scouting out the area around it and spitefully planting a few extra booby-trap surprises for the first infantry patrol to enter the area after his departure. Whether that infantry patrol belonged to his side or the enemy's was a matter of complete indifference to him.

Two days later, at the fifth target location on his list, he finally got the reaction he had been hoping to provoke out of the enemy all along.

He had taken up position a few kilometres short of the target location – the burnt-out shell of a Golgotha heavy bomber – and watched patiently through his binox as the enemy deployed into the surrounding shell-churned terrain from a hovering atmocraft. They were good, Venner could see. He could tell by the way they handled themselves, swiftly and silently melting into the nearest cover as soon as they hit the ground. One of them wasn't quite as good or experienced as the others, landing clumsily and fumbling with the release catch on the harness of his anti-grav jump-pack. Venner shot him in punishment, sending a steel jacketed screamer slug straight through the faceplate of his lightweight chem-suit from a range of over two thousand metres.

After that, having announced his presence to the rest of the enemy sniper troupe, he was ready to begin the hunt in earnest.

He had counted five soldiers: all of them doubtlessly well-equipped, well-trained and highly motivated. To be anything less would have ensured their deaths long before now. Nu Earth was a completely unforgiving combat arena, and ruthlessly weeded out the weak and the unlucky. Venner had served in similar sniper troupes, and knew well enough how they operated. Three, or perhaps even four of the remaining enemy snipers would act as bush-beaters, there to flush the prey out of hiding.

They would move forward, scout out the terrain, try to draw the target – him – out of hiding, trying to trick him into revealing his position. Depending on the situation and the responses of their prey, they would try either of two strategies. The first would be to pin him down, bracketing his position with pinpoint accurate sniper fire and forcing him to engage in a deadly long-range sniper duel. Meanwhile, their victim's attention and return fire was fixed on them, the leader of the troupe, the master sniper, would be moving round behind him somewhere, looking for the perfect spot from which to make his kill shot.

The other strategy, which often depended on a panicked response from a less experienced target, was for the snipers to aggressively go on the attack in precise, set patterns, flushing the target out of hiding and herding them straight into the sights of the waiting master sniper. Both strategies were equally valid. Venner knew both of them intimately, both as a bush-beater and master sniper team leader, and knew dozens of ways to circumvent either of them. For this situation, he presented himself to his hunters as the panicked quarry, allowing them to adopt the second of the two strategies.

They had hunted him across the battlefield for a day and a half, with Venner careful never to slip entirely from his pursuers' perception, even on several occasions giving away his location long enough to allow two of them to take speculative shots at him. On another three occasions they had launched seeker-bots to find him. The small anti-grav drone devices buzzed across the face of the battlefield, bathing mud-filled craters, abandoned trenches and the jagged remains of bombed-out ruins and fortifications with probing scanner fields from their multiple target-detection systems.

Venner had evaded the drones with contemptuous ease. The material of his lightweight chem-suit, fabricated in research labs on a world many light years from here, baffled many of the drones' systems, blocking out his body heat signature and defying most of the normal methods of life sign detection. Using breath exercises that would have been familiar to snipers centuries ago, he was careful to control his breathing. On the few occasions the drones' search paths brought them drifting past his position, Venner knew that they were equipped with scanners that could detect the presence of human breath exhaled though a respirator out into the toxin-filled atmosphere of Nu Earth. At one point, one of the drones passed almost within touching range of Venner, but he kept his position, fighting the urge to reach out and smash the irritating, buzzing little thing out of the air – his contempt for an enemy who would dare to try and use such toys against him going up a few more notches and further feeding his growing kill-hunger.

He had killed the first of his pursuers a few hours later, finally tiring of the game he had been playing with them.

By this point, he had worked out their patterns of movement as they closed in on where they foolishly and mistakenly believed him to be; even more foolishly believing that they were driving him forward into the prepared killzone where their master sniper controller patiently lay in wait. Venner had allowed himself to be driven back in that direction, recrossing territory that he had first travelled across in his journey towards the listening post. Venner had mentally mapped out the area here the first time he had travelled across it, instinctively looking for danger areas and vantage points – his sniper's instincts automatically reducing the confused battle-scarred landscape to what it had now become – a hunting zone where cover, position and angles of fire were all that mattered.

He had a fairly shrewd idea where the master sniper would be: in the turret of the gutted giant Nordland Blackmare tank that lay in the centre of a wreckage field of a years-old battle between opposing forces of armoured assault vehicles. That was where he would have situated himself, in a protected position with a commanding view of the surrounding terrain, and he wasn't foolish enough not to credit a skilled, experienced opponent with any less intelligence than he believed he had himself. The bush-beaters were another matter, however. Younger and less experienced than their team leader, lured into a sense of false security by their prey's apparent unwillingness to stand and fight – and secretly eager to make the killshot for themselves and rob their team leader of his prize – they had willingly allowed themselves to be duped, and Venner intended to make them pay the full price for their fatal error.

He picked off the one on his left flank with a shredder slug, an easy shot from a range of more than four hundred metres. After playing cat-and-mouse with the young idiot for an hour or so, he had led him to believe that he was hiding amongst the shorn-off stumps of a group of petrified trees in a middle of a mud field some two hundred metres from Venner's actual position. When the bush-beater had crawled out of his own hiding spot to find a better shooting position behind the nearby wreck of an APC, Venner had been ready and waiting for him.

The shredder slug carried out its designed task, breaking up into a hail of razor-edged micro-missiles which shredded through chem-suit and flesh, incapacitating but not killing its target. His chem-suit ripped in a dozen or more places, the air pipe to his backpack respirator severed, flesh punctured by multiple wounds and his exposed skin blistered as the biochemical agents in the air went to work; the enemy sniper fell to the ground, writhing and screaming. He had an open radio link to the remaining sniper troupe, and his comrades heard every sound of his death agonies. He screamed in pain as his lungs burned away from the poison air he breathed into them; the flesh-destroying biochemical spores burrowed into him and spread like wildfire within the rich warmth of his bloodstream.

The one on the right flank was the first to break, the screams of his comrade echoing in his chem-suit's radio headset as he came running to his aid. His path took him along a shallow, smooth-walled gully that had probably once been an infantry trench before some kind of heat weapon had scoured through it and melted its walls into blackened glass. Venner had been through it earlier, anticipating that this would be the most direct route the sniper on his right flank would take if provoked into rash incaution, and had seeded the trench with micro-mine booby traps. A short series of shattering explosions from the direction of the trench-gully instantly informed Venner that his plan had paid off.

The third and last remaining bush-beater was either too scared or more cautious and experienced than his two dead comrades. Dug into a good vantage point on the crest of a large shell crater three hundred and twenty metres away, he had a fix on Venner's position and began peppering it with shots. His fourth shot blew the head off the figure in a chem-suit crouched in the overhang beneath the remains of the chassis of a blown-apart self-propelled gun. The man relaxed, raising his head to get a better look at the body of the enemy that had just killed two of his friends. It was then Venner killed him with a single shot fired from the new position he had fallen back to, even before the booby traps in the trench-gully detonated. The other position he had been happy to abandon, leaving behind a chem-suited corpse of the Souther infantryman that he had set up to look like a sniper lying in wait. Now, with the bush-beaters all disposed of, there was only the master sniper left to take care of.

Venner fired off a single shot. It ricocheted off the side of the Blackmare's turret, letting the sniper inside know that his enemy had a fix on his location and daring him to try and move.

Venner himself moved forward, cautiously and carefully, hugging cover, following the series of blind spots that his mental map of the area told him would exist as seen from the vantage point of an observer inside the tank wreck. He figured he could probably get safely within three or four hundred metres of the enemy sniper's location. He then would find a good firing position amongst one of the many tank wrecks strewn around the area, and only then would the real battle, a battle of true patience and bitterly hard-won experience, begin. It would be a battle where the first mistake from either marksman would almost certainly be rewarded with instantaneous death. It was the kind of battle Venner lived for, nothing less than a test of true skill and experience.

Venner was still about eighty metres short of the closest tank wreck when he felt the touch of death upon him. The material of his chem-suit – lightweight, more like a second skin than the crude, bulky outfits worn by most of the participants of the war on Nu Earth – was run through with thousands of strands of delicate monofilament wiring. Sensitive to infrared or electronic scanning, such as the kind cast out by the hi-tech precision scopes on a sniper rifle, they gave the wearer an instant warning that an electronically-sighted weapon was being aimed at him. Venner received that warning now – a burning sensation pierced his heart as the network within his bodysuit detected an

infrared targeting beam playing across the front of his chest –
the monofilament wiring instantly heating up in reaction.

Venner threw himself aside as he heard the crack of a rifle
shot from somewhere off to his left. The shot whizzed past
him, blowing apart the semi-petrified remains of a Souther
infantryman corpse that lay half-buried in the ground
behind him.

The enemy sniper was close, he realised, probably within
thirty metres or so. Too close for Venner to even begin to
think about running for cover or raising his own rifle and
returning fire. Before he'd moved a few metres or even spotted a target to return fire on, his opponent would have
compensated for his first miss and nailed him with his second shot. He had been tricked, he knew. His opponent had
foreseen Venner's assumption that he would have sought
shelter in the Blackmare's turret and moved position once
Venner started picking off the rest of the troupe. If indeed
he had ever been in the Blackmare in the first place, Venner
thought bitterly.

Venner was a man who valued skill, who valued finesse,
who valued a challenge and the thrill of the hunt. More
than anything, though, he was a man who valued his own
life. Abandoning any further claim to skill and finesse, he
reached for the pistol-like weapon that hung from his equip-
ment-laden belt. He raised and fired it in the general
direction the sniper's shot had come from, just as he imagined the enemy marksman would be drawing a bead on him
to take that second and surely fatal follow-up shot.

The ugly, blunt-nosed pistol weapon in Venner's hand
exploded, firing out a hail of deadly missiles which buzzed
through the polluted air, seeking out the telltale heat signature from the hidden sniper's body and carbon dioxide
traces from their respirator-filtered breathing. The weapon
was crude and imprecise, critically short-ranged and liable
to malfunction under the notoriously variable atmospheric
and temperature conditions of Nu Earth. It didn't need to be
deadly accurate, though. Each buzzing missile was proxim-
ity reactive, programmed to explode into a hail of
flesh-tearing shards whenever its simple target systems

detected it was close enough to something that may or may not have been its intended target.

Venner dived for cover, his weight crunching through the frozen chemical frost that coated the ground on this segment of no-man's-land, as he sought to evade both the sniper's shot and the blast effects of his own weapon.

His chem-suit's advanced sound filters protected him from the worst of the series of short, roaring explosions that followed. When the explosions faded away, those same filters immediately picked up a sound that they had been pre-programmed to detect and amplify: the sound of a human being in pain, calling for help.

Venner quickly retrieved his rifle and stalked towards the source of the sounds, wary of a trap. As a sniper, he himself had used autobot drones to broadcast similar sounds in the past, luring in enemy troops to capture or finish off what they thought was an injured enemy. The analysers in his chem-suit's micro-processor systems informed him that the moans sounded authentically human, with no sign of any electronic origin. A few seconds later, the evidence of Venner's own eyes confirmed it.

The enemy master sniper lay in the shadow of an upturned Souther light tank, one that had taken a direct hit from a firebeam weapon, judging by the gaping, smooth-edged wound melted through the armour of its hull. The man had been hit multiple times by the explosive shards, and lay groaning on the ground, his blood bubbling furiously as it bled out through the rips in his chem-suit and reacted fiercely with the toxic elements in the air around him. He would die soon, either from shock and blood loss, or, more likely, from exposure to the leftover remnants of whatever biochemical weapon had once been used on this portion of the battlefield.

He raised his head groggily, watching as Venner walked towards him. He wore the trademark featureless, spherical black helmet that marked him as one of the so-called "black domers", a master sniper who had more than a thousand confirmed kills to their credit. Venner was delighted. This would be the fourth black domer he had killed.

The two snipers looked at each other.

"How many?" asked Venner, shocked at the sound of his own voice. It had been the first time in over a week he had heard it, and it sounded unfamiliar to him, especially when talking in the harsh, guttural language of the enemy.

"Twelve hundred and fifty-three," answered the Nort sniper, unable to keep the betraying hint of pride out of his voice, even at a time like this.

"Not bad," grunted Venner. The Nort nodded in acknowledgement, as one equal to another. Then Venner shot him through the heart. The man deserved respect and a quicker, cleaner death than the one he had been facing.

"But nowhere near good enough," the Souther added, bending down to search his opponent's corpse for some kind of identification. The other kills were strictly small-fry, but to receive a confirmed kill on a black domer he would have to bring back proof of his status and identity. He had to strip off the man's chem-suit to find it, finally managing to take a scan-reading off the barcode tattoo on the back of the corpse's neck.

An hour later, the atmocraft arrived to pick him up. His real mission over, he hadn't troubled himself to double back and destroy the last listening post, but he had its coordinates precisely mapped. Some petty glory boy in an artillery unit somewhere could proudly claim the credit for its destruction, assuming the Norts hadn't dismantled and moved it on elsewhere in the meantime.

Sitting back in the pressurised interior of the atmocraft, he checked his suit's own internal chem-count meter twice against the read-outs on the wall panel beside him before breaking the seals on his suit's neck brace and taking off his helmet. He sat back for a moment, breathing deeply and relishing the nearest thing to clean, unfiltered air that he'd tasted in over a week.

The two other Southers in the cabin with him shifted nervously. One of them, the atmocraft's crew chief, busied himself with some pointless maintenance task, clearly feeling uncomfortable in the presence of the Souther Security

Service's most notorious assassin. The other, a young female intelligence officer, did her best to retain an aura of command authority in the face of a man who – no matter what junior rank his service record said he possessed – vastly outclassed her in terms of experience, ability and appetite for death.

Venner smiled, spotting the data-port in her hand and its winking green light showing that it had information waiting to be downloaded.

"Another job for me?" he asked, indicating the device in her hand. "Show me."

"You need to rest," she told him. "Once you're back at base and have been fully debriefed, we'll–"

"Show me." The smile left his face.

She handed the device over. Venner pressed his thumb against its small ID plate and tapped in his authority code. The screen blinked into life, information scrolling across it at a rate matching the movement of his eyes as he studied the new mission briefing. A name came up, and then a visual image.

The smile returned to Venner's face, and he sat back, contentedly resting his head against the panel behind him. Someone at Milli-com wanted someone here on Nu Earth dead, and, since they had given the job to Venner, then that was exactly what was going to happen. Venner knew the target's rep. He was a notoriously tricky bastard, this one, and had been reported dead several times before, but somehow always managed to survive. Milli-com didn't have any leads on his current whereabouts, and so Venner would have to rely on his own skills and resources to track him down, at least to start with.

Yes, this one was going to be a real challenge, Venner thought, returning his attention to the screen, thinking of everything he had heard about the target's history. And besides, he reminded himself, this particular piece of renegade scum had had it coming to him for a long time.

TWO

Rafe rode the caustic jet streams, guiding her fighter craft through the gauntlet of ice fragments, chem-vapour, acid rain squalls and hurricane-force winds that ran rampant up here, twenty kilometres above the surface of Nu Earth. The damage done to the face of the planet – entire mountain ranges levelled by early nuclear exchanges, forests destroyed, vast swathes of land burned into sterile desert, seas reduced to tideless lakes of toxic sludge – had caused huge and disastrous climactic changes to the environment, and not just on the planet's surface.

If the grunts on the ground thought they had it bad, Rafe considered, then they should try waging a war up here, in a poisoned, shifting void where sudden extremes of temperature could shatter the metal of your wings or grill you alive in your cockpit. Clashing chem-clouds sometimes spontaneously combusted into sheets of flame and violent atmospheric storms could unleash barrages of craft-destroying lightning blasts more deadly and accurate than any kind of enemy anti-aircraft fire.

And that was just some of the natural hazards Souther combat pilots had to face up here. Added to that were the Norts, and their determined efforts to sweep the skies of Nu Earth clear of any Souther presence.

From the ground, radar-directed missile and lascannon batteries looked upwards and scanned the thick, blanketing veil of chem-cloud cover in search of enemy targets. Up here, among those same clouds, Nort patrols of ugly, lethal, stub-winged Grendel and Gorgon fighters hunted remorselessly for Souther air vessels, while every bank of polluted chem-cloud might conceal a hidden field of aerial mines, or one of the much-feared Barrakuda missile-drones that the Norts released in their thousands into the upper atmosphere of Nu Earth. Stealth-equipped, notoriously difficult to detect and kept aloft by a compact but powerful anti-grav motor, they drifted among the highest banks of chem-cloud, programmed to home in on the radar and energy signatures of Souther craft.

Higher still, many kilometres overhead in low orbit, where the outermost fringes of the atmospheric envelope ended and true space began, the hunter-killer satellites lay in wait. Endless series of them, strung out in variable, ever-changing orbits, encircling the planet in deadly, looping patterns. From up there, they looked down on the world below, probing the thick belts of chem-clouds with questing scanner beams, searching for aerial targets. Every Souther pilot lived in terror of them, waiting for the screaming, electronic alert sound in their helmet earphones that would tell them their craft had blundered into the detection cone of one of these orbital weapons, and then waiting for the hail of radar-guided missiles that seconds later would be unleashed down upon them.

The Nort pilots ran the same gauntlet, Rafe knew. For every piece of ordnance the Norts deployed against Rafe and her comrades, the Souther weapons designers had something to match. For years now, the war on Nu Earth had degenerated into nothing more than a brutal and bloody war of attrition. For every new weapon or tactic devised by one side, the other was sure to develop a countermeasure or create their own imitation version of the enemy's weapon soon enough. The knowledge that every pilot lost and craft downed would almost invariably be matched by an equivalent loss to the enemy was of little consolation to the pilots on either side.

The casualty statistics for the air war on Nu Earth were supposed to be a closely-guarded secret, known only to the planners and strategists at Milli-com, but every Souther pilot was intimately acquainted with the cold, hard fact at the heart of those numbers and equations. The average life expectancy for a combat pilot in the Nu Earth theatre of operations was just a little over thirteeen months.

Rafe had been flying combat missions non-stop for more than three years. When she was in the cockpit, flying search-and-destroy missions, routine combat patrols or whatever other low survivability duties her asshole of a squadron commander had dreamed up for her, she thought about little else than surviving the mission intact – without her and her craft being fragged or vaporised by any of the multitude of forms of instantaneous death on offer in the skies over Nu Earth.

Every day she returned safely to base to climb back out of the cockpit of her Seraphim fighter was an added bonus, the relief of her continued survival tempered by the knowledge that tomorrow or the next day she would have to climb back into the cockpit and do it all over again.

There was a soft warning *bleep* over her helmet intercom, coming from the navigator position in the cockpit space behind her.

"I see it, Gabe," she told the occupant of that space, flicking on the heads-up sensor display inside her helmet visor. It showed a fiery mass plunging down through the atmosphere many kilometres away. More evidence of the war that raged not just in the skies of Nu Earth or on the ground beneath them, but also in the heavens overhead.

"What do you think, Gabe? One of ours, or one of theirs?"

"Difficult to say," buzzed the voice of her copilot/navigator. "It's too far gone into re-entry to be sensor-recognisable, but I'm guessing it's one of theirs. Our killer-sat units have been targeting Nort orbital platforms in this sector for the last few days now. All part of Milli-com's big new push, I guess."

Rafe watched the sensor display for a few more seconds. The destroyed Nort device, probably one of the small three-man surveillance and orbital bombardment monitoring stations the Norts used more and more frequently these days, was far enough away to be no danger whatsoever to her and her craft, but a couple of dozen tonnes of burning, super-heated wreckage was going to put a serious dent in someone's day when it hit the ground a few minutes from now.

"Gabe. Track its trajectory and send an impact warning down to–"

A double-*beep*, almost smug-sounding, alarmed in her helmet intercom. Typically, her navigator was already at least one step ahead of her.

She sighed to herself. "What would I do without you, Gabe?"

"Beats me," buzzed the voice from the empty seat behind her. "There'd be no one here to look out for your cute blue ass, so I guess you'd really be deep in the tox-sludge without a chem-suit."

Gabe – or the Wachowski-Linder Industries GABRIEL-302 auto-drone flight unit, as his manufacturers called him – was a prototype sentient copilot/navigator programme specifically designed for use with the Seraphim fighter. He and Combat Flight Pilot Second Rank Rafaela Blue made a perfect combo, everyone agreed. None of the other pilots in the squadron could be persuaded to fly with some box of chips and wires sitting there as their copilot and, equally, none of the navigators wanted to share a cockpit with a blue-skinned genetic freak like Rafe.

Correction, she reminded herself: a blue-skinned *female* genetic freak.

"GI Dolls." That's what they had called her and the others, and probably still did, behind her back. "Milli-com bed warmers." "Command staff stress release units." "R&R Commandos." Those were favourites too, homing in on the generally-held suspicions about why exactly the Milli-com top brass had wanted female as well as male Genetic Infantryman beings created, and what exactly the female version's non-combat duties at Milli-com had entailed.

Rafe had heard them all, all the sniggering jokes and comments, and tended not to react too well to them.

Which was why she was flying solo now, and dumped with every shitcan mission that came across her squadron commander's desk. That was what happened, she reminded herself, when you put three of your supposed comrades into the base infirmary – one of them a flight commander nursing a broken arm and fractured jaw – after a forthright exchange of views one night in the pilots' mess.

She half-smiled at the memory. One thing was for sure after that little incident, she remembered. It was the last time anyone ever called her any of those names. At least to her face. The fact that it had happened the day after she had been officially confirmed as the highest-scoring Souther ace pilot in this whole campaign sector had only made things all the sweeter.

It was also the reason, she had to ruefully remind herself, why her enraged squadron commander simply hadn't been able to have her recycled all the way back to Milli-com.

After the destruction of the entire genetic infantryman regiment at what had infamously come to be known as the Quartz Zone Massacre, the GI program had been deemed an official failure; the plug had been pulled on any future attempts to use genetic science to create armies of super-soldiers purpose-designed to wage war in the unique combat conditions on the surface of Nu Earth. That left just the so-called GI Dolls – and one last remaining and particularly resilient example of the male of the species, she reminded herself – and no one seemed quite sure what to do with the contingent of female GIs that had been created in the gene genies' bio labs at Milli-com. The near-critical level of mounting losses to the war had finally forced the military planners' hand, however, and the female GIs had been individually assessed and reassigned to regular duties throughout every branch of the Souther armed forces.

Like many of her gene-sisters, Rafe's assessment scores showed an almost preternatural level of intuitive ability and aptitude for machine interface and information categorisation. However, while most of the others found useful roles serving in the vast pools of data assimilators and battle strategy assessors that made up a great part of the million-strong command staff of Milli-com, further testing had revealed Rafe to be almost uniquely qualified for one particular job...

"Yessir," she breathed to herself. "Flying the friendly skies of Nu Earth. Working nine-to-five in the most hazardous combat environment on the most dangerous war world in an entire galaxy full of people busy shooting at each other! Why, it's just about everything a gal grown in a test-tube ever dreamed of!"

There was a querying *bleep* on her helmet comm.

"Nothing, Gabe," she replied. "Just thinking aloud."

Her copilot's designers might have equipped their creation with a personality matrix that seemed to have stuck on a default setting marked "love-struck lecher", but an understanding of good old-fashioned human irony seemed to be have been beyond even their programming abilities.

Another comms alert lit up on her visor display, calling for her attention. "What you got for me, Gabe?"

"Radio intercept," chimed the reply. "An aerial distress call, coming from right in our neighbourhood."

She checked the radar display, unsurprised to see nothing there. The high-level chem-clouds were so dense in some parts of Nu Earth, and contained so much radiation, sensor-scrambling or radar-blocking trace elements, that on occasion the first warning you had that you might not be alone in the skies was when you came cruising out of a cloud bank and suddenly had to take emergency evasive action to avoid a midair collision with a patrol of enemy fighters. Or alternatively, a flight of your own side's troop landers that someone forgot to tell you would be flying in your vacinity on the same day.

Just another extra little thrill that added to the general excitement of flying the friendly skies above Nu Earth, she reminded herself.

"One of ours, Gabe?"

There was a brief pause in response to her question. The airwaves of Nu Earth were awash with coded signal traffic from both sides, much of it designed to jam out the communications frequencies of the other side. It could take a highly-trained human operator years to get to grips with the complexities of the invisible landscape of Nu Earth's radio-wave environment.

Gabe – his powerful processors scanning through thousands of frequencies on a bewildering number of wavebandss, and comparing the collected data to the information held in his daily-updated memory files – accomplished the required task in a few brief seconds.

"Affirmative, hon. It's a command rank frequency, Pershing-level priority. It's kinda strange, one of the older code variants that no one's really used much in the last few years, but it's still registered as valid and non-compromised by the Nort crypto-breakers. Give me a few more moments, babe, and maybe I can–"

"Gabe..." There was something more than a distinct note of impatience in Rafe's voice.

The navigator unit couldn't properly imitate the uniquely human sound of a sigh of resignation, but Gabe's vox-programmes did the best they could. "Got a signal-lock on the source. Intercept course plotted. Feeding it through to you now."

The data flickered across her visor display but even before her mind had properly assimilated it, her GI intuitive senses had already kicked in and she was bringing her craft's main thrusters online and swinging the fighter around to the required new heading.

"Sounds like some useless piece of Milli-com brass maybe got closer to the action than he wanted to. C'mon, Gabe, time to go earn our daily hazard pay."

"They've started paying us now? When did that happen? Did I miss a squadron memo or something?"

Rafe's reply, couched in terms that breached several directives from Milli-com on the use of inappropriate terminology over official Souther military communications channels, was lost amidst the crescendo roar of the fighter's thrusters blasting into full, fiery life.

THREE

They found the source of the distress call without much trouble, and a little extra something else. Three Nort fighters, Grendel-class patrol interceptors, who were either the cause of the distress call, or, like Rafe and Gabe, had picked up the signal and zeroed in on its source, no doubt eagerly anticipating the promise of easy prey.

Gabe had picked up their radio chatter – voices barking excitedly at each other in the harsh, guttural tones of the language of the Norts – while he and Rafe were still some distance away. Forewarned of the presence of the enemy craft, Rafe had climbed another thousand metres into the cover of a dense layer of rust cloud and then cut power and throttled back, coming in on the Norts in a manoeuvre that was half gliding, half controlled fall. Cutting the flow of power to the Seraphim fighter's engines would reduce the telltale energy signature that might betray its presence to the Nort craft, while the rust cloud – a swirling vortex composed of millions of tiny fragments of battlefield debris swept up into the upper atmosphere by cyclonic strength winds – would shield her approach from the Norts' radar senses.

It was a dangerous manoeuvre and other, more cautious pilots would have actively sought to keep out of a rust cloud, but Rafe knew her craft and her own abilities, and was confident that both would see them safely through.

The Seraphim bucked wildly, buffeted by the wind forces lurking inside the rust cloud. There was a frantic drumming sound, so loud and intense it quickly merged into one big hammering rumble, as rusting flecks of debris bounced off the fighter's armoured skin.

"Probably going to need a new paint job when we get back to base," Gabe observed. Rafe said nothing, but suspected that Gabe's personality matrix processors had probably been chewing over the concept of irony a little more during the ride in.

"Warning light on the starboard intake," he noted. "Probably debris sucked into the engine cowling." By the time Rafe had looked to check, the warning status had changed to two small flashing amber lights.

"I see it," she confirmed. "So when do we start worrying?"

"Probably at four," came the reply, just as the third warning light came on and something inside the cockpit started beeping urgently.

"What about five?" asked Rafe.

"There is no five," Gabe informed her. "About ten seconds after warning number four, the engine explodes, taking most of the wing with it, and we take the short, fast route to finding out whether the grunts at ground level have it any worse than we do up here."

"I know my crate. It'll hold," said Rafe, wondering if Gabe's personality matrix had advanced enough yet to know a bluff when it heard one.

It was at that moment they broke out of the rust cloud and saw the targets ahead of them. Nort Grendels, four of them, which was one more than she and Gabe had been expecting, going by the three separate voice patterns Gabe had positively identified from their radio chatter.

"Guess the fourth one must not be such a big talker," said Rafe, as she hit the boosters again and sent her Seraphim diving down into an all-out attack manoeuvre. Gabe's comms receptors broadcast the Norts' shouted exclamations and squawks of horrified surprise, which were instantly drowned out a moment later by the roar of explosions.

One of the Nort fighters vaporised in midair, struck by one of the missiles launched from the rocket pods on the wings of Rafe's fighter. The destroyed craft fell away, reduced to little more than burning fragments, fragments that might ironically one day be swept up from the ground during a cyclone storm to become part of another rust cloud.

The other Nort fighters frantically peeled away, evading the same fate as their comrade. Another of Rafe's missiles got a semi-lock on one of them, and exploded as near to its target as possible, peppering the Grendel's hull, engine and wings with shrapnel. The Nort dived towards the cloud layer below, his tail fin partially shredded and one engine trailing black smoke. Gabe tracked him with the Seraphim's targeting systems and opened up with the rear turret quad-lasers, blowing away the remainder of the Nort fighter's tail section. The Grendel – an ugly, blunt-nosed thing, typical of the Norts' pragmatic approach to military design – corkscrewed crazily through the air and then dropped like a stone, disappearing into the cloud layer below. Like every other Nu Earth airman, the Nort pilot would be equipped with a grav-chute and a chem-resistant flight suit, but even if he managed to bail out of the stricken craft, he must have known his chances of surviving the journey through the dense and highly toxic chem-clouds would be minimal.

In the Nu Earth air war, there were very few lucky escapes and no prizes at all for merely being second-best.

The remaining two Nort fighters were running ahead of the faster, more agile Souther aircraft, pushing hard with their afterburners, chasing after the target that had drawn them here in the first place. Rafe could see it now, a lightly armed command transport. Its hull shape showed the familiar lines of Souther design, although Rafe couldn't quite recognise what type and model it was. On cue, Gabe chimed in with the results of his vessel ID scan. "It's a junker, hon. Mostly composed of the airframe of an old Buffalo Class Type IV atmo-shuttle, but with a few other pieces added in."

Rafe frowned. "Junkers" were common enough on various parts of Nu Earth. Craft built from the salvaged remains of battle-destroyed wrecks. They were mostly used by off-world mercenary units and the so-called scavenger packs, small bandit armies composed of deserters and renegades from both sides of the war.

But what the hell was a senior Souther command staff officer doing flying about in something as undignified as a junker?

"Coded transmission hidden inside their craft ID beacon checks out, hon. They're definitely carrying someone with VIP status," reported Gabe, almost as if he could read her mind.

"Not for much longer," said Rafe, watching as the two remaining Grendels streaked towards the vulnerable shuttle craft.

It was a miracle that the shuttle had survived this long. Rafe suspected that the Grendel pilots' plan had probably been to capture the Souther craft and its human cargo intact, sending out radio warnings that they would blow it out of the sky unless it landed now in Nort-controlled territory.

Now, however, with Rafe arriving on the scene, the Norts had apparently abandoned this plan and now wanted to destroy the shuttle and whatever VIP passengers it might be carrying.

She pushed her Seraphim hard to gain on the Norts and their quarry, locking onto the nearest of the Grendels. Missile lock-on tone pinged loudly in her helmet speakers, but she didn't fire, knowing if a missile missed its initial target then it could easily mistakenly lock onto the shuttle craft as its secondary alternative target. Instead, her finger went to the firing stud of her fighter's main guns. The finger hovered there, waiting patiently for the right moment to unleash the power of the four forward-firing lascannons slung beneath the Seraphim's nose cone.

The Seraphim jolted violently as it rode the turbulence from the engine wash of the two Nort fighters. Close enough to feel the heat from your target's engine thrusters meant close enough to fire and Rafe's finger stabbed down on the trigger stud just as, a moment too late to save itself, the Nort fighter directly in front of her deployed its rear defensive measures.

A hail of small objects fell away from the tail of the Grendel, just as Rafe's lascannon bolts ripped into it. Anyone watching might have thought the hail of objects were part of the Nort fighter, fragments blown off by the lascannon hammer-blows which smashed apart the Grendel's entire rear section in one furious burst of fire, but Rafe knew better.

"Scatter mines!" she called in warning to Gabe, wrenching at the flight controls in an effort to evade the hail of explosive devices coming flying towards them.

Their fuses were proximity-sensitive and they exploded all around the Seraphim, filling the air with fragments of flying shrapnel as the Souther craft tried to weave a course through them.

Rafe heard warning alarms sound. Shards of metal tore through the cockpit floor and she felt something punch into her lower leg. Wetness spread there, inside her flight suit, to be cut off a moment later as her enhanced GI body detected the damage to it. The coagulants in her better-than-human bloodstream stopped the bleeding almost instantly. Any other pilot would also be terrified by the fact that their cockpit had been holed and that its interior was now possibly contaminated by the deadly toxins that were ever-present in the Nu Earth atmosphere, but Rafe's GI immunity system made her invulnerable to the worst of just about anything the planet's super-polluted environment had to throw at her.

Despite the agony from her leg wound – it would be a few more seconds before the chemically-boosted contents of her bloodstream would manufacture enough stimulants to kill the pain. As the damage alerts lit up her instrumentation panel and filled the comms channels of her helmet speakers, Rafe kept her attention locked on the task of saving her craft. Only GI reactions allowed her to jink her fighter out of the path of the flaming, expanding mass of wreckage that was all that now remained of the enemy Grendel.

Her Seraphim wasn't out of danger yet, however. Something – Rafe caught a brief glimpse of a tattered, burning ragdoll thing still strapped into its pilot's chair – struck the cockpit canopy with enough force to leave a spider's web of deep cracks in the thick layer of armoured glassteel. Shocked, Rafe lost control of her craft for a split-second. By the time she had regained control and piloted the Seraphim safely through the last of the wreckage cloud, the last remaining Grendel had successfully acquired its target.

It swept in from beneath the slower-moving shuttle craft, raking its underbelly with a devastating close-range volley of fire from its twin banks of wing-mounted quad-cannons. One of the shuttle's engines stalled and exploded. Rafe could clearly see the bright streaks of armour-piercing tracer shells passing through the shuttle's underside and then exiting out through its topside, causing untold damage to the ship's vulnerable internal systems and even more vulnerable human components.

The shuttle dipped abruptly, then fell away. Only one of its landing thrusters was left functioning amidst the fiery scrap yard wreck of its destroyed underbelly. Rafe could see it firing wildly and could well imagine the panic in the shuttle pilot's mind as he fought to bring his crippled craft down on a controlled descent into the midst of whatever further dangers awaited it at ground level.

The victorious Grendel peeled up and away, going into a textbook banking turn that would bring it back on course for a return pass over the shuttle. Whatever ideas the Nort pilot had about returning to finish the shuttle's destruction ended in a blazing fireball as Rafe locked onto the Nort plane and despatched a seeker missile after it.

She followed the shuttle down, listening in to the pain-wracked voice of the pilot or copilot in its bullet-riddled cockpit.

"Mayday, mayday, this is Buzzard Three-One… We are going down. Repeat… Going down. We are going down…"

The mayday, weak and barely audible, ended in an abrupt electronic squeal as the shuttle's cannon-damaged comms array blew out. Souther military protocol and natural human compassion to a comrade pilot told Rafe to follow it down and get a confirmed fix on landing zone,

even if that so-called landing zone ultimately turned out
to be nothing more than a wreckage-strewn crash site.
The colourful spectrum of system alert warnings on the
display panel in front of her said otherwise, however. Rafe
was at the controls of one seriously sick machine. Four
confirmed kills officially made this a very successful
patrol mission, but she hadn't exactly got away
unscathed.

The display on her helmet visor was showing their number two engine on the starboard wing as an official goner,
their hull was perforated in more than a dozen places – and
bleeding either air or power from most of them – and the
Seraphim's scanner senses were blinking on and off with an
independent life of their own.

"Time to turn for home and park this crate on the ground,
Gabe. But, first, I need you to–"

"Already there, hon. I've tracked that shuttle as far down
as I could and now I'm projecting its most likely landing
area, based on its last known course and trajectory. Wait,
coming through now."

There was an uncharacteristic pause from the navigator
unit. When it spoke again, Rafe understood the reason for
its momentary hesitation.

"It's Nordstadt, Rafe. Those poor suckers are going to
come down right in the middle of hell. There's something
else too, hon..."

"Spit it out, Gabe."

"The command codes in the shuttle's distress signal. Like
I said, they were kinda old, but they still checked out as
valid. I've dug further in to the files and those codes are
coming up as flagged. Restricted, under S-Three authorisa-
tion. We're supposed to report in any contact with any craft
identifying itself by those code protocols."

Rafe swore. If going down over Nordstadt wasn't bad
enough, then now whoever was in that shuttle also had the
S-Three bloodhounds on their trail. And then she suddenly
remembered something else.

"So we gonna do it?" prompted Gabe. "We gonna tell S-
Three all about it when we get back to base?"

Rafe thought about it, a horrible realisation growing inside her. To have come so close, and not have known it at the time...

"No, Gabe, we're not. We're going to tell somebody something all right, but it's not going to be anyone at S-Three."

"Babe?" Gabe was getting better and better at the quizzical tone, she noticed.

"'Buzzard', Gabe. That's what I'm talking about. Search through those big memory banks of yours and then tell me if that word means anything to you."

FOUR

Nordstadt.

From the air, it seemed to stretch out forever. A vast sea of shell-cratered rubble, dotted with scattered archipelagos of still-standing ruins, which were the bombed-out and artillery scarred remains of vast blocks of buildings. Twenty years after the first shells fell in Nordstadt, they were still fighting for these prizes. At night, from the position of the reconnaissance drones flying kilometres overhead – or from the spy satellites and orbital weapons platforms looking down from space – the flashes of explosions and the flickering choruses of las-fire from endless night attacks looked like angry waves of light lashing against the stony shores of these few remaining island fortresses.

The fighting never stopped on Nu Earth and nowhere was that more true than here, in Nordstadt, the former capital of the Greater Nordland Territories on Nu Earth.

Twenty years ago, at the outset of the war, Grand Marshal Hague, a man whose name was now a curse on the lips of Souther troops all over Nu Earth, conceived a daring plan to secure the planet for the Southern Confederacy. His target was Nordstadt, the largest city on Nu Earth, and the key to the Norts' control of the planet's large northern continent. Hague's plan was simple, if audacious; a massive troop drop from orbit right into the seat of Nort power on Nu Earth. At the same time, four entire Souther armies would launch an armoured thrust through the Nort front lines hundreds of kilometres away. They would push deep into the Nordland-held territories and drive hard to reach

Nordstadt itself and link up with the tens of thousands of troops there that had dropped down from orbit.

The plan, which had violently polarised opinion in the command councils at Milli-com, succeeded better than even some of its advocates had secretly hoped or expected. The orbital drop losses were heavy, just as had been privately predicted, but the troops, all veterans, were drawn from the ranks of legendary para-drop regiments like the Red Shells, the Pegasus Guard and the Orbital Eagles. They dug in hard and withstood the Norts' bruising attempts to dislodge them from the several vital areas of the city that they had seized in the opening hours of the offensive. Likewise, the ground attack element of the plan also brought heavy losses, as entire Nort and Souther armoured divisions smashed into each other in clashes of mutually assured destruction. Hague's planning and bloody-minded determination ultimately prevailed however, as the Nort front line collapsed and columns of Souther tanks and troops carriers swept across the Nort heartlands, brutally overwhelming any opposition in their path as they drove relentlessly onwards towards Nordstadt.

Twenty-two days and an estimated seven hundred thousand Souther lives later, the battered, beleaguered survivors of the orbital drop emerged from their strong points amongst the rubble to gratefully embrace their colleagues amongst the first Souther armoured reconnaissance units to reach the city, and Nordstadt was officially declared to have been captured.

If only things had been that simple.

Despite the propaganda rush to celebrate the bravery of the orbit-drop troops and to hail Hague's plan as a triumph, the Norts still hadn't been entirely dislodged from the city. They still remained in control of several large areas of it, and now, like the Souther paratroops before them, they dug in and prepared to hold out for as long as they could.

Hague's plan depended on the Norts' resolve breaking after the collapse of their main front line and the capture of their showpiece city. Now, though, Nordland propaganda made all it could of the bravery and tenacity of the defence forces in Nordstadt, and Nort resolve stiffened rather than weakened, aided by the off-world reinforcements arriving on Nu Earth far sooner than the Milli-com planners had expected.

Hague's plan, its shortcomings exposed, swiftly began to fall apart.

The Norts continued to hold out in Nordstadt. Better than that, they managed to retake entire parts of the city in an orbit-drop ironically almost identical to the one first carried out by Hague. Worse still, from the Souther point of view, Nort counter-attacks began to apply immense pressure on the corridor that the Souther armoured forces had driven through enemy territory – the same corridor which the Souther forces in Nordstadt now depended on for reinforcements and resupplying.

Desperate to regain the advantage, the Souther generals realised that Hague's plan had failed and looked to other ideas. The generals requested other prize objectives and to deliver the knock-out victory blow that had seemed so tantalisingly possible in those early stages of the war. Nordstadt was just the first entry in a litany of names that would soon become grimly familiar to any student of Nu Earth warfare.

The Dix-I Front. The Magno Line. Tambuk. Nu-Krimea. Fort Neuropa. The Quartz Zone. Sevastipolitan. The Neverglades. The Battle of the Kashan Gates.

Untold millions of dead. Years of waste. Reworked versions of short-sighted strategies that had already failed in previous actions. All the evidence of a conflict sinking into a crushing war of bloody attrition, with both sides increasingly willing to feed entire armies into the meat grinder in a frantic search to open up the slightest advantage over the enemy.

Over the intervening years, there were other battles, other conflicts flaring up all over Nu Earth, new fronts to consume the attentions of the strategy planners on both sides of the war. Throughout it all, however, Nordstadt remained, a festering sore for Norts and Southers alike; an open, raw wound, consuming men and materials at a truly terrifying rate.

The lines of battle changed and then changed again. The besiegers became the besieged and found themselves the besiegers once again. One side and then the other launched yearly fresh offensives to finally drive the enemy from the city and raise their own victory flags over what little remained of Nu Earth's largest and proudest city.

Its tallest towers and spires were shattered by artillery bombardments. Its parks and gardens were churned into mud fields by shell fire and the heavy treads of armoured vehicles. Its wide boulevards were left choked with the rubble heaps of collapsed buildings and the burned-out wrecks of columns of military vehicles. Its giant factory complexes were gutted by infantry battles that raged for weeks on end, and its suburbs and sprawling patterns of worker habs were levelled by waves of bomber attacks and orbital missile strikes.

Nordstadt, the city, had been destroyed a dozen times over, but Nordstadt, the target objective, remained intact in the minds of the military planners of both sides, long after it had ceased to hold any remaining strategic worth as the main struggle for Nu Earth moved on to other prizes and other killing fields.

With Nordstadt, however, too many lives had already been expended for either side to admit that it was no longer an objective worth fighting for. To the Norts, it held deep significance as a symbol of their national defiance, their first foothold on the one-time paradise of Nu Earth, a city now reduced to ruins but still holding out against the treacherous Souther enemy. To the Southers, it was also a symbol, a reminder of how close they had come to outright victory in those earliest days of the war. The Norts would never willingly give up one inch of the bloodstained earth their city stood on. And there were many on the planning staff at Milli-com who saw the ravaged metropolis as a crucible, a place where Nort forces could be endlessly drawn in and destroyed in a particularly brutal microcosm example of the relentless war of attrition that was now being waged all across the galaxy.

Nordstadt must be held at all costs and the invaders driven once and for all from its sacred soil, Nort propaganda had preached for the last twenty years.

Take Nordstadt for good, the Souther strategists believed, and Hague's plan would finally be validated. The Norts had attached such mythic significance to the place that their resolve would break at last and victory on Nu Earth, and on many of the other battle planets in the galaxy beyond, would swiftly follow the city's final fall.

And so the gruesome stalemate had continued for two decades, with every year bringing a new Nordstadt "Final Victory" offensive which would consign hundreds of thousands of more human lives to their fate in the slaughterhouse the city had become. Despite the propaganda boasts, none of the generals and planners could see an ultimate end to the carnage. No one could see the much-heralded final victory that would once and for all drive the enemy out of their hiding places and bolt-holes amongst the rubble of Nordstadt.

All this, however, was about to change. The strategists on one side conceived a plan that would indeed finally end the battle for Nordstadt, in a level of callous mass butchery that had never before been contemplated.

FIVE

"Clear!"

Sergeant Hanna Coss lowered her binox-scanner, satisfied after several minutes of careful searching that there were no unexpected nasty surprises waiting out there for her and her squad. No human heat signatures or the telltale oxygen/carbon dioxide exchange traces from a chem-suit breathing apparatus that would signal the hidden presence of a Nort sniper or ambush patrol.

At her command, the first two members of the squad stepped warily out of cover and began the dangerous journey across the open ground of the street in that familiar half-jogging, half-crouching gait that had come to be called the "Nordstadt Two-Step". They reached the comparative safety of a shattered doorway on the other side of the street, its stone surround scorched and pockmarked with the impact burns of multiple las-rounds. They gratefully crouched in the cover it offered, using their las-carbines to scan the surrounding terrain for signs of danger.

It was only after a further thirty seconds, when one of them – Mckenna, who, at the age of twenty-three and with two years of combat experience under his belt, qualified as a grizzled old Nordstadt veteran – signalled the all-clear, that Hanna allowed herself to partially relax. She signalled for the next two members of her squad to cross: Verns, and the kid who had only joined the unit last week. She'd detailed Verns to nursemaid the kid until he'd learned at least some of the moves he would need to have a half-decent chance of surviving his Nordstadt tour of duty.

Hanna was annoyed because she could never remember the kid's name, confusing him with the other rookie they got sent last month, the one who tripped that Nort plasma-mine over in the ruins of the Chancellery building. The blast had vaporised the rookie along with Handley and Lindermann and there hadn't been enough human remains to fill an ammo satchel.

Hanna wouldn't have time to familiarise herself with the new kid's name because he and Verns were still only halfway across the street when the Nort mek struck.

It was an Amok, a Nort battle droid, and it came rearing up out of a rubble pile on the other side of the street. It had been months since the Norts had last been reported using any meks in Nordstadt. Hanna guessed it must have been lying dormant for at least that long, its power cells slowly running down, its systems damaged by the weight of the falling masonry that had buried it in some previous battle. Dozens of Souther patrols had probably passed through this area in that time, so Hanna guessed it was just her squad's dumbass luck to have inadvertently triggered something in the droid's failing detector systems.

It rose from the rubble heap, its motive gears growling and roaring as it shrugged off the weight of a tonne or so of fallen stonework. It raised and fired the chaingun weapon built into its left arm and Verns and the rookie disappeared in a sudden red splash, shredded into pieces by the impact of hundreds of high-velocity las-rounds. After that, it turned its attention to the other two troopers sheltering in the once comforting shelter of the doorway.

One of them, Hassey, the less experienced of the pair, took aim at the machine with her carbine, but her wiser partner simply grabbed her and hurled them both backwards into the room behind them. A second later, the doorway and the area around it were obliterated by another furious volley of chaingun fire.

The mek started stalking towards their new hiding place but then stopped in its tracks as several las-rounds ricocheted harmlessly off the back of its armoured head. It turned, its gears growling in anger, seeking the source of this new annoyance and it was only then that Hanna looked dumbly at the rifle in her hands, realising with some degree of incredulity that she had been the one who had fired. Like the trooper on the other side of the street, she had known that the standard Souther infantryman's las-carbine was as good as useless against an armoured Amok battle droid, but that hadn't stopped her from instinctively trying to save the lives of the soldiers under her command.

She watched, dumbly, with almost a sense of resigned detachment, as the mek drew a bead on her and raised its chaingun arm to fire. At least with a chaingun duel her death would be pretty much instantaneous; even if there were only a few more body parts left to ship home than that of the kid who stepped on the plasma-mine.

Despite her resignation, she flinched at the sound of the hissing chatter of las-weapons before she realised it was the sound of las-carbines and that the rest of her squad were all around her, subjecting the Nort droid to a withering hail of covering fire intended to save her life.

The Amok staggered under the impact of multiple las rounds. Presented with so many different targets, its logic processes damaged and until now long-dormant, the droid wasted a few precious moments in processing this new information and decided on a new course of action. This extra time was a gift Hanna didn't intend on similarly wasting.

"Grenades!" she shouted. "Whatever you've got, use 'em! Sweeney, where's our squad lazooka support?"

She looked round in search of the hapless Sweeney. Specialist First Class Dwayne Sweeney, who bitched and moaned every step of every patrol about the weight of the heavy lazooka weapon he had to carry, who had contrived on three different occasions to accidentally lose the thing, and who had been told by Hanna, only half-jokingly, that she would shoot him the next time it happened. And there he was, kneeling on the ground and expertly taking aim at the Nort droid as Jansen, his loader, fumbled to release the charge setting on the shell-like power cell he was slotting into the back of the lazooka tube.

The Amok was firing again and the air around Hanna and her squad buzzed with the heat of high-velocity las-rounds whipping past them. One of the rounds struck Jansen full in the face, exploding through her chem-suit's helmet visor and she was hurled backwards, dead before she hit the ground. Hanna ran forward to Sweeney's position, knowing the lazooka was their only chance against the mek. More las-bolts whipped past her, one of them painfully scorching the armour plating on her shoulder, and she heard a scream and the sickening sound of las-rounds searing into human flesh, but she didn't have time to see who else in her squad had just been hit.

She was at Sweeney's position now, chaingun fire chewing up the ground around them as she grabbed the fallen power cell and slammed it into the loading breach, twisting the setting ring to full charge and arming the weapon. She rapped hard on Sweeney's shoulder guards, giving him the required double-tap "weapon hot" signal.

It wasn't necessary. Sweeney pulled hard on the firing trigger as soon as he felt the first rumble of pent-up energy pass through the lazooka, and a blast of high-density las-power blasted out to blow the mek's head off.

It stumbled back, blinded, but still not out the fight. Its sensor systems may have been located in the head unit, but its CPU and power cell hearts were housed in the more heavily-armoured chest section. Sweeney targeted that next. His next shot blew away the thick layer of armour and the one after that reduced the entire thing to a burning heap of fused metal.

Hanna rapped on her lazookaman's suit armour again – three taps, "job well done" – and reluctantly turned to survey the remains of her squad. Verns, Jansen and the new kid were all dead and the scream she had heard had come from Singh, who had lost the lower part of his left arm to another hit from that damned chaingun. Mortjik was down too, struck by shrapnel from the exploding droid. He was lying on the ground, writhing and moaning, his hands grasping at the bloody puncture holes in his chem-suit, more in an attempt to protect his exposed flesh from whatever deadly toxins might be in the air than to staunch the flow of blood from his wounds.

Babic and Ludlow were already bending over him. "Get those suit patches on him now!" bellowed Hanna, desperate not to lose another man to this botched encounter.

There was one small blessing to the fighting in Nordstadt; neither side had used chem and virus weapons in anywhere near the same level as they had in other parts of Nu Earth in the earliest years of the war. Therefore the tox-levels in Nordstadt were well below Nu Earth standard. Had this been anywhere else – the Dix-I Front, Nu Sevastopol or any of the battle zones bordering the Scum Seas, then Mortjik would have been a dead man seconds after he was hit.

One thing was clear, though. With more than a third of her squad down, this mission had just been reclassified as an official clusterfrag.

She activated her helmet comm, opening a channel to some rear echelon radio operator sitting safe in a hidden oxy-dome back at Regimental HQ.

"Sundance Sierra Seven reporting. I have casualties: three dead and two wounded requiring immediate med-attention. Requesting permission to scratch mission and return to base."

"Permission granted, Sierra Seven. Bring your people in."

Hanna shut down the comms link – the Norts sometimes used high-flying atmocraft which the Souther troopers called Bigears to track Souther radio comms and then launch homing missiles down upon the signal's source – and turned to her squad, supervising as they began unpacking the two lightweight collapsible stretcher-bags to carry their two wounded comrades back to base.

"Look sharp, people. Mission's over. We're going back home."

She checked the readings on her digi-map, tracking a return route back to their company base in the tunnels beneath an old maglev subway station. Her eyes flicked to the marker that designated their mission objective. They had been about three kilometres distant from it when they had ran into the mek. Three kilometres. It didn't sound far, didn't look far on the screen of her digi-map, but in Nord-stadt three kilometres might have well been the distance between you and the dark side of the moon. No way her squad could have covered that distance, not in the shape they were in.

She turned again, looking in the rough direction of the target objective. All she could see was the usual Nordstadt landscape of rubble, bombed-out shells of buildings and the ever-present hazy shimmer of chem-cover. All she could hear through her helmet speakers was the usual Nordstadt ambient drone of the distant crackling of small arms fire and the rumble of artillery.

Hanna sighed and put away her digi-map. Somewhere out there, a shuttle had come down and Hanna and her squad had been sent to find and investigate the crash site. No one seemed very sure if it had been one of theirs or a Nort crate. One thing was sure though; whoever those poor bastards were, they were on their own now.

He had always been a natural born survivor, so it came as little surprise to him that he should have survived this too, falling out of the sky in a blazing wreck, smashing headlong into a rubble landscape of blackened, burned-out ruins.

Naturally, the others who were in the shuttle with him hadn't fared as well as he had, he thought, but then, that was always the way of such things, it seemed.

Two of his bodyguards had died instantly, reduced to shredded meat when a blaze of cannon fire from the attacking fighter had torn through the floor of the rear pas-senger cabin. The pilot had done well to nurse his crippled craft down in a semblance of a controlled crash landing manoeuvre, but he was dead too. His last useful act had been to engage the emergency auto-grav systems, cushion-ing the ship from the very worst of the impact as it belly-flopped into the ground, but that hadn't been enough to save his own life as the shuttle had ploughed for another hundred metres or so through the rubble, its journey abruptly ending as it buried itself nose-first into the rein-forced rockrete wall of a bunker emplacement. This secondary impact had smashed the shuttle's cockpit section as if it had been made of cordwood, killing anyone still left alive in it. The deaths of the pilots mattered little. They had already served their purpose and that was all that was important to the survivor.

His last remaining bodyguard was dead too, speared through the chest by the metal shaft of a support strut that had shattered free during the initial impact of the landing. His adjutant – a petty, obsequious man who had preyed on his nerves for some time – would follow the rest of the dead crew soon enough.

The adjutant was lying on the buckled metal of the floor of the cabin, still strapped into the acceleration chair that had so singularly failed to protect him. He lay there, crushed between the floor and the crumbled remains of a bulkhead wall that had collapsed in a collision with some obstacle on the shuttle's ploughing course through the rubble.

He was still alive, the inside of his faceplate splattered with coughed-up blood from his crushed lungs. He was making feeble struggling movements, emitting sounds of piteous gratitude as the figure of his commander bent down over him. The survivor could barely contain his contempt for the man; the pitiful fool actually thought he was trying to help him!

The pathetic sounds of gratitude soon changed to noises of shock as the dying man quickly divined the survivor's real purpose. Hands expertly searched the pouches and pockets of the man's chem-suit, stripping him of anything that might be useful to his commander's continued survival. Digi-maps, valuable bars of barter metals, a suit patch kit, ration packs, las-weapon power mags, a wideband communicator, it all went into the survivor's own equipment pouches to join the treasures he had already stripped from the corpses of the bodyguards. Best of all was the man's personal sidearm; a Nevsky-model Nort las-revolver, which the survivor had long ago noticed as being irritatingly superior to his own sidearm.

Satisfied with his haul, the survivor clambered out of the shuttle through a wide gash in the hull, casually ignoring the increasingly feeble sounds of distress from the cabin behind him. Stepping away from the wrecked ship and dismissing the whole crash event from his mind, he activated his helmet systems, scanning the surrounding area for any signs of immediate threat.

He knew he had come down somewhere in Nordstadt, and was familiar with the reputation of the place as a killing zone without equal in the whole of Nu Earth, but even this wasn't enough to cause him any undue concern. He had survived everything else and he was supremely confident in his ability to survive here too. Not just to survive, but–

He winced, a bolt of pain shooting through the raw-fleshed, flame-transformed mask that was all that remained of his face. His suit's med-systems registered the fact and administered the required dosage of medication into his bloodstream. It was enough to dull the pain, but never fully vanquishing it, in keeping with the preset instructions he had fed into the med-applicator unit. The pain of his wounds, the bitterness of the memory of how he had come to lose his face and his hatred of the creature that had caused those wounds, was what gave him the vital edge that had allowed him to survive for so long. Once, he had held real power and position, but now he was little more than a scarred, hunted freak. A wounded animal, fleeing from one bolt-hole to another, pursued by–

There was a warning bleep from his suit systems. He looked up at the scene in front of him, through the infrared vista projected onto the inside of his helmet visor.

He saw them moving forward through the rubble, maybe two dozen or so of them, with presumably a similar number closing in out of sight from behind.

He had been instinctively reaching for his sidearm, but now he relaxed, recognising his would-be attackers for what they were.

Scavengers. Filthy rabble scum, looking to strip the wreck and its occupants, living and dead, of everything they could.

He smiled and raised his hands in the air. This was going to be far easier than he would ever have dared hope.

SIX

"How many shuttle drops you think there's been in the last week?"

"Sarge?"

They were sitting outside the entrance to the company HQ oxy-dome, her and Ludlow, resting and enjoying the sensation of not being shot at. Hanna was staring up into the sky, watching the blazing contrails of the transport and supply shuttles lifting off and landing at the main Souther defence zone twenty kilometres away across the city.

Mortjik and Singh had been handed over to the medics. Mortjik would be back on his feet in a few days time, she had been told, but Singh had already been shipped out by company hopper to the main defence zone, and would probably be on one of those shuttles later today or tomorrow, on his way out of Nordstadt for further med-treatment. His wound would be evaluated and he would either be invalided out of military or, if possible, fitted with a prosthetic arm and redeployed back into frontline service, although probably not Nordstadt. Either way, Hanna didn't think they'd be seeing him again anytime soon.

She pointed up at the contrails. "The shuttle drops. Is it my imagination, or have there been less of them every day for the last week or so?"

Ludlow looked and then shrugged noncommittally. "Couldn't really say, sarge. Everyone knows about General Ghazeleh's tank boys pushing in from the south to open up the land road again and us getting ready to break out and link up with them. If we're gonna do that, then we're gonna need more shuttle drops, not less. Maybe they're shipping the fresh meat in through another safety zone, the one in the north-west quad, maybe."

"Maybe," said Hanna, thinking the exact opposite. If there were extra reinforcements coming into the "Stadt", then they sure as hell weren't seeing any of them here. The company CO had just told her he had no replacements coming through from Regimental HQ to plug the gaps left by the week's toll of casualties. Castle's and Aldubi's squads had taken a heavy beating in a serious firefight with at least half a company's worth of Norts three days ago and, to try and bring the rest of his squads back up to strength, he was collapsing the remains of those two units into the others. Hanna's squad was to get Harlech and Marcos who were both fairly well experienced veterans, but that still left her squad three troopers short after this morning's action. The other squads in the company were similarly running under strength.

She looked up into the sky again, counting contrails; she was sure that there were supposed to be more than she had been seeing. Her gaze went higher into the darkness of falling night, into the heavens above Nu Earth where the generals were, secure in their command satellites, and where orbiting observation posts looked down on everything, sending details of the war's progress back to the strategists at Milli-com. All she could do was hope that someone up there knew what they were doing.

"Roger, Super Six-Two, you are cleared for take-off."

Halmada hit the ignition on his shuttle's belly thrusters, lifting it off the deck of the underground hanger and sending it floating effortlessly up the wide tunnel shaft, even before the heavy blast doors overhead had finished rumbling open. It was the kind of manoeuvre he had performed countless thousands of times in his life: first as a freelance commercial shuttle pilot working the asteroid mining operations in some of the outer systems, and later, after he was mandatorily drafted in response to the war effort's acute need for experienced aircrew, doing it here on Nu Earth as a pilot for the Souther military.

He had two sons and a son-in-law in the service with him. Juan, his eldest, had followed in his father's footsteps and was now serving on the spacer crew of the big interstellar armed transports, thank God as he was generally well out of danger. His son-in-law was an artillery officer right here on Nu Earth, but it was the youngest boy, Philippe, whom Halmada worried about the most. He was an infantryman fighting on one of the war worlds in the Karthage system, eighty light years from Nu Earth. Juan had been told by a spacer colleague who had just come back from that sector that the fighting was heavy there, and none of them had heard from Philippe in over three months. Every time Halmada took off in a shuttle like this, with the cargo compartment behind him full of the broken and bleeding bodies of soldiers seriously injured in battle and being evacuated up to an orbital med-base, he thought of his younger son. He and wondered if somewhere on that other war front, he might be lying there wounded, maybe even dying, on the deck of a shuttle just like this one.

They were out of the shaft now, accelerating rapidly up into the sky before the Nort long-range artillery gunners could draw a bead on them. The ride up into orbit at this speed would be rough on the injured men behind him, but the alternative was to cut speed and increase all their chances of being blown out of the sky by Nort anti-aircraft missiles or any prowling fighters that might be up here waiting for them.

Normally, after the injured had been unloaded, he and his three-man flight crew would rest for six hours and then do the whole thing again, loading up with troop reinforcements, supplies or ordnance, or sometimes all three at once. They would then fly back down to Nordstadt to deliver their cargo and pick up more wounded for delivery back up into orbit.

Back and forth, between Nordstadt and the orbital bases. Flying an average of three times a day in and out of the worst combat zone on Nu Earth, with only one day in ten off for some much needed rest and relaxation, and sometimes not even then. You'd have to be insane to calculate the long-term survival odds of the situation, and the picture-covered wall of remembrance in the aircrew mess, plastered with photographs of all their dead or missing comrades, showed just how lethal those odds truly were. Still, day in day out, Halmada and his crew kept on at it, knowing that, until General Ghazeleh's armoured divisions could make the crucial breakthrough past the ring of Nort ground forces around Nordstadt, these shuttle flights were the only link between the outside world and the Souther forces cornered inside the besieged city.

Except even this final link seemed to be slipping for reasons Halmada and his comrades didn't understand. They were flying only twice a day now, and carrying a lot less troops and supplies down each time. Hell, a couple of times this week, they had even flown down with their holds completely empty.

Troop reinforcements. Ammunition. Food and med supplies. These things were the lifeblood of the Souther army in Nordstadt and these were the things it was now secretly being apparently starved of. All of the aircrews realised this and none of them were happy about it, but the hanger decks of the orbital bases were swarming with armed, grim-faced military policemen and, far more significantly, nameless, ever-watchful officers whose uniforms bore no unit or divisional insignia. The shuttle crews knew when to keep their thoughts to themselves. There didn't have to be any insignia on those uniforms for anyone to know those wearing them belonged to S-Three, the Souther military's secretive and much-feared intelligence and covert ops service.

There was a black bag operation in motion. A state of permanent martial law had been declared years ago for all personnel serving in the Nu Earth theatre of military operations, and summary executions weren't unknown. Halmada and the others knew enough to just carry out the orders they were given, fly their shuttles and not ask any questions. Which was exactly what the spooks from S-Three wanted.

They were at the atmospheric envelope now, the point where Nu Earth ended and the blackness of true space began. Nordstadt and its attendant horrors were far below them, lost beneath the impenetrable murk of the chem-cloud cover. Halmada thought of his son Philippe, maybe fighting in a hellhole just like the one down there, and then he thought of all the other tens of thousands of Souther troops trapped in Nordstadt. He prayed that the generals who consigned them all to fight and die in these places knew what they were doing.

General Fyalla Ghazeleh raised his binox and watched the entire might of his three divisions' mobile artillery batteries fall on the Nort positions. Giant plasma-bomb shells exploded like starbursts, turning night to day and incinerating everything within a three hundred metre radius of their point of impact. Howitzer-launched seeker missiles buzzed angrily through the air, searching out Nort tanks dug in hull deep into carefully prepared defensive positions. Waves of incendiary shells turned lines of trenchworks into rivers of fire, while volley after volley of high-explosive rockets blew apart bunkers and hard shelter blockhouses.

Ghazeleh was a general of the old school. "Blood and Guts Ghazeleh" they called him at Milli-com, while his own troops took pride in being led by the man they had nicknamed "Fighting Fyalla". Ghazeleh was happy to lay claim to either title. Yes, he pushed his boys hard – and girls, he reminded himself, although the idea of sending women into combat had never rested easy in the mind of this particular old warhorse – but they went into battle knowing their commander would never willingly throw their lives away for nothing.

If only other Souther commanders thought as he did, he angrily thought to himself. Especially those vainglorious jackasses at Milli-com.

"Beg your pardon, sir?"

It was the voice of his executive officer Colonel Garr, standing beside him on the hull of his command tank. With a start, Ghazeleh realised he must have said that last thought aloud in his trademark blunt growl.

He chose to ignore the man for a moment, preferring to concentrate on the far more pleasing spectacle taking place in the view through the imaging sights of his binox. The Norts had pulled back to their prepared defensive positions almost on the edge of the horizon, but that wouldn't save the slimy bastards from one final pasting courtesy of old Blood and Guts Ghazeleh. Normally, the spectacle of Norts dying by the hundreds would be more than enough to warm the old veteran Nu Earth warrior's heart, but tonight it wasn't even enough to take the edge off the cold, bitter anger that now filled him.

"Beg your pardon, sir," continued the executive officer, "but how long do you intend to keep the bombardment going?"

Ghazeleh lowered the binox, favouring the man with the kind of contemptuous glance that was another Blood and Guts Ghazeleh trademark.

"Until we've not got one bastard shell or rocket left to fire," he growled. "We've hauled the whole bastard lot of it this far with us, so we might as well let the Norts have it all before we turn tail and run back in the direction we came from."

The orders had come through from Milli-com an hour ago. Executive command priority: Abandon advance immediately. Break off all contact with the enemy and fall back to rejoin main Souther front line at original start-up position.

Just thinking about the meaning behind this sudden communiqué only further fed Ghazeleh's anger. His original orders were to forge a path through the territory the Norts had retaken in their last offensive and break the enemy's grip around Nordstadt, relieving the besieged Souther forces currently trapped there. It had been a daunting order, some might have said near impossible, but achieving the near impossible had been a career speciality for Fighting Fyalla, and now his armoured columns stood within fifty kilometres of the outskirts of Nordstadt. The Norts were mobilising reinforcements to resecure their weakening stranglehold round the city, but one final lightning push now, Ghazeleh was convinced, would be enough to smash through and link up with the encircled Souther army in Nordstadt.

Now, as far as Ghazeleh was concerned, the communiqué he had received from Milli-com was nothing less than an execution order served on every Souther soldier still fighting in the city.

The executive officer beside him shifted uneasily and nervously cleared his throat. Ghazeleh had known for months that the man was an S-Three undercover operative, no doubt put in place to report on the latest heretical utterances of the politically suspect old veteran. He imagined tonight would give the little toad enough material to open up a whole new dossier on him.

"Beg pardon again, sir, but our orders from Milli-com were quite explicit. We are to break off contact with the enemy immediately and withdraw back to the main lines."

Ghazeleh didn't lower his binox as he replied, trying hard to keep his legendary temper under control. "I read them too, colonel. But tell me, why are we here? What is the purpose of everything we're doing?"

"Sir?"

The man's tone was half-puzzled, half-humouring. He probably thinks I'm starting to go senile too, thought Ghazeleh. Another exciting new chapter to be added into that dossier of his.

"Why are we fighting this war, man?" This time Ghazeleh didn't try to hide the anger and impatience in his voice.

The man's answer was textbook perfect, straight out of the lecture halls of the military academies on the main Souther homeworlds.

"Sir, to defeat the enemy and drive them off the surface of Nu Earth. If we control Nu Earth, then we control the interstellar transit routes through this system's black hole warp gate. By possessing those routes and denying their use to the enemy, we will have gained an immeasurably significant advantage over the enemy elsewhere throughout the galaxy."

"Exactly, colonel. We're here to beat the crap out of the Norts and the best way I know how to do that is by killing as many of the bastards as I can, while making sure they don't do the same thing back in return. Trust me, colonel, when I tell you that in almost twenty years of fighting this bastard war on this bastard planet, I've discovered that doing the best thing possible to win this war and following explicit orders from those stupid pricks in Milli-com aren't necessarily the same thing."

The executive officer blanched and hastily withdrew. Probably memorising every word of what I just said, thought Ghazeleh, so he can get it all down word-perfect in the report he's going to write on me tonight.

"Keep firing," he told his artillery officers. "If we have to withdraw, then I want the Norts to at least get a taste of what would have happened to them if Fighting Fyalla and his boys had been able to stick around to give them a proper fight."

The artillerymen grinned in pleasure at their general's words and hurried off to make sure his orders were carried out. Ghazeleh refocused the settings on his binox, zooming in past the artillery bombardment still raining down on the Nort positions and instead looking beyond towards the darkness behind the Nort positions. He could see the dim glow of it just over the edge of the horizon, highlighted intermittently by the flashes of artillery duels probably just as fearsome as this one. The darkness of the sky above it was broken by flickering lines of light from anti-aircraft and rocket batteries.

It was Nordstadt, the glow of the battles going on there clearly visible to the naked eye, and it was only fifty kilometres away.

He lowered the binox and mumbled a silent prayer to himself. If he couldn't do anything to help the poor bastards trapped there, he prayed to the merciful god of his desert nomad ancestors that there was still someone else out there who could.

SEVEN

He didn't have a name – not really. His designation, the serial code that marked him as just another piece of military hardware and was branded even into his cellular structure, was Bio-Subject GI 3627218/R2. That had been his given name even before he had emerged as an infant clone from the gene genies' flesh tanks. It had been the only name he had been allowed to answer to in those first formative years in the testing labs and barrack levels of Milli-com where he and his clone-brothers began the process of being forged into living weapons.

And it was there, formed up into four-man fire teams under the watchful supervision of overseers who were part military training instructors and part prison guards, that he and his clone-brothers began to give themselves names of their own.

As clones, they were supposed to be indistinguishable from each other. Physically, that remained true. They all had the same weirdly unnatural blue skin tone that was a factor of the natural immunity their genetically-enhanced systems equipped them with to combat the toxic environmental conditions they would encounter on Nu Earth. They all had the same, harsh war-mask facial features and they all had the same blank, pupil-less eyes that allowed them to see through dense banks of chem-mist and which so unnerved many of the ordinary human personnel they came into contact with during their years of training.

It was psychologically, however, that they differed from each other.

It was a development their creators hadn't foreseen, but in training it quickly became apparent that no two of their creations were as exactly alike as had been expected. Some showed distinct personality quirks while others showed a marked aptitude for certain specialist skills and abilities.

Their overseers picked up on this and to amuse themselves, started assigning pet names to some of their charges in the same way hunters would give names to particular favourites amongst a pack of hunting dogs. The Genetic Infantrymen, with an attitude of perverse pride, claimed these joke names for themselves, turning the insult against their custodians.

Names and specific personalities began to develop. Sniper sharpshooters received names like Deadeye, Gunnar, Triggerman and Topgun. Stealth & Infiltration specialists were Pointman, Silencer and Shadow, while demolitions experts became Boomer, Fuseman and Cracker.

There were other names too which were more appropriate to personalities: Eightball, Hardball, Strike, Mainman and Topper.

And Rogue. Above all, there was the one they had quickly come to call Rogue.

He had been one of the first to rise to prominence amongst the GI Regiment trainees, swiftly establishing himself as a natural leader, a soldier to whom the other GIs instinctively deferred. He would have been a natural choice for fire team leader if it hadn't been for the instinctive renegade streak that ran through him, warring constantly with the obedience programming that was coded into his DNA.

It was the overseers who gave him his name and he had done everything possible to live up to it, sending one of his instructors to a two-week stay in med-bay after a dispute on the firing ranges. The penalty for such an offence was literal recycling back into the gene genies' flesh tanks, but the commanding officers in charge of the GI Regiment had made an exception in Rogue's case. Their task had been to create and train a cadre of living weapons and GI 3627218/R2 was a living weapon without equal, even in an entire thousand-strong regiment of such weapons.

The rest of the legend would come later. The Quartz Zone Massacre and the destruction of the entire GI Regiment during their first real baptism of fire. The against-all-odds survival of one sole GI and his quest to find the man who had betrayed them all. His roaming mission across the surface of Nu Earth, searching for the elusive, so-called Traitor General.

It was a legend known to every Souther soldier on Nu Earth whether they believed in it or not. The legend of the solitary, superhuman figure of vengeance who roamed no-man's-land, accompanied by the dead voices of his comrades.

It was the legend of the Rogue Trooper, the last of the Genetic Infantrymen.

EIGHT

Rogue dived for cover, acting on the verbal warning from Helm. A second later, high-velocity lines of las-fire stitched fiery patterns into the ground where he had been crouching. It had taken him more than three hours to cover barely four hundred metres of war-torn terrain, ghosting past a series of hidden detector drones and underground robot sentry posts on the way. He had got far on luck and stealth, but he must have triggered some other hidden auto-guard device that neither his own enhanced senses or Helm's scanner systems had detected in time.

Stealth and intuition might have got him this far, but now it was time to bring his other abilities into play.

"Bagman."

It was a statement, not a question, because he knew Bagman would already be waiting for the cue. Bagman, who was always there to watch his back in the old four-man fire team unit they had been part of, and who was still there now, his personality-encoded biochip slotted into place in the armour-cased equipment pack Rogue wore on his back.

"Got you covered, Rogue," buzzed the voice of his dead comrade from the biochip's speech modulator.

A series of small, flat disc objects flew out from an ejection port just over Rogue's shoulder. Micro mines.

They spread out in a wide arc, detonating in close sequence as soon as they struck the ground and creating a deadly barrier of flame and shrapnel in a crescent shape twenty metres in front of Rogue's position. The limited blast waves and the flying shrapnel would do little to damage the robot sentry guns, but the explosions would be enough to confuse their electronic senses for a few moments and a few moments was all Rogue needed.

"Helm?"

The biochip in his helmet slot was linked into the helmet's compact, but powerful comms and scanner systems had already tracked the necessary target information. In life, Helm had been the team's pointman. In death, or its equivalent in the strange electronic limbo state of a living personality surviving as a memory code recorded onto biochip circuitry, he still fulfilled the same role for Rogue and his other two fire team comrades.

"Target one at ten o'clock, thirty-one metres distant. Target two at three o'clock. Picking up two more of the sentry guns we passed on the way in, now coming online behind us."

"Gunnar?"

The rifle weapon in Rogue's hand loaded with the biochip of the fourth member of the original GI fire team, was waiting for his cue.

"RPG shell in the pipe and ready to go, Rogue."

"And I've got your back," confirmed Bagman, as Rogue heard the whine of his backpack's servo-arm mechanism being activated.

Rogue fired the RPG attachment slung underneath his rifle's main las-barrel, confident that Bagman would take care of the danger behind them. The missile shot away, unerringly finding its target. The closest sentry gun position disappeared in the incandescent flash of a gamma bomb explosion.

Moments later, the sound of the detonation was echoed by a similar blast from somewhere behind him, as the plasma sphere grenade Bagman had hurled out took care of one of the targets. True to his word, Bagman was watching Rogue's back. That was how he had died, during the nightmare of the Quartz Zone Massacre, taking the impact of a lethal blast aimed at Rogue. Even as a memory recording stored on a biochip board, Bagman was still there to watch his clone-brother's back.

Rogue was up and running, on the move, defying the two remaining sentry guns' ability to track and kill him.

Designed specifically for Nu Earth combat conditions, the sentry guns' targeting programmes were set to detect and zero in on slow-moving, human targets wearing the bulky, cumbersome armoured chem-suits standard to all Souther front-line infantry. A Genetic Infantryman target, fast moving, unencumbered by any kind of chem-suit protection, his speed and reflexes boosted to para-human levels, was a different proposition entirely.

The sentry guns' twin lascannons chattered loudly, filling the air all around Rogue with noise and the hissing passage of volleys of las-bolts. Their aim was textbook precise, achieving everything their programming parametres demanded, but the blasts of las-fire struck the space where their scanner senses told them their target should have been split-seconds after Rogue had vacated it.

Their target gave them no time to correct their programmers' mistake. He jumped, twisting in midair, firing another rifle-launched missile into the chem-murk behind him, blowing apart a sentry gun. Even before he had hit the ground again, his enhanced GI reflexes and instincts were already going to work on zeroing in on the position of what was now the last remaining enemy target.

He hit the ground, the plasti-flesh material of his skin protecting him from the jagged shards of half-buried shrapnel and rusting war debris that would have spelled instant death to anyone wearing a chem-suit. Las-fire from the sentry gun tore up the ground behind him, tracking remorselessly back to where he now lay. It would be on him in moments and then the benefits of even his toughened GI skin would make little difference. The concentrated fire from the sentry gun's weapon would tear him apart just as it would for any other flesh-and-blood target.

"Zeroed in, Rogue," confirmed the voice of Gunnar as Rogue took aim with the rifle. "Fire capacity now set to max."

In life, Gunnar had been the squad marksman and he was still able to put his skills to good use, figuring out the required range and most effective firepower setting even before Rogue raised the sight scope to his eye.

Alone, his marksmanship skills were lethal. Working in tandem with Rogue's, they were straightforwardly devastating. The GI rifle chattered in Rogue's hands, spent power cartridges flying from its ejection port as it cycled through the magazine clip at a terrifying rate. On its own, one las-round from the weapon would make little impact on the sentry gun unit's armoured housing. Fired together, at a rate of several hundred a minute, their combined effect would be more than enough to get the job done.

Multiple las-rounds smashed like hammer-blows into the sentry unit's rotating turret top, melting and cracking its armour. One drilled through to the unit's sensor core, instantly rendering the weapon blind. Two more struck its power feed, severing it. Robbed of power, the chattering of the sentry gun's rapid-fire auto-las weapon instantly cut out. A moment later, the whole unit exploded as its damaged power core fractured apart.

Satisfied that the threat from the sentry guns was over, Rogue was already up and moving even before the last burning pieces of the destroyed auto-defence unit had struck the ground. He could see his objective buried in the ground ahead of him. To the untrained eye, or the spy-cams of any roving Souther reconnaissance craft or orbiting surveillance satellite, it looked innocuous enough; just another debris heap or mound of shellfire-scooped rubble in a typically Nu Earth battle-scarred scene strewn with such landmarks. It was Helm's sensors that had first picked up the whispering traces of voices in the ether which had eventually led them here, and it was Rogue's combat intuition and enhanced, eerily inhuman GI eyes that had finally picked the object out from amongst the surrounding terrain.

It was a Nort comms-post, camouflaged to blend in almost perfectly with the battlefield environment around it. The airwaves of Nu Earth were filled with radio traffic, much of it deliberately designed to jam out the enemy's own communications transmissions. Add in the interference from the many high-level radiation zones that blighted large areas of the planet's surface and the communications-scrambling effects of the violent storms that constantly raged across one part or another of its upper atmosphere, reliable long-range communications soon became a problem for both sides, even with all the hi-tech means at their disposal.

There were thousands of these comms-stations dotted everywhere across the surface of the planet, gathering in the faint ghost-whispers of damaged communications signals, filtering out the worst of the interference affecting them and then boosting them on towards their intended final destination. Any one of Rogue's endless journeys across the no-man's-land wastes of Nu Earth normally brought him within the telltale electronic footprint of at least one enemy comms-station, but as a rule he generally passed up on the opportunity of hunting down and destroying them. They were low-priority targets in the one-man mission that had taken him from one end of Nu Earth to the other and, as he suspected he was just about to find out, any attempts to attack one carried certain inherent dangers all of its own.

The sensitive comms equipment inside and the crew manning it were protected from the inhospitable exterior environment by a dome-seal; a las-shielded pressurised bubble which offered an atmospheric safe haven, allowing the men inside to work unencumbered by the need for chem-suits. An RPG launched gamma missile would still be enough to blow the dome open, instantly killing everyone inside from the effects of exposure to the lethal Nu Earth atmosphere, but for reasons of his own, Rogue needed to capture the comms-station's facilities intact.

"Dispensing seal-burster, Rogue."

"Read my mind, Bagman," said Rogue, taking the compact missile-like device and slotting in onto the firing attachment at the front of his rifle.

They would now be panicking inside the dome, he knew. Alerted by Rogue's triggering of the auto-defences, they would be scrambling into chem-suits and grabbing weapons and ammo packs.

"Picking up a mayday call, Rogue. The bad news is, they definitely know who's out here knocking at the door," warned Helm.

"Stak! Nain! Genetik Infantryman!" sniggered Gunnar, putting on a stereotypical Nort accent straight out of the very worst kind of Souther propaganda war-viddies.

"Doesn't matter who they try to call for help," growled Rogue, raising and firing his rifle. "By the time anyone gets here, these slugs are going to be history."

The seal-burster shell blasted through the skin of the dome, opening a catastrophic breach in its carefully maintained pressurised environment. Clean, immeasurably precious air rushed out, the lethal toxins and pathogens of Nu Earth's atmosphere seeped in.

By the time Rogue stormed in through the airlock a few seconds later, just about everyone inside the dome was dead. Their corpses lay on the floor in the familiar positions of agonised contortion caused by exposure to the raw poison of Nu Earth's atmosphere.

One of the Norts had been arguably fortunate enough to get his chem-suit on and sealed up in time. He flayed towards Rogue, screaming incoherently in his native tongue, managing to snap off one panicked and poorly-aimed shot with the officer's pistol in his hand.

One shot was all he got. A carefully aimed double blast from Gunnar took him square in the chest and blew him backwards away from the comms equipment. His corpse sprawled on the floor alongside those of his comrades.

Rogue took off his helmet and laid it on the workspace beside one of the comms array units.

"Clock's ticking, Helm. Do your thing and let's get out of here before someone shows up in answer to that mayday call."

NINE

They were in and out of the comms-station in less than two minutes. Another few minutes' of fast cross-terrain movement at GI speed brought them to the half-buried wreck of a giant artillery tractor that they had already selected on their journey in as a good emergency fall back position. It was a few minutes after that they heard the sounds of the airstrike as a flight of Nort atmocraft gunships wiped the comms station off the face of the earth. Afterwards, when the smoke and heat of the incendiary charges had cleared, a group of Nort hoppers came in and dropped two full platoons of troops into the area. Rogue watched for a few minutes as they nervously spread out their search as the hoppers hovered overhead, circling in a wide concentric pattern and scanning the jumbled terrain below with searchlights and gun targeters.

Rogue knew that the Norts had a whole wing of their military intelligence division dedicated to hunting him down and destroying him. As soon as the men in the comms-station had identified him and got their mayday out, Rogue knew from past experience that the Norts' response would be swift and brutal. That was why he had to get out of there as soon as possible.

To the men fighting in the Souther armies, he was mostly a myth, the Nu Earth legend of a soldier who not only survived but thrived on the poisoned battlefields, the trooper who had gone renegade to find and kill the traitor responsible for the deaths of his comrades. Many of them doubted his existence, an idea that the Souther military police, the so-called and much detested "Milli-fuzz" were keen to encourage, while at the same time actively hunting for Rogue themselves, desperate to finally get their hands on a soldier who had long ago been classified as a renegade and deserter. To those Souther troops who had encountered him, he must have still seemed fantastical; an eerie, ghostly figure who emerged from out of the chem-mists to give them much-needed support against a Nort ambush or assault. And then, as soon as the battle was over, disappeared back into the mists as mysteriously as he had first appeared.

To the Norts, though, he was something else. A figure of terror and superstition. An inhuman, seemingly indestructible gene-freak creature who prowled the battlefields of Nu Earth, killing Norts wherever he went. Rogue had heard some of the rumours whispered about him in the Nort trenches: about how he drank the blood of his victims, how the very gaze of those blank, inhuman eyes of his could kill, how the Souther genetic scientists had designed their abomination creations to survive by feeding on the flesh of corpses left on the battlefield.

Monster. Renegade. Ghost. Gene-freak. Deserter. Nu Earth urban legend. No one ever said life would be easy as a genetically engineered super-soldier.

Rogue scanned the shape of the closest hopper craft through his rifle's telescopic sights, his expert marksman's eye easily picking out its most vulnerable target points. The pilot's head was clearly visible through the glass of the cockpit. The power feeds to the side-mounted anti-grav thrusters. That under-armoured maintenance hatch in its underbelly, giving him a clear shot straight through into the craft's power core.

The hopper skimmed closer, maintaining a level twenty metres above the ground. Rogue kept it fixed in his sights, waiting for any sign that the Norts aboard had detected his hiding place. Confident that, if need be, he could down it with one well-aimed burst of shots.

The hopper retreated off to the left, moving to rejoin the other craft in the main search area a kilometre away in another section of the battlefield. Satisfied at last that they weren't going to be found, Rogue relaxed and left Gunnar perched in the hatchway of the upended tractor vehicle's driving cab compartment as he slid back down to rejoin Helm and Bagman in the rear cargo hold.

"Okay, Helm. What you got?" he asked, pushing aside the virus-eaten, skeletal remains of one of the vehicle's original crew.

They had picked up the first traces of the radio transmission half a day ago. Helm's comms systems routinely picked up hundreds of such ghost signals every day, and he just as routinely blocked most of them out, bringing to Rogue's attention only those that were of any tactical significance to their immediate situation. This one, however, had been different.

For starters, it had come in on an obscure Souther military command frequency that hadn't been used officially in years. It was the frequency reserved for use in communications between Milli-com and the now dead and destroyed Genetic Infantryman Regiment. Secondly, it had contained enough of the correct GI code signals for Rogue and the others not to automatically dismiss it as bait for another Nort trap. Over the years, the Norts had used various bogus radio signals to try and lure them into carefully prepared ambushes and Rogue and his comrades were well used to such tricks.

This didn't seem to be the case here, however. The signal was badly distorted and heavily code-scrambled and Helm's processors only had limited success in cleaning it up. One word of what little he had been able to make out had still been enough to persuade them to break off from their current route and take a dangerous detour towards the nearest comms-station that Helm's sensors could detect.

Buzzard.

Just one word, but to Rogue and the others, it had all the impact of the dry, deadly crack of a sniper shot.

Now Rogue listened in quiet anticipation as the transmission, cleaned up and filtered through the more powerful equipment they had found in the comms-station, played back through the speech unit of Helm's biochip.

"Guardian Angel to Blueboy, this is Guardian Angel looking to return a solid blue favour to a friend out there on
rogue mission walkabout. Have possible fix on Buzzard for
you, Blueboy. Buzzard's wings are clipped and he may be
on the ground and looking for a new nest. Buzzard's last
known location at the following coordinates..."

"You hear that voice, Rogue?" broke in Bagman, excitedly.
"And she's calling herself Guardian Angel! You thinking
what I'm thinking?"

Rogue chose his next words carefully. Bagman's biochip
had been damaged in a firefight several years ago. Ever
since then, Bagman's personality matrix had been erratic, to
say the least. Still, Bagman was a brother GI who had died
saving Rogue's life and Rogue never allowed himself to forget that fact.

"I hear it too, Bagman. It's the voice of that GI Doll, the
one we helped out back in the Volg Wastes."

It had been over a year ago. They had gone to the aid of
a downed Souther fighter pilot who was on her own against
an entire Nort patrol platoon. Rogue had helped even the
odds against her, although from what he had seen, she had
been more than capable of looking after herself. They had
never met face-to-face, communicating only by radio as
Rogue gave her the covering fire she needed to dig herself
out of trouble. Rogue had vanished back into the mists as
soon as he knew she was safe and that her rescue pick-up
was on the way, but she was a fellow GI and she must have
realised her mystery ally's identity.

And now here she was all this time later, calling herself
his guardian angel and returning the debt of gratitude from
that day in the Volg Wastes.

"Buzzard? You think it's really him?" asked Helm.

Buzzard was the codename of the man they only knew as
the Traitor General, the Nort double agent who had been
responsible for the destruction of the GI Regiment at the
Quartz Zone Massacre. They had tracked him down to
being one of the generals among the staff of an orbiting
Souther command satellite called Buzzard-Three, but he
had escaped and suffered serious burns in the process.

Since then, they had hunted him all over the face of Nu Earth, following up every rumour of his survival, pursuing him from one bolt-hole to another, flushing him out of hiding each time, only to see him slip away out of their grasp yet again. His cover amongst the senior levels of the Souther military had been blown after the destruction of Buzzard-Three and the reported deaths of all aboard it, but in the chaos of the war on Nu Earth, it had been easy for him to find other places to hide, and other identities to hide behind.

The last time they had encountered him, he had been posing as a brutal interrogator called Buzzard in a Nort prisoner of war camp. He had escaped from them there too, and after that they had lost the trail, becoming involved in some of the larger events of the war around them.

But now they had picked up the scent again, and the hunt was maybe on once more. Assuming, Rogue reminded himself, that the information they'd received was genuine.

"She's Genetic Infantry. Solid blue," he said in response to Helm's question. "If there's no one else we can trust, at least we can still trust our own. GIs don't lie to other GIs."

Solid blue. It was the phrase the GIs had always used strictly among themselves, first in the years of harsh training in Milli-com and then during the nightmare carnage of the Quartz Zone Massacre. "Blue-skinned freak" was the most common epithet used against them by their instructor-guards, but the close brotherhood of GIs had typically turned the insult on its head, adopting the intended slur as a badge of pride.

Solid blue. The ultimate guarantee of loyalty from one GI to another. Rogue might have suspected that the message was a trap cleverly laid by the Norts or even the Souther Milli-fuzz, but as soon as he heard those words, he knew it was genuine.

"Bagman, dispense digi-map. Let's see where those coordinates we've just been given–"

"Already there," interrupted Helm. "It's Nordstadt, Rogue. If that info's right, then the Traitor General's gone to ground right in the middle of the biggest clusterfrag on the planet."

Rogue digested the information. Nordstadt was over two thousand kilometres away from their present position, with half a continent and several of the very worst battle sectors on Nu Earth between them and it. To get there would be near impossible. To do it alone and on foot would have to be thought of as certain suicide.

Rogue picked up Helm and hefted Bagman onto his back, scrambling back up the slope of the floor of the tractor wreck to retrieve Gunnar.

"C'mon, guys. Let's go hunt a traitor."

Rafe made her way out of the squadron's comms room, Gabe floating ahead of her and acting as lookout. He had downloaded his personality matrix into a smaller, portable drone-shell from its hardware base aboard her Seraphim fighter, which was now safely parked in a hardened shelter craft bay below ground. His drone body, a small floating orb, looked hardly any different from any of the other kinds of messenger and security drones that were a common sight on any Souther military base, and would hardly have merited a second glance from anyone still about at this hour.

It was just about night cycle now on the base, when the sun went down on this side of Nu Earth and the black hole that was the main objective of the entire war hung high in the night sky, casting its eerie black glow down on the ravaged face of the planet below. No one seemed to know how the superstition had started, but for years Nu Earth combat pilots thought the black hole symbolised bad luck, and when it filled the sky on nights like this, as few night flight missions as possible were conducted. "Black sun rising", they called it, and the tradition seemed to be one observed on the Nort side as well. No one flew a mission if they could help it on nights like this, and so most of the base was locked down and its personnel enjoyed a rare twelve hours of very welcome rest and relaxation.

Rafe, however, had more important things to do than try to join in the drinking, gambling and bull sessions now going on in the pilots' mess.

She had gone looking for Burke, the squadron's signals-man, two hours ago. It hadn't been difficult to find him. He was in the main mess bar, where he usually was when he was off-duty, and it hadn't been difficult to bring him round to her way of thinking. Like everyone else, he would have heard the barracks room jokes and whispers about what special abilities the GI Dolls were supposed to have been trained experts in. He was back in his bunkroom, uncon-scious from the effects of a potent mixture of alcohol and pills. Rafe had matched him drink for drink in the mess and back in his room when she had produced the bottles of sedative-laced scotch. However, when your enhanced GI constitution allowed you to gargle cyanide and breathe in the most lethal viral agents without any ill-effects, it would take more than two-and-a-half bottles of scotch and a gen-erous handful of med-kit sedatives to put you out of action.

When he woke up tomorrow, Burke would have the king of hangovers. Rafe doubted that he would actually be able to remember anything about what happened – not that any-thing had, she reminded herself, or not the kind of action Burke had been hoping for – but no doubt his overactive imagination and the need to boast to his buddies would do the rest, and her reputation around the base would plum-met even further. The elite combat pilots traditionally didn't fraternise socially with the enlisted personnel, never mind go back to their private quarters with them and engage in whatever unlikely feats of sexual gymnastics that Burke's imagination would later conjure up.

Rafe didn't care. She had got everything she had wanted from the creep after plying him with booze and pills and the once-in-a-lifetime thrilling prospect of bedding a real, live GI Doll. He had told her everything she wanted to know: the entry code to the comms room and the day's signals password. His security passcard to log in and activate the equipment she took from his pocket after he had finally slumped down unconscious onto the bed.

Once they were in there, Gabe had done the rest, con-necting into the comms equipment, negotiating his way through the levels of security buffers to access the higher bands of command-reserved communications frequencies. He had found the one they were looking for, one of the long, unused GI Regiment comms channels and used it to send out Rafe's prerecorded message. The whole procedure had been necessarily hasty and clumsy. They had left enough telltale electronic fingerprints all over the comms room database files for any even halfway-rigorous security check to turn up evidence of what they had done, but they had still managed to do everything they had set out to do. The alert message to the Rogue Trooper was out there now, hidden among the mass of other Souther military traffic that was beamed out all across the planet and beyond every day. Protected by the correct code protocols that Gabe had hacked into and used to scramble-encrypt Rafe's words, the message would be authenticated as properly valid by the Souther communication network's security systems and relayed all across Nu Earth.

Using Burke's passcard, she left the restricted comms wing and re-entered the main corridor of the base's admin block. She had done everything she could. Now all she could do was pray that Rogue was still out there somewhere and able to pick up her message.

And hope that there was no one else out there listening in who might try and stop him.

TEN

Venner was getting a feel for the Rogue Trooper's thinking. Just by tracking the GI's movements from afar, he had been able to get a real sense of his target's abilities, and how he was able to put them to such deadly effective use on the battlefields of Nu Earth.

It had been almost two weeks since they had picked up the transmission. Acting on a vague hunch, he had directed the techs to maintain a watch on the old GI comms frequencies. The techs complained that those channels hadn't been used in years, but within a few days, Venner's hunch had paid off and they had intercepted a message intended for the Rogue Trooper. It was more than Venner could ever had hoped for. He didn't much care who sent it, or why. That would be the task of other, lesser servants of the Souther military intelligence machine. All he cared about was that it confirmed that his main mission target was still out there, and gave a possible fix on his location for him; everything depended on what the Rogue Trooper did next and for the last twelve days. Venner had been sifting through the reams of communiqués, field reports, combat zone despatches, intelligence reports and radio-intercept transcripts that flooded daily through S-Three's extensive comm-channels capabilities.

It was a daunting mass of information, but through experience and a hunter's intuition for the signs of his prey, Venner soon found what he was looking for.

In Bullrun Sector, a roving Souther infantry company probing forward into Nort territory found a Nort bunker complex with all the enemy troops dead or missing. One of the company scouts reported glimpsing what he reported later to be a "figure not wearing a chem-suit" walking off into the chem-mists.

Two days later, a Souther listening post intercepted an emergency signal from a Nort supply depot. The signal was garbled, comprised mainly of the voice of a panicked Nort radio operator with the jumbled sound of gunfire and explosions in the background. The voice was abruptly cut off by the sound of gunshots. Venner had heard the sound of that distinctive brand of gunfire before, in tapes in the S-Three records library. It was the sound of the unique make of rifle that had been issued only to the Genetic Infantry Regiment and, as far as Venner knew, there was only one man on Nu Earth still using that very special kind of weapon.

The techs hadn't been able to trace the source of the transmission, but the information kept on seeping in, and soon enough the course of the Rogue Trooper's journey became readily apparent.

More Nort radio intercepts and spy-sat visual data confirmed the trail of hit-and-run destruction he left in his wake as he travelled across the Nort-held terrain of Kursk, Romstein and Tannhauser Sectors. He had crossed into Souther territory three days ago in Vanguard Sector, helping to repulse a Nort armoured attack on a section of the frontline. A battalion commander attempted to arrest him as a listed deserter after the battle but was prevented from doing so by his own men. In the confusion, the Rogue Trooper disappeared as usual into the banks of chem-mist.

There were suspicions afterwards that the Rogue Trooper had crossed the Scum Sea aboard a Souther military transport, reaching the planet's main northern continent and covering almost a thousand kilometres distance in a matter of hours. A Souther atmocraft pilot was still under interrogation over the issue and had insisted he didn't know anything about the renegade stowaway his transporter had been carrying. Venner had seen the man's record and thought otherwise. The pilot had fought and been wounded in the notorious Dix-I Front campaign, where it was said that it was only the Rogue Trooper's actions in various areas of the battle-front which prevented that defeat from becoming a full-scale military disaster for the Southers.

Whatever the truth of the matter, the Rogue Trooper was confirmed as being positively sighted on Souther territory on this side of the Scum Sea yesterday when a Souther half-track patrol spotted him twenty kilometres into no-man's-land. They duly reported the sighting only after they had returned to base. Reading between the lines of their subsequent report, Venner had quickly spotted why they had been so slow in reporting the encounter; the Rogue Trooper had almost certainly saved them from a Nort lazooka squad that had been waiting out there in ambush for them.

Their unit's exasperated commander had sent more patrols out into no-man's-land to find the renegade. Predictably, of course, none of them found anything, assuming they had actually tried looking.

By this point, Venner himself was on the ground, on the Genetic Infantryman's trail. Which was what had brought him here, to the burnt-out ruin of a Nort watch station on the banks of a wide stretch of toxic, irradiated sludge that had once been a fast-flowing river a couple of kilometres in on the wrong side of the no-man's-land divide.

The men with him were uneasy, nervous at being on the ground this long in Nort-held territory. Or maybe, Venner smiled to himself, they were just afraid at being around him.

"Headcount?" he asked the young captain who had dutifully come trotting up to him with the results of his squad's search of the area.

"Twenty-seven so far, sir," the young man answered nervously. "Most of them like these ones here."

Venner looked dispassionately down at the Nort corpses lying sprawled at his feet, admiring the skill involved in their killing with the grudging respect of one professional appraising the handiwork of another.

Most of them had been killed at extremely close range, their respirator tubes severed or their chem-masks ripped off. Their deaths would have been almost instantaneous, caused by exposure to the virus-laden air around them. One had been killed by a single vibro-knife thrust through the heart. Venner doubted if any of them would even have had the time to realise who or what had killed them.

He turned round, looking at the river behind him. The Rogue Trooper could have crossed the river at far safer, less well-monitored points than this, but Venner had seen the files on GI psychology and knew the Genetic Infantryman was genetically programmed to principally do two things; take Nort lives and whenever possible save Souther ones. Venner now had proof that this programming still held true, and he filed the information away for later use. An enemy, no matter how skilful and lethal, who followed certain pre-set and predictable patterns of behaviour, was an enemy with a built-in weakness.

He studied the scene, imagining how the assault would have happened. The Rogue Trooper would have waited until sunrise to make the crossing. The rays of the newly risen sun would have reacted with the chemicals in the water, creating a dense, early morning tox-mist from the river that would have covered his approach. The toxins and acids in the water would have been no problem to a soldier with chem-resistant skin and any sentries on the riverbank would have been dealt with swiftly and silently as soon as he waded ashore. The two-man crew of the watchtower would have been dispatched with two almost instantaneous shots from that ingenious rifle of his, and after that he would have been in among the rest of the Norts before they even knew he was there.

Venner studied the scene before him, his mind painting in the bloody details of the brief, relentlessly brutal battle that would have followed. A plasma sphere grenade hurled into the first of the bunker shelters instantly incinerated the Nort troops who were probably still sleeping inside. A long, ripping blast from his rifle would have taken care of the Nort bodies that came spilling out of the second bunker and the occupants of the third bunker, the ones lying on the ground around Venner, he killed with his bare hands or with a vibro-knife.

Again Venner remembered the information in those files that had been beamed through to him from his patrons in Milli-com. A Genetic Infantryman was the deadliest close-combat killer on the face of Nu Earth, his reactions and killing speed far outclassing any mere human opponent in a bulky and cumbersome chem-suit. Venner shifted his stance, feeling the reassuring weight of the sniper rifle slung across his shoulder. He didn't care how dangerous the Rogue Trooper was since he didn't have any intention of allowing the blue-skinned gene-freak to get within any-where near striking range of him.

"Captain."

"Sir?" The reply was immediate. Again, Venner smiled. Technically, the young officer outranked him, but Venner was the top assassin of S-Three's much-feared Special Exec-utive Branch, and in such matters, rank insignia counted for very little indeed.

"Gather up your men, captain. We're leaving."

The young officer was hesitant. "Sir, my mission briefing was to help you gather intelligence on where the Genetic Infantryman deserter was heading next. I-I'm not sure we've done that yet, sir."

Venner favoured the man with one of his glances. The officer looked away quickly, unwilling to meet the gaze of the sniper's dead, grey eyes.

"I've known all along where he was going, captain."

The master sniper's gaze passed on towards the edge of the horizon. He couldn't see it, but he knew it was there, exactly one hundred and sixty-three kilometres to the north.

"He's going to Nordstadt, captain, and so am I."

PART TWO
CRUCIBLE

ELEVEN

Milli-com.

Hidden in a secret hyperspace location, deep in the very heart of Souther-controlled space. Three whole fleets of Southern Confederacy Navy battlecruisers patrolled its approaches and the firepower of the station's own defences was enough to make even the most determined enemy think twice about attempting a direct assault. Early warning stations monitored every hyperspace gateway leading to it, and most of these pathways were sown with minefields, the safe routes through them known only to the most trusted pilots of the ships of the Confederacy Navy. In more than twenty years of unremitting warfare with the forces of the Greater Nordland Territories, it was the proud boast of the men and women of the Southern Confederacy military that the enemy had never once mounted a successful attack on Milli-com.

For the crews of Souther ships on final docking approach, their first glimpse of the station as it loomed massively out of the shifting depths of hyperspace was always an awe-inspiring sight. It appeared as a giant artificial moon, orbited by rings of sub-satellite docking platforms and defence stations bristling with gun turrets and weapon batteries. Hundreds of craft came and went every day, arriving from and departing to points throughout the galaxy, and the station's enormous size dwarfed even the largest of the Navy's mightiest battleships and troop transports.

More than a thousand decks, they said. The largest man-made object ever constructed, containing more than a

million personnel. Planners, strategists, propaganda
experts, military intelligence officers, weapons designers
and research scientists, all of them engaged in the deadly
business of a war that had grown to engulf the entire
known galaxy.

Information flowed ceaselessly into Milli-com from
hundreds of different war fronts. There, it was dissected
and disseminated, filed away and compared with other
reports. Staffs of thousands of data assimilators studied
and assessed all this information, forwarding the most
relevant of it to those further up the chain of command.
Eventually, the information was transmuted back into
orders which flowed back out to the hundreds of war-
torn worlds in the galaxy beyond. There, Milli-com's
commands would be put into action, and the results of
those actions would see more information flowing back
into Milli-com, starting the whole process again, and
sending countless more hundreds of thousands of
Souther troops into battle to fight and possibly die. Safely
insulated from the carnage happening on the war fronts,
the staff of Milli-com viewed the struggle only as lists of
casualty figures and reports of the latest territories
gained or lost that appeared daily across their info-
screens.

Of the long-term engagements being fought on hundreds
of worlds, few merited more than one Strategy & Planning
deck on Milli-com. The vast majority shared deck space and
resources with the command staff of at least one other bat-
tlefront. There were several decks from where dozens of
minor engagements, dismissively termed as "bush wars" by
Milli-com's upper command staff cadre were being supervised at the same time.

One war zone was different, however. Unique in the set-
up of Souther military command, nine entire decks of
Milli-com were solely dedicated to the task of winning the
war on Nu Earth.

No one could remember the last time the sound of the popping of champagne corks had been heard on the main

strategy bridge of Milli-com's Battle Sector Nu Earth command decks. Certainly, there had been precious little to celebrate in the last twenty years, as the war degenerated into a bloody stalemate punctuated by a series of even bloodier failed attempts to break that stalemate.

White-jacketed mess orderlies circulated through the assembly of several hundred command level staff officers, dispensing glasses of champagne and trays of delicately spiced canapés. The noise in the main strategy bridge, normally no more than a low hum of whispered conversations and the quiet crackle of hundreds of incoming radio communiqués, had now risen to an excited hubbub of self-congratulatory chatter, punctuated by an increasing number of loud, barking laughs. Laughter too was generally an unknown sound in this place, since the war on Nu Earth and the endless casualty figures and battle reports that filtered through these decks had given scant cause for any light-heartedness over the years.

But now all that was going to change, Daniels thought, helping himself to yet another glass of champagne from the tray of a passing orderly. He sipped it thoughtfully, scanning the surrounding crowd for any sign of the foxy little brunette signals lieutenant from Deck 375. He had sent her an invitation to the party, dressing it as a friendly gesture from one Milli-com comrade to another, but both of them knew what it really meant. Consequently, he had rearranged his duty shifts several times to ensure that they "accidentally" bumped into each other in the officers' commissary.

The resulting lunches they had shared together had been a pleasing distraction from the business of winning the war, and had increasingly left Daniels in little doubt about where the relationship might ultimately be heading. Inter-rank fraternisation of the kind he had in mind was officially frowned upon by Milli-com Command, but the rigours of this war surely drained on a man's spirit, Daniels reminded himself, and sometimes a fellow needed a little extra-curricular R&R. Especially when his wife and family were safely more than two hundred light years away...

Then he saw her, coming out of one of the elevator exits and showing both her holocard invitation and personal ID disc to one of the black-uniformed Milli-com security agents stationed there. The security man scanned both items with a handheld checker, comparing their contents with the confidential information now scrolling across the inside of his helmet's data visor. Grudgingly satisfied that she wasn't a Nort assassin or – even worse – an uninvited gatecrasher from the lower ranks, he stepped aside and allowed her to pass.

She walked down the steps that led onto the main bridge floor, looking around her with a slightly questioning smile, no doubt searching for any sign of the dashing Strategy Division colonel at this prestigious gathering.

Daniels studied her for a moment, his mind momentarily dwelling on the pleasures no doubt to come later tonight, his eyes equally dwelling on the chief sources of those pleasures. She was wearing earrings and a few subtle but highly effective touches of make-up – cosmetics were officially frowned upon by Milli-com Command, not that anyone seemed to be willing to take any notice of such minor infringements. She seemed to have selected a dress uniform that was a size too small for her slender frame, the dark material of her tightly buttoned and belted trousers and tunic emphasising the contours of her hips and breasts, giving Daniels a deeply pleasing preview of those assets that had first drawn his attention to her in the first place.

Checking the details of his own uniform, the gleaming colonel's stars on his epaulettes, the row of polished decorations and service awards on his tunic breast, he stepped forward to greet her, his most charming and dashing senior officer class smile fixed on his lips. She was turning her head in his direction and he increased the pace of his dashing stride towards her, drawing in his slight paunch an extra vital inch or so. He forced himself to undergo weekly sessions in the officers' gym, but it was a constant battle against the temptations of the hospitality on offer in the senior officers' mess, and–

"Damn fine show, eh, Daniels? And what about this champers? Damn good stuff. It's a '72 vintage, if I'm not much mistaken."

Daniels turned, his heart sinking as soon as he had felt the first insistent tug on his elbow. Major Xavier Sisca-Morgan was a notorious ass and an idiot of the highest order. He was, however, also unfortunately the nephew of Field Marshal Sisca-Morgan, commander of the Karthage campaign being waged from another deck twenty-two levels below. If Major Sisca-Morgan realised that people were only willing to give him even the time of day purely on account of who his uncle was, then the braying fool certainly gave no indication of it.

Daniels did his best to keep his smile fixed on his face while he forced himself to respond to this most unwelcome of interruptions to the night's pleasures.

"I'm sorry, major, I don't think I quite follow…"

Daniels watched, his anger growing, as the grossly corpulent Sisca-Morgan took a slurp from his champagne glass and noisily swilled its contents around inside his mouth. Daniels felt it was definitely to Sisca-Morgan's advantage that only the Milli-com security personnel were allowed to go armed on the strategy bridge. If Daniels had had his regulation sidearm on him, he wasn't certain he couldn't be held responsible for his actions, no matter who the uncle of his would-be victim might have been.

"Yes, definitely the '72," concluded Sisca-Morgan, swilling down the rest of what had clearly been only one of many glasses of the night. "Such a fine vintage, and so rare too, ever since those damned Norts attacked the vineyard worlds in the Grenoble system. Such barbarity! I tell you, Daniels, it takes things like that to remind you what it is we're fighting this war for!"

Sometimes Daniels managed to ask himself if his years of working in Milli-com, far removed from the real horrors of the actual warzones, hadn't perhaps made him callous or at least flippant to the realities of the carnage of the war they were all engaged in. At such times, it was almost reassuring to encounter fools like Sisca-Morgan, if only to remind himself of just how far he still had to fall before he became a complete officer class horse's arse.

"Indeed, my dear Sisca-Morgan," he managed to say with only the barest veneer of politeness. "Why, just imagine how much less the tragedy would have been if those damn Norts had decided to lay waste to something that really mattered, like say, a major centre of population in one of the core systems, instead of a few miserable and thinly populated agricultural planets. We might have lost a few billion people, but at least we would still have the benefit of this year's latest grape crop to aid the war effort. Now, excuse me, major, but I've just seen General Vallo and I really must have a word with him about the latest intelligence reports."

With that, he was gone, leaving behind him a Major Sisca-Morgan whose facial expression was set in a perfect "O" of astonishment. Daniels's thoughts were on the main prize of the night. That foxy, curvaceous signals lieutenant from Deck 375. For the moment, at least, all thoughts of the damage he might have just inflicted on his command staff career were temporarily forgotten. Tonight belonged to the pursuit of more immediate and pressing concerns.

He couldn't see the girl, but he didn't think it would take him long to track her down. After that, there would be a few drinks, some jokes and maybe a few only slightly exaggerated tales about the important role he had played in the planning of Operation Hammerfall, the event they were all here to celebrate tonight. Then, after that, back to his private quarters, hopefully, where he already had a bottle of champagne on ice. And then, after that…

"Ah, Major Daniels. Just the man I was hoping to bump into."

Daniels turned, ready to give short shrift to this latest obstacle in the path of tonight's pleasures. He stopped short, the brush off excuse dying on his lips as soon as he saw the colour of the uniform of the officer beside him. Strategy & Planning personnel like Daniels wore dark green. Communications & Signals staffers like his intended sleeping partner for the night wore dark blue. There were hundreds of people in the room wearing both kinds of uniforms. The man beside him was different, however. He wore the neutral grey of the Southern Security Service. The much-feared S-Three; guardians of the Souther military's precious hoard of secrets and black bag intelligence operations, the less of which Daniels knew about the better, in his opinion.

As was customary with S-Three officers, the man's tunic bore no name tag or identifying insignia other than the rank stars on his shoulder epaulettes, but Daniels didn't need to see any name tag to know the identity of the man now talking to him.

"Colonel Marckand," he stammered, taking a gulp of champagne in a desperately unsuccessful attempt to disguise his obvious unhappiness. No conversation with any S-Three office was ever that welcome, particularly if the S-Three operative was one of Marckand's notably grim reputation.

"Excuse me, colonel," continued Daniels, "but I really must have a word with General Vallo about the latest intelligence reports. Perhaps, later we can talk, when I've finished my urgent business with the general?"

Marckand smiled. The change in expression didn't improve the look of his features, not with those three, long raw-edged parallel scars that scored through the skin of one side of his face, running all the way from his jaw and up into his hairline.

"General Vallo left fifteen minutes ago, Daniels, so I'm afraid your conversation will have to wait. As will your other urgent business with that attractive young thing from Deck 375."

Daniels gulped down more champagne in panic. Goddamn S-Three, snooping into everything! Keeping tabs on everyone! Wasn't there anything that happened here on Milli-com that they didn't know about?

"What is it I can do for you, colonel?"

Again Marckand smiled. "Operation Hammerfall. An audacious scheme. Some might say controversial, even.

Others might even say ruthless and cold-blooded. You're certain of its chances of success?"

Daniels relaxed somewhat now, feeling himself to be on safer ground. They had spent months planning this operation and he was intimately familiar with every detail of it. Dozens of senior officer careers, Daniels's included, depended on its outcome, and all involved were supremely confident that medals and promotions would be coming their way once it was all over.

"We certainly think so, colonel, and so does Grand Marshal Cohen. If you want to discuss the matter with him, I'm sure he'll be amenable to keeping our colleagues in S-Three fully informed of the situation."

Almost on cue, there was a burst of laughter from the far side of the room. Daniels followed the intelligence officer's cold gaze, seeing the grand marshal standing there with a group of his cronies, few of them below the rank of two-star general. Even the man standing attentively behind the grand marshal and responsible for keeping his cognac glass topped up was a full-blown colonel. The figure beside the grand marshal was tall, beautiful and blue-skinned.

One of the so-called GI Dolls. Officially, she was designated as the grand marshal's aide and bodyguard, but while the diaphanous evening gown she wore left little to the imagination, Daniels couldn't see any sign that she was wearing any kind of hidden sidearm beneath the clinging, transparent material of the garment. Or indeed, that she was really wearing anything else at all. The grand marshal stood with his cognac in one hand and his other hand blatantly pawing at the buttocks of his female GI companion while he laughed and joked with his cronies. Perhaps that's what he's doing, Daniels pondered somewhat bitterly; searching her for hidden weapons, to assure himself that his bodyguard was indeed armed in readiness to protect him. If the esteemed grand marshal remained true to form on these occasions, then a few cognacs later the public body search he was currently conducting of his bodyguard's figure would soon move onto even more intimate areas.

"Oh, I don't think we need interrupt the grand marshal, especially when he seems to have other pressing business in hand at the moment," commented Marckand, with the hint of a knowing smirk on his scarred features.

Daniels found his glass suddenly empty. Before he had fully registered the fact, Marckand had plucked it out of his hand and replaced it with another full one from the tray of a passing orderly. And now they were moving, the S-Three man laying an arm round his shoulders and leading them off to a quieter part of the room. The crowd parted before them, highly decorated staff officers instinctively shrinking away from the presence of the grey-uniformed intelligence man. Daniels risked a helpless glance behind him, searching desperately for his lieutenant from Deck 375, but it was too late. He was already in the clutches of the man from S-Three.

"No, Daniels, I was wondering about the security implications of Operation Hammerfall. It must have been quite a feat to plan such a huge operation and not allow any hint of it to leak out. Surely our old friends in Nordland must have some hint of what's going on?"

One part of Daniels – the part that hadn't already consumed half a dozen glasses of champagne and a few pep pills to give him the courage to dazzle that foxy little signals thing with his wit and charm – knew that he shouldn't be talking about this. Another, even more sober, part wondered if the S-Three man hadn't slipped something into that last glass of champagne, some devious substance brewed up by the S-Three chemists to loosen the tongues of interrogation subjects. But it was too late, and Daniels found his pride in what they had accomplished in planning this momentous operation all too willing to come surging to the surface.

"Oh, they know we're planning something in Nordstadt, but they've got completely the wrong idea about what it is. That's the genius of what we've been cooking up all these months, misdirecting the enemy as to our true intentions."

A questioning, silently encouraging look from Marckand was all it took to bring the rest of it to spill out.

"Of course, it's been impossible to hide the depletion of manpower in the Nordstadt sector, but the Norts have no idea of the true situation. We think that they believe we still have over two hundred thousand troops on the ground in Nordstadt. In fact, the real figure is almost less than half that."

"And how has this been achieved? The Norts haven't noticed any evidence of an evacuation operation in Nordstadt?"

Daniels allowed himself a brief smile of smug pride. "They haven't noticed it because there hasn't been one. We've done it all through natural wastage. Our wounded and KIAs are airlifted out of the battle zone as normal, but the supply shuttles are running mostly empty on the return journey, with only the barest minimum in reinforcements being brought back into the warzone. Our killed and wounded casualty rates run at about six thousand a week in Nordstadt. It hasn't taken that long to run our strength down to our current levels just by letting the war take its natural toll."

"And the Norts still haven't realised this?"

Another smug smile from Daniels. "We have dozens of signals units in place, sending communications back and forth between non-existent forward combat units and equally non-existent command centres. If the Norts are listening into our communications, and of course they are, then the amount of standard radio traffic they're intercepting tells them we're still there in force."

"And the Norts have taken the bait?"

This elicited an even greater smile of satisfaction from the strategy officer.

"Absolutely. Hook, line and sinker. They know we're in a weakened state in Nordstadt, but they don't know nearly the full extent of it. They've been moving in reinforcements for months now in the build-up to their next full assault. They're obsessed with Nordstadt. It's like some kind of Holy Grail to them and they'll do anything to drive us out of the place for good. That's the whole linchpin to Hammerfall, the realisation that the Norts have such a massive

strategic blind spot when it comes to anything to do with
the place. Say what you want about old Cohen, but he was
the first one to see the opportunity and have the courage to
seize it. If we'd only launched Hammerfall years ago, then
God knows how many lives we could have–"

"Exactly how many enemy troops are we talking about?"

Daniels's lips went dry at the question. Just thinking
about the enormity of what was about to happen was still
staggering when you stepped back to contemplate it. He
eagerly accepted the full champagne glass that Marckand
pressed into his hand.

"According to the latest intelligence reports? Roughly one
million, two hundred thousand Norts, most of them sitting
hidden in reserve positions all round the perimeter of the
Nordstadt crucible, and all of them waiting for the final
assault order. That figure includes a confirmed count of six-
teen entire divisions of their finest Kashar and Kashan
Legion stormtroopers and four divisions of their Nordska
Guard armoured elite. They've been building up their
assault forces for months now, ever since they first detected
our slowdown in feeding fresh reinforcements into the city.
They think we're suffering a failure of confidence in continuing to hold Nordstadt and now they're taking full
advantage of that fact. Of course, that's exactly what we
want them to think and the more troops they think we've
got there, the more of their own troops they're willing to
commit to take the city."

"And our own forces in Nordstadt, what do they know
about what's really happening?"

Daniels looked around him, checking to see who might
be eavesdropping on the conversation. This was one of the
most contentious points of Hammerfall, one of the parts of
the plan that had caused the most controversy, and more
than a few senior officers within Milli-com Command to
resign their commissions in disgust at what was being pro-
posed. When it was first suggested, it had caused Daniels
some soul searching of his own, but now he was convinced
it was a sadly necessary sacrifice. In war, one sometimes
had to be willing to make harsh decisions such as those.

involved in the successful execution of Operation Hammerfall.

"They know a fresh enemy offensive is coming, of course.
It would be impossible for them not to have been made
aware of the build-up of Nort forces around them. They
know that they are the bait in a trap. However, for the pur-
poses of operational integrity, it has been regretfully
necessary to conceal the full extent of the mission details
from every Souther soldier still involved in the Nordstadt
Crucible campaign, from the lowliest infantry trooper to the
most senior army group commander."

"So what do they think is going to happen?"

Daniels glanced around again before answering.

"When the main Nort offensive begins, the commanders
of our forces in Nordstadt have been led to believe that we
will then commence a massive surprise troop drop from
orbit, taking the Norts by surprise and trapping the greater
part of their vanguard inside the city, where it will be encircled and destroyed. At the same time, they have been told
that General Fyalla's armoured divisions will break through
the Nort lines to link up with them, opening up a secure
land bridge with the main element of our ground-based
forces."

"And, of course, none of this is actually going to happen."

Daniels's reply came straight out of the carefully prepared
preamble to Operation Hammerfall's original mission statement.

"Regrettably not. As many command staff and specialist
military personnel as possible will be evacuated prior to the
ultimate commencement of Hammerfall, but for the pur-
poses of the success of the operation, it is unfortunately
necessary that the greater part of our forces remain in place
within the Nordstadt crucible to draw the enemy forces on
into the final closing of the trap."

Daniels continued on, perhaps pre-empting the usual
moral problems with the strategy behind Hammerfall that
had troubled so many other staffers aboard Milli-com.

"Trust me, we've run through all the available alternative scenarios a thousand times already and Hammerfall

is still the best of the bunch. I mean, let's be honest. We're engaged in a war of attrition here, there's no getting around that fact, and in a conflict like this, the only thing that counts is killing more of the enemy than they can kill of yours. That's what we're doing with Hammerfall. Of course, the loss of so many Souther lives is regrettable, but it's a sacrifice we're willing to make. I mean, just look at the payoff. A hundred thousand of our boys for well over a million Norts? Including some of their most elite divisions? No, you can't argue with those kind of figures, no matter how ruthless the strategy might seem. If Hammerfall succeeds, and I've staked my career on the fact that it will, then the effects on Nort morale could well tip the balance once and for all in our favour in the war on Nu Earth. The Norts won't shrug off a million plus casualties so easily, and the complete loss of Nordstadt to them could well prove to be a devastating blow to their psychology, one they might never properly recover from."

Daniels broke off, suddenly aware of how loud and excited his voice had become. Even here, in this select gathering, it still wasn't wise to talk too openly of some of the most contentious points of the Hammerfall operation. Marckand's next question, however, cut directly to the most secret part of the plan.

"And when does all this happen?"

Daniels looked around them before risking a reply. Luckily, no one seemed to be paying any attention. In fact, it was almost as if the high-ranking S-Three officer inhabited his own personal dead zone, one that didn't need any scan bafflers or void generators, or any of the other sophisticated anti-surveillance technology routinely employed by the Souther security services. Those at the party seemed all too willing to simply blank the presence of that grey uniform out of their awareness.

"In two days time, according to all our best intelligence assessments and our monitoring of the notable increase in recent Nort radio traffic. They're on the move already, filtering advance storm units through into the outskirts of the city. These might look like nothing more than the usual probing attacks of our defences, but we know just how big the build-up of forces in their rear echelons is, and we're confident that this is really a move forward to secure start-up positions for the imminent main assault. After that, once the attack begins, the countdown to Hammerfall begins."

"And how long will that countdown be?"

"Twelve hours," replied Daniels, without hesitation. "That's how long we anticipate it will take them to completely overwhelm our outer defences and bring the main bulk of their assault units forces into the city, converging on all directions on the remains of our own forces who will by then be trapped and completely encircled in the centre of the city. That's when we launch Hammerfall. After that, Nordstadt and everyone in it, including over a million Nort troops, will simply cease to exist."

"Impressive," nodded Marckand. "Thank you, colonel. You've been most instructive. If you ever need a favour from S-Three, please don't hesitate to contact me. By the way, I think I see your little friend from Deck 375 just over there, talking amiably to our heroic comrade Major Dion."

Daniels looked round in utter consternation, following the direction indicated by Marckand. True enough, there she was, deep in smiling, laughing conversation with Dion. Major Dion was a Southlands Special Forces battalion commander in the Karthage campaign, and had just returned from there to recover from wounds suffered in his latest frontline heroics. His handsome face and war time exploits were all over the propaganda channels at the moment, and he was one of Milli-com Command's golden boys, held up to the civilian population of the Southern Confederacy as a shining example of Souther military daring and heroism. Even the fresh wound marks on his face and injured arm tucked inside the tunic of his dress uniform only seemed to add to the man's glamorous warrior mystique. Daniels cast envious eyes on the decorations on that tunic breast. There, set amongst a host of valour-in-battle awards, sat the Southlands Cross. Beside it was the gleaming platinum and diamond disc of the Confederacy Medal of Honour, which untold billions of people all across the galaxy had seen Confederacy President Markus pin onto that tunic only days ago in a special live propaganda broadcast from the steps of the Presidium Palace. Daniels's collection of decorations looked extremely poor in comparison, especially since absolutely none of them had been won in actual battle with the enemy.

From the way she was talking to the dashing young hero major, it was clear to everyone that Dion had made yet another victorious conquest tonight. At one point she glanced round, perhaps catching sight of Daniels's face in the crowd, but then quickly looked away again, turning her attention back to Dion and giggling loudly at his latest witticism.

Daniels turned away in dejection, but looked around in surprise as soon as he realised that Marckand had somehow managed to completely disappear in the few moments that Daniels's attention had been directed elsewhere. Oh well, he decided, the S-Three man's vanishing act was no great loss. Especially not now that the rest of his night had already been so completely ruined.

Downhearted, angry and embittered, Daniels wandered off in search of one of those orderlies and the trays of drinks they all carried. If he wasn't going to get laid in honour of Operation Hammerfall tonight, he was sure as hell going to do everything he could to ensure that at least he was going to get very, very drunk indeed.

Marckand made his way through the press of bodies, pausing only once to put the untouched glass of champagne he had been nursing all night onto the tray of a passing orderly. Most people suddenly found something else to occupy their attention as he passed into view, while a few brave souls managed to direct a few weak and insincere half-smiles and words of greeting in his direction. He ignored them all. He had accomplished what he had come here to do. Now it was time to get out.

He quickly crossed the bridge floor, sweeping into one of the smaller conference rooms there.

"Gentlemen. If you please…"

That, and the grey uniform, was all it took to clear the room in moments of the gaggle of young junior officers who had been in there. The air in the small room was heavy with the cloying scent of halo-sticks and many of the men and women had the telltale glassy-eyed look of halo-weed intoxication. They fled the place without even a second glance, probably terrified that the S-Three man would have them all rounded up and sent to the Nu Earth war fronts for possession of an illegal contraband substance.

Alone in the room, Marckand activated his palm communicator. The voice of Costello, his second-in-command, responded moments later. As with all of the most secure areas aboard Milli-com, the strategy bridge deck was heavily scan-shielded, jamming out all personal communicator frequencies in the interests of military security, but the device Marckand used was S-Three technology, overriding all the standard security buffers.

Marckand got straight to the point. "The operative, is he in place yet?"

"We received word from him two hours ago. He's in Nordstadt now. Is there a problem with the timing of this Hammerfall operation, colonel? Do you wish to abort mission and pull our man out of there?"

Marckand thought about it for a moment and then made his decision. "No, maintain mission status. Operative is to acquire and eliminate primary and secondary targets, as per original mission parameters. And, Costello?"

"Colonel?"

"I've just been given to understand that things are going to be getting very hot in Nordstadt very soon. Make sure our operative knows that, no matter what happens, he is to complete his mission. Give him whatever assurances you have that we'll pull him out of there as soon as his task is over."

There was a slight pause before Costello answered. "Understood, colonel."

Marckand considered his options on the elevator ride back down to his private quarters. He had been recruited from the regular military into the Southlands Security Service twelve years ago, although he had been a Nort double agent for three years even before that. There had been a small but significant cabal of Nort double agents working at Milli-com then, most of them men like him. Men who, while having some natural sympathies for the racial supremacy doctrines that had propelled the Greater Nordland Territories to such heights in so relatively short a time, had taken a cold-blooded look at the war in its earliest days and come to the seemingly inescapable conclusion that, ultimately, Nordland would be the victor of this war. The Southern Confederacy had the advantage of greater resources of manpower and territories, but it was the Norts who had supremacy in terms of technology and the sheer fanatical will to dominate and destroy.

Marckand and those others did not think of themselves as traitors. Rather, they saw themselves as mercenaries, selling their loyalty to the side that would inevitably emerge as the stronger of the two. Of course, they would be well rewarded for such loyalty after the war was over, and this was where their so-called treason would serve their fellow Southers well.

After they had won the war, the Norts would still need reliable and trustworthy servants to act as governors and administrators of their newly conquered Souther territories, and this was where Marckand imagined that he and his fellow collaborators would have a mutually rewarding role to play. Mediating between the Norts and their new Souther subjects, he would be able to protect his fellow Southers from the worst excesses of Nordland barbarities. However, there would have to be sacrifices made amongst those elements of the Souther populations who regrettably remained hostile to Nort rule or who contravened the Norts' most ruthless policies on racial purity. Marckand and his fellow collaborators would have blood on their hands, that couldn't be denied, but they reassured themselves that the carnage would be a lot worse without them being there to negotiate with the Norts on behalf of their defeated fellow Southers.

But, of course, the war had lasted longer than anyone could have anticipated and the prospect of that early Nort victory had long since faded away. Marckand had cursed his early naivety in those days, but it was too late to go back and change things now. He had been responsible for feeding vital secret information to the Norts for years, and his bloody fingerprints were all over various Souther missions and offensives that had ended in spectacular failure after encountering Nort resistance which was either far greater than expected or, in some instances, where there simply shouldn't have been any Nort forces in the first place.

He no longer considered himself a Nort agent now. Indeed, over the last few years, he had gained a formidable reputation within S-Three for his single-minded zeal in hunting down and eliminating cells of Nort spies and sympathisers within the Souther military. The fact that many of these Nort agents had been put in place by Marckand in the first instance was not a fact that he chose to share with his fellow spy-hunters.

Now, almost everyone who had ever known of his double-agent status was dead. Of the original senior collaborator cabal, only himself and one other was still alive. All the others died in a series of freak accidents or mystery assassinations, all of them conducted by Marckand and his pet killer, Venner. Only once had Marckand almost been uncovered, when a rival spy-hunter agency had managed to discover the activities of one of the cabal members and get to them before Marckand. Luckily, he had managed to have his collaborator comrade transferred into S-Three custody. After that, it had been a simple matter to arrange the prisoner's unfortunate escape, although, instead of the hidden shuttlecraft promised by Marckand, it had been the waiting gunsights of Venner's sniper rifle that the prisoner had come running towards.

And now only one of his old collaborator cabal comrades remained, although it was the one who was the most cunning and ruthless of them all, possibly even

more so than Marckand himself. The man was a pale
shadow of his former self, though. A nameless and disfigured renegade, on the run on Nu Earth, fleeing from
one wretched bolt-hole to another, pursued by his own
personal spectre of death. Marckand knew something of
the reputation of the blue-skinned killer that pursued his
old traitor comrade. It seemed more than likely that this
renegade Genetic Infantryman would eventually find and
kill his target, but the man he was pursuing was a nat-
ural-born survivor and seemed to have a knack for
slipping through his pursuer's fingers. Marckand couldn't
take the risk that the traitor would ultimately survive the
war, or that the Genetic Infantryman, in his endless pursuit of his quarry, might somehow find out about the
existence of another high-ranking traitor in Milli-com.
That was why Marckand had set Venner on the trail. The
assassin was an extra safeguard, sent in to ensure that
events transpired in exactly the way Marckand wanted
them to.

And now he had an additional safeguard too. Operation
Hammerfall. If the Genetic Infantryman or Venner didn't get
their man, then Hammerfall surely would. It would be a
pity to lose such a useful tool as Venner, of course. It was
rare to find an assassin as skilled and as completely and
solely dedicated to the business of killing as Venner was,
but ultimately, sacrifices had to be made, just as that fool
Daniels had said to him earlier on. And, besides, Venner
knew far more about some of the reasons behind the missions Marckand sent him on than was strictly healthy for
either of them.

Which brought Marckand's thoughts round to the sub-
ject of Costello. She knew nothing of his past as a
double-agent, naturally, and she had served him loyally
and competently enough over the last few years, but
there had been something in her tone tonight that Marckand hadn't liked. That slight but fatal hesitation before
she confirmed his order that Venner was to be lied to and
then abandoned to his fate in Nordstadt. An underling
who started questioning their superior's orders was an

underling who might start looking into the possible reasons behind those orders, and that Marckand couldn't risk
at all.

He had arranged enough tragic accidents for various comrades and underlings over the years. Perhaps it was time to
arrange one more for poor and too-curious-for-her-own-good
Captain Costello.

It sat invisibly in a far-flung orbit around Nu Earth, far
removed from the normal transport routes and debris fields
around which the main action in the orbital war revolved.
Hammerfall, protected by dense banks of scan-bafflers and
null-shields, undetectable to all but the most probing enemy
searches.

The weapons platform was fully automated, since the
designers of Operation Hammerfall put their faith not in
weak and fallible human personnel but in the cold, unemo-
tional machine minds of computer programmes and
maintenance droids to carry out the appointed task, when
the time came.

The station hung in a fixed position, watching the disc
of Nu Earth revolve far beneath it. Its scanners and missile targeters were fixed on one small area of the planet's
surface, and every time that area came round towards
them during the latest cycle of the planet's orbit, Hammerfall One's machine systems went to work. Range
coordinates were rechecked and recalibrated. Atmospheric conditions were assayed and any necessary
changes to missile flight systems were programmed in.
Targeter systems tracked the target area as it revolved past
below them, waiting patiently for the order to launch
from Milli-com Command, waiting just as patiently as
they watched the target location slide away out of sight,
disappearing round into the far, sunward side of the
planet.

It watched and waited, this hidden and most secret of
weapons platforms, equipped with a battery of twenty
high-speed ballistic missiles that could reach the surface
of Nu Earth in a matter of minutes, each of those missiles

carrying a nuclear warhead of devastating explosive yield.

It watched and waited, this angel of death. Waiting for the order to wipe the city of Nordstadt off the face of Nu Earth.

TWELVE

"Left fire team, forward! Watch out for Nort fire from those towers just beyond that burned-out smelter. Ludlow, give them covering fire! Goddamn it, Sweeney, why aren't I hearing that lazooka of yours firing already?"

Intense volleys of las-fire swept back and forth between the buildings, seeking out the men and women sheltering amongst them. Las-rounds cracked off stone and steel, leaving behind fused burn holes and blackened scorch marks. Rockets screamed overhead, followed moments later by a series of shattering explosions fifty metres behind Hanna's position. The Norts had brought up a missile launcher vehicle, one of their infamous "Zell Orchestras", as the Souther troops called them, naming the weapon after one of the Norts' most brutal and ruthless war marshals.

A building, part of the steelworks' old admin block and already listing badly from damage sustained in some long ago previous engagement, collapsed under the impact, toppling to the ground in a thunderous hail of stone and dust. Vesper and her squad had taken up position there only a few minutes earlier. Hanna hoped to hell they had managed to get out of the place in time.

The building collapse brought a momentary lull to the firing. A squad of Nort stormtroopers, unmistakable in their black and gold chem-suits, took advantage of the moment, running out into the broadway directly in front of Hanna's position, making for the dense cover of the tangle of thick steel girders on the other side of the street.

"Kashan Legion bastards!" Hanna yelled to the squad members around her. "Frontal fire! If those scum want to take back their precious sacred soil of Nordstadt that much, then they're going to have to pay for the privilege."

Her eight squad members opened fire as one, emptying their mags in seconds. Six Norts fell to the ground instantaneously, cut down by a volley of las-fire. The remaining three turned and tried to sprint back into the safety of the cover they had just left.

One of them almost made it. Hanna picked him off with a single round that sent him sprawling back to rejoin the bodies of his comrades.

Another of the Norts, injured but alive, started crawling back towards cover, screaming in pain and shouting for help. Babic, the squad's best marksman, put paid to him before he had covered much more than a few metres by exploding his head with a single expertly-aimed las-round.

Babic grinned in ruthless pleasure. Hanna glanced at him, countenancing the act with a single approving nod. The members of the Kashan Legion, and their brother scum in the Kashar Legion, were special cases. Both elite Nort units prided themselves on never taking prisoners and had been responsible for many notorious war crime incidents during the course of the war on Nu Earth. Souther troops, whenever they found themselves in battle against the Kashans and Kashars, were only too happy to return the favour.

The other Norts in place in the surrounding cover responded quickly to the deaths of their comrades.

Rapid fire las-rounds lashed down upon Hanna's position, coming from a Nort heavy weapon team situated in a covered walkway spanning the breadth of the street ahead of them. Hanna and her squad hugged the rusting hulk of the overturned steelworks tractor rig that formed the centrepiece of their makeshift street barricade.

Las-rounds from the heavy weapon, a tripod-mounted Nort strubber gun capable of pouring out fire at a rate of two thousand rounds a minute, blasted apart the material of the barricade, stripping away layer after layer of cover in search of the Souther infantry troopers cowering behind it.

Further up the street, Sweeney leaned out of cover of the doorway he had been sheltering inside, bringing his lazooka up to bear. The strubber gunner spotted him, immediately switching away from the barricade target and swinging his aim towards this new danger. Hanna and her squad cringed in fear behind the remains of the barricade as hundreds of las-bolts flew past their heads, ripping up the street behind them by churning up its rockrete surface as they tore a path directly towards Sweeney.

The lazookaman fired just before the trail of strubber rounds reached him, the walkway and the heavy weapons team it contained disappeared in a molten flash. The remains of it came crashing down into the street. Norts instantly ran out to seize control of this newly-offered piece of cover but Hanna and her troops were ready for them. Fire from three squads beat into the Nort position, driving them back again and leaving more Nort corpses strewn on the ground.

Repulsed a second time, the remaining Norts still sheltering in the cover of the buildings at the far end of the broadway began to pull back, probably hoping to regroup and try and find another way through or around the Souther strongpoint. Souther las-fire sent them on their way, picking off a few unlucky stragglers.

Hanna breathed a sigh of relief. The Norts had been probing forward in strength in this sector all day. Radio chatter from other units told her that everyone else was experiencing exactly the same kind of deadly pressure that her platoon had been undergoing, although some of them hadn't withstood it as well as her people had. The Norts had seized the high ground of the giant slag heap mounds west of here, and no one had heard any word from Third Platoon since it went in to join the ongoing battle inside one of the three cavernous smelter sheds that made up the heart of the steelworks.

For the moment at least, the battle here was over. Maybe now they could get a chance to send their wounded back to company HQ.

"Sarge? You feel that?"

She did. A rumbling in the ground beneath their feet. "Probably just the shock waves from an artillery bombardment going on somewhere else," she told Babic. "Let's just hope it's the Norts getting a pummelling and not any of our people."

But the rumbling grew stronger. A pile of rubble nearby shifted and then tumbled to the ground. Nervous faces behind chem-suit visors looked uncertainly at their squad leader.

"Earth tremors! It's an earthquake, maybe. Some new kinda Nort weapon!" panicked Shore, one of the new recruits from the remains of Fifth Company who had joined them only last week.

"Don't be ridiculous," Hanna told him. "The Norts come up with some weird ordnance but even they're not dumb enough to try using something like that."

The rumbling grew stronger. There was a crash from up the street. Hanna turned to see the steel-reinforced wall of a large storage shed smashing itself to the ground. Panic seized her.

Jesus, maybe it was an earthquake! Maybe the Norts really would be willing to destroy their precious Nordstadt...

With a clanking roar of metal and engine gears, the first Nort Blackmare tank smashed its way through the remains of the toppled wall, shrugging off the tonnes of shattered wall sections and steel girders that bounced harmlessly off its front and top armour. A moment later, a second Blackmare bludgeoned a path through the same breach, widening it even further. Nort infantry and smaller armoured vehicles poured through the gap in the wake of the two Blackmares, sheltering in the protective cover of the two leviathan tanks.

Each Blackmare weighed hundreds of tonnes. They were the most powerful armoured vehicles on Nu Earth, far outclassing anything the Southers had to counter them. One Blackmare alone was more than enough to deal with for an entire armoured company of Carter class Souther tanks.

The first Blackmare rumbled down the broadway like a mobile earthquake, its massive, metres-wide treads crushing apart and then pulverising to dust even the largest pieces of rubble in its path. The turret, larger and heavier than any whole normal tank, swung slowly round towards the Souther position.

"Tank shock," they called it. The terror that seized the hearts and minds of infantry of any kind when confronted with the reality of a tank assault. Hanna had faced a Nort armoured attack before and recognised all too well the feelings of panic now welling up within her and her squad. If even their own tank crews were afraid to go up against the monster Blackmares, then what chance did an ordinary infantryman stand, armed with nothing more than a standard las-carbine and a satchel of plasma sphere grenades?

The tank continued to rumble forward. The turret continued to turn. The ordinary infantry trooper side of her was paralysed with fear, overwhelmed by the sheer scale of the thing bearing down on her. The platoon leader side of her, however, knew she had to do something to save the lives of her and the troops under her protection, and quickly.

"Abandon position. Scatter! Find what cover you can!"

They ran. Seconds later, the Blackmare's ten metre long main barrel fired.

The explosion vaporised most of the barricade, tossing the twenty-five tonne tractor rig up into the air as if it was nothing more than a child's toy. The blast took out the buildings on either side of the street, collapsing them inwards and further adding to the carnage.

The bodies of Souther troops were hurled, mangled and on fire, through the air or were crushed beneath tonnes of falling masonry from collapsed buildings. The blast picked up Hanna and hurled her fifteen metres down the street. She landed hard, feeling pain explode in her left leg. Dazed and fighting the urge to black out into welcome oblivion, her first instinct was to reach out to take hold of her las-carbine, but it was long gone.

A long crack ran down the length of her face-plate, partially obscuring her vision. She saw Babic lying nearby. Or, at least, his upper half. There was no sign of his legs and lower torso. Her ears rang in the aftermath of the explosion but through the sound-haze she could still hear the urgent alarm tone of her chem-suit systems, warning her that her suit's integrity had been breached and she was now in danger of exposure to the unfiltered hazards of the poison atmosphere of Nu Earth.

Ignoring the warning, she tried climbing to her feet, intending to find a weapon – any kind of weapon – and at least go down fighting. Her injured left leg gave way under her and she collapsed back to the ground, sobbing in pain.

Hanna rolled over, feeling the ground shaking beneath her. She looked round and saw the Blackmare climbing over the mountain of rubble that was all that remained of those collapsed buildings. The monster bore remorselessly down on her and she saw the crawling figure of an injured Souther trooper die screaming beneath those enormous grinding tracks. She reached down and fumbled with the release catch of her pistol holster, determined to at least die with a weapon in her hand, no matter how useless it might be.

What happened next was something Sergeant First Class Hanna Coss would never forget for as long as she lived.

The Kashan tank grenadier troops riding on top of the Blackmare cheered in triumph as they watched their Souther enemies scatter before them. A few fired shots to pick off some of the wounded in the tank's path, but most were content to cling onto the handholds on the tank's hull and turret and to allow the giant beast its rightful spoils. They were still cheering when the blue-skinned figure who, impossibly wasn't wearing a chem-suit, leapt ten metres down from the rooftop of a nearby building and landed amongst them.

The plasma sphere that Rogue had dropped just before he jumped cleared a landing spot for him. The explosion didn't even scratch the Blackmare's topside armour, but it was more than enough to take care of the Kashan tank grenadiers riding on the platform behind the main turret.

He landed moments later amongst the carnage of dead and dying Norts. Gunnar chattered in his hands, sending the bodies of the grenade explosion survivors spilling lifelessly

down the steep sides of the tank's hull. A second blast
cleared most of the Norts riding on top of the turret.

Rogue clambered up the turret ladder sending another
Nort falling towards the ground twelve metres below with a
single kick.

Ascending on to the turret, he ducked to evade the
buzzing las-sword blade swung at him by a Kashan Legion
kapten. Even through the protection of his scaled synthi-
plastic skin he felt the heat from the weapon's blade as it
crackled centimetres past the flesh of his back. He coun-
tered the attack with the butt of his rifle, smashing it into
his opponent's face and caving in the visor of his chem-suit
helmet. The Nort officer fell off the turret with a gurgling
shriek, choking on a noxious mixture of his own blood and
Nu Earth's air. He hit the steep, armoured slope of the
Blackmare's front and then fell screaming beneath the
grinding tracks.

Rogue blew the turret hatch with a seal-burster, leaping
down into the turret interior to deal with the crew.
Unprotected by chem-suits or breather masks, the men
manning the tank's main turret gun were easy prey to the
poisoned air that came rushing into the vehicle in the
wake of the seal-burster blast. Those who were still alive,
choking and partly paralysed from the effects of exposure, proved even easier prey to Gunnar's vibro-knife
bayonet attachment.

Rogue kicked open the hatch in the turret room floor
and stepped back smartly as a volley of shots ricocheted
up the ladder shaft from the tank's main control room
below. The Norts down there probably as many as fifteen
of them, manning the Blackmare's various weapons and
power systems, had breather masks on and were now
waiting for him. Rogue reached back and grabbed the
three strange oblong-shaped grenade devices dispensed to
him by Bagman's claw-arm.

Needle-bombs, picked up on a raid on a Nort supply base
on the long, hard journey to Nordstadt. Rogue was glad
he'd hung on to them. Now he'd found the perfect opportunity to use them.

CRUCIBLE 115

He pulled the fuses and dropped them down the ladder shaft, slamming the hatch shut immediately afterwards. He heard a scream of panic from below, cut off abruptly by a series of three sharp whiplash sounds as the needle-bombs detonated, instantly turning the interior of the tank's control room into a slaughterhouse.

Each of the devices was packed with thousands of razor-sharp metal splinters wrapped around a high-density explosive core. When one detonated it sprayed the splinters out in a circumference of a hundred metres or more, perforating everything within that range. The grenades were designed for open air use against concentrations of attacking troops, to be dropped by low-flying aircraft or laid in by mortar bombardment. One splinter hit on its own was rarely enough to kill, unless it pierced a vital organ. Dozens of such hits, however, would reduce a chem-suit to tatters and cause death either by atmospheric exposure or massive blood loss. Used properly, they could break up an infantry attack in seconds. Used inside the confines of the metal-walled interior of a tank cab, they were nothing short of gruesomely devastating.

The Blackmare's crew weren't so much killed as ripped to shreds. The sprays of needles tore human bodies apart as if they were made of wet paper. Needles by the hundred penetrated control panels and operating systems, shattering delicate internal components. They struck power feeds and electric cables, causing multiple blow-outs. The huge war machine ground to a halt, its crew dead, its control systems destroyed.

Rogue opened the floor hatch again, glancing at the scene below.

"Nothing moving down there, Rogue," confirmed Helm. "No life signs, no audio pick-up of any trace of human heartbeats."

Rogue looked down and saw a metal floor slick with thick sprays of human blood. More blood dripped from the bottom rungs of the ladder. The entire interior of the space had been redecorated in shades of wet crimson. He dropped the hatch with a clang, satisfied that the bombs had done their task.

He reached for Gunnar, picking him up and gently removing the precious GI biochip from its slot in the side of the rifle. The Blackmare's main gun and turret power systems were still operational and a winking green light on a console board showed the gun was armed and ready to fire, with a large-calibre las-shell already loaded and in the pipe.

Moving quickly, he prised open the casing of the weapon's targeting computer and yanked out a handful of small circuit board chips. The device died with a quiet electronic squawk, the green status lights on its master console fading away to nothing. A second later, it hummed with life again as Rogue slotted Gunnar's biochip into the place of the missing circuit boards.

"Okay, I'm in, Rogue. Let's do it," Gunnar's voice sounded different, strange and harsh, filtered through the speech modulator of the Nort computer.

Rogue smiled. One Nort Blackmare down, one more to go.

Hanna couldn't believe it when she saw the blue-skinned figure leap onto the top of the Nort tank and wipe out almost two full squads of elite Kashans in as much time as it would normally take her to change ammo mags on her las-carbine. She still didn't believe it when she saw him vanish inside the turret and then, again in roughly the time it would take to swap las-round clips, the giant tank came shuddering to a dead halt, stopping just a few terrifying metres short of where she lay helpless in its path.

There was a loud, rumbling crash from behind the dead Blackmare and Hanna watched in horror as the second Nort tank started to crest the rise of the rubble mound blocking the street behind her. Nort infantry and smaller armoured vehicles swarmed after it, eager to avenge the mysterious loss of the first Blackmare.

Then, as Hanna watched, the turret of the first tank began to revolve, turning away from the Souther positions to point directly back down the street towards the advancing Norts.

What happened next was something else she would never forget.

"Target in sight," reported Gunnar. "Range, fifty metres and closing. Multiple secondary targets well within range of impact blast radius on primary target."

Rogue looked through the targeter scope. The enormous metal bulk of the second Blackmare entirely filled the scene in front of him. He saw the armoured slopes of the target's front and turret rise up in front of him as the Blackmare laboriously climbed its way up the rubble slope. He saw the faces of the Kashan tank grenadiers clinging onto the vehicle's sides. A shot now would probably be a kill shot, but they would only have this one chance and Rogue couldn't risk wasting it on a shot that might only disable the Nort tank or, even worse, simply just ricochet off its metre-thick reinforced front armour.

"Hold your fire, Gunnar. Wait for my order."

The front of the Blackmare reared up as it crested the top of the rubble mound.

"Wait…"

Rogue tracked down with the targeter scope, seeing the Blackmare's vulnerable underbelly slide into sight as the tank crested the rise.

"Wait…"

The tank sat at almost a thirty degree angle, its treads grinding rubble boulders into dust as they fought to push it over the top of the crest.

"Wait…"

Any moment now, it would tumble forward as it made it over the top, and charge down the other side of the slope towards them. Its own turret gun was pointing uselessly up into the air, but once the tank cleared the rise and levelled off, it would be targeting them almost immediately.

"Wait…"

Rogue scanned the underbelly of the target, looking for weak spots. Although it was the Blackmare's most vulnerable spot, the armour there was still thicker than the frontal armour of most other tank vehicles on Nu Earth.

"Wait…"

The Blackmare lurched forward, its front end descending, its underbelly slipping out of sight as it cleared the rise and started its descent of the other side of the rubble heap.

"Fire!"

The concussive roar of the Blackmare's turret gun was almost enough to knock Hanna unconscious. She saw the shot strike the second Blackmare square in the underbelly, just as the tank tipped back and forth at the fulcrum of its attempt to negotiate the top of the rubble mound.

It penetrated through, exploding inside the vehicle's hull, destroying it and instantly killing everyone aboard, both those inside it and those clinging on to its exterior. Pieces of tank and the bodies of the Kashan grenadiers riding on its hull were blown high into the air. The explosion knocked the massive body of the tank backwards, sending it sliding back down the slope and into the midst of the troops and vehicles following on behind. A whole platoon of Kashan stormtroopers died beneath its tracks. Two Firespitter flame-gun tanks and an APC full of more Kashans were crushed like matchwood by the weight of the sliding juggernaut.

It exploded a second time when it hit the bottom of the slope, the fires raging inside it setting off its fuel tanks and munitions stores. The effects on the Nort troops and infantry gathered there was catastrophic. Those that weren't consumed by the explosion were crushed under tonnes of masonry from yet another unstable building that came collapsing inwards onto the street from the effects of the blast wave.

The detonation of the munitions blew off the Blackmare's turret, sending it flying into the air atop a billowing column of flame and smoke. It came crashing down to earth a seemingly impossible one hundred and forty metres away, landing right on the heads of the Norts at the rear of the attack wave. The Kashan Legion battalion commander died along with many of his troops, as the shattered, burning mass of the turret rolled right over the top of him and his command vehicle.

Hanna saw all this and still didn't believe it. She still didn't believe it when she saw the blue-skinned figure climb back out of the turret of the first Blackmare, slide nimbly down the front of the vehicle and leap a full eight metres down on to the ground.

Rogue hit the ground with a thud, his GI legs braced for an impact that could well have broken ordinary human bones.

He took off running, pursued by las-shots from those few Kashans who had made it over the top of the rubble heap and so escaped the same fate as their comrades on the other side. He wasn't worried. In less than thirty seconds, most of these scum would be history because thirty seconds was the time setting he had fixed on the demolition charge he had dumped down the turret's shell supply shaft just before he vacated the Blackmare. It was still back there, ticking away among the stacks of shells in the munitions store buried deep within the Blackmare's hull, and when it blew the effects would be identical to those that put paid to the other Nort tank.

Rogue still wasn't worried. Running at GI speed, he would be far away when it blew and the destroyed hulks of the two Blackmares would be more than enough to effectively block off this broadway from any further Nort armoured advances. If the Norts wanted to find an open route through into the city's steelworks sector, then they would have to look for it somewhere else.

A shout from Bagman, however, quickly signalled a sudden change to Rogue's escape plan.

"Eleven o'clock, Rogue. One of ours, injured but still alive. She's lying directly in the blast radius when that Nort junk pile goes up!"

Rogue saw her, a wounded Souther Infantry sergeant, struggling to stand up despite the pain from a broken left leg. He changed course without thinking, reaching her in a few strides, scooping her up into his arms without even breaking pace.

She grunted in pain from the sudden movement but didn't cry out. A good trooper, was Rogue's instinctive judgement. He had arrived at the battle scene to see enough of her squad's stand against the advancing Kashans to know that she was an able squad leader, someone who the Southers would need in the days to come, in what was clearly the beginning of a major Nort offensive to retake what was left of Nordstadt.

Rogue kept on running, Nort las-rounds striking the ground around him. Answering fire from the Souther troops at the other end of the street crackled through the air over his head. Rogue changed direction again, making directly for the safety on offer there.

The limp body in his arms stirred. Hanna looked up into the face of her saviour.

"You… you're the Rogue Trooper," she said, incredulously. "I… I thought you were just another Nu Earth legend…"

"You better pray he ain't, lady, 'cos, right now, he's the only thing between you and a one-way ticket to Palookaville."

Hanna realised the leaks in her suit must be more serious than she thought and that she had gone chem-happy, because she could have sworn the weird-sounding, electronic-modulated voice she just heard had come from one of the Genetic Infantryman's pieces of equipment.

"Ten seconds till boom time, Rogue."

Now Hanna knew she was spacing out from breathing in too much chem-cloud air, because that voice definitely came from the helmet on the Genetic Infantryman's head.

Rogue cleared the two metre high barrier of the secondary barricade with a single vault, shouting out in warning to the Souther troops gathered there.

"Fire in the hole! Heads down, Southside."

He laid the semi-conscious form of Hanna down in front of an astonished company medic. "Her left leg's broken and her chem-suit's leaking in at least two places. Get some suit patches on her and give her a shot of whatever anti-pathogens you've got in your med-kit."

A second later, the Blackmare exploded in a titanic blast that put paid to the remaining Norts and sealed off the

broadway once and for all. The Souther troops behind the
barricade cowered in shock as the roaring blast wave rode
over the top of them.

When the dust cleared and they dared to look up again,
Rogue was long gone.

THIRTEEN

The news was soon all over Nordstadt. The unofficial radio chatter between one Souther unit and another was full of it.

"…swear to god, I saw him with my own eyes. The Rogue Trooper. Three metres tall he was, with skin that deflected las-rounds like they was light summer rain."

"Took out almost a whole Kashan armoured division, I heard. Blew up six Blackmares in a row with that fancy GI super-rifle of his and left a Nort general strangled to death with the air pipes of his own chem-suit…"

"…a sign of god, I tell ya. Now that the Rogue Trooper's here, there ain't no way the Norts are ever going to take this place. They might as well pack up and head for home right now…"

"…been given some kinda special amnesty by the top brass at Milli-com, that's what some guy at Divisional HQ told me. They orbit-dropped him in to raise hell behind the Nort lines and this is just the start of it. Yeah, now Rogue's here, you know that the rest of our reinforcements can't be too far behind…"

The radio chatter filled the Souther airwaves, the news leaping from one unit to the other. Even just knowing that the Rogue Trooper was there with them, and that he had already made his presence felt among the Norts, was enough to give the hard-pressed Souther forces fresh hope. The Norts had pushed in to seize several of the city's out-lying sectors, but once word spread of what happened in the steelworks sector, the Southers started fighting back with renewed vigour. The Nort advances into the north-west hab district and the harbour sector were stopped dead in their tracks, while a counter-attack by the remains of the 161st Souther Light Infantry Division, with armoured support from the Third Barbary Zone Rangers, actually succeeded in completely driving them back out of the territory they had seized that day in the flattened ruins of the southern factory sector. The Nort advance faltered and then stopped altogether as Nort High Command deemed that any further losses of the scale they were now starting to suffer were unacceptable at this opening stage of the offensive.

A glance at the map of Nordstadt confirmed their thinking. Despite the setbacks, they had still succeeded in seizing over seventy per cent of the intended target territory, and their grip around the centre of the city was now measurably greater. They listened in to the chatter on the Souther radio frequencies, hearing the excited whoops and hollers of the Souther troops as they celebrated the day's victories.

Let them have their moment of celebration, the Nort generals smiled to themselves. Let them think their precious Genetic Infantryman will be enough to turn back the tide of men and machines that will soon come sweeping over the Souther positions and take back Nordstadt for good. They would all learn differently soon enough.

Others were listening in too, and what they learned was exactly what they wanted to hear.

Venner sat in the sixtieth floor of one of the smashed glass towers of what had once been Nordstadt's main financial district. The building had doubtlessly once been far taller, possibly as high as two hundred storeys or more, but twenty years of unrelenting warfare had been more than enough to reduce it to its present height.

As it was, it was still probably one of the highest points in the city, no doubt prized by both sides and changed hands dozens of times over the course of the conflict so far. The corpses of the building's most recent occupants, the half dozen members of a Nort observation unit, lay scattered about him. Venner had scaled one of the building's elevator shafts, easily bypassing the booby trap devices set in place there long ago by one side or the other. The Norts hadn't even known he was there until he struck with pistol and knife, and he had killed them all before they could send out a warning.

Venner scanned the terrain and easily picked out details of the day's battles. As night fell over Nordstadt, Nort and Souther artillery batteries traded retaliatory bombardments. The Souther rounds fell on the territory lost to the Norts in today's assaults, while the Nort guns pummelled the retreating Souther forces as they dug into their new defensive positions. One whole manufacturing sector on the other side of the river was ablaze, torched by retreating Souther troops to block the enemy's advance through it. Souther incendiary shells continued to fall, feeding the blaze even further and frustrating any Nort attempts to negotiate a safe route through the heart of the inferno.

Atmocraft from both sides buzzed through the night skies above the city. Low-flying bombers made attack runs over troop positions and higher-flying spotter craft directed in fire for the artillery batteries. Fighters flew amongst them, picking off targets almost at will. In the few minutes that Venner had been watching, he had seen eight flights end either in flaring midair fireballs or as blazing comets sent crashing earthwards into the rubble below. The Norts seemed to be getting the worst of it, and any of their bomber squadrons attempting to fly over the Southers' inner defence perimeter were met with intensive barrages of anti-aircraft fire from which few managed to escape.

After months of relative inactivity, at least by Nordstadt standards, the battle for control had flared back into life with a vengeance.

As Venner watched, he listened into the radio communications of both sides, his assassin's instincts sifting through the mass of chattering voices for the information he was looking for. It didn't take him long to find it.

Swiftly, he tapped out a short message on his wrist communicator keyboard, sending up a code-protected transmission to a null-shielded S-Three comms-satellite in orbit overhead. The satellite, which appeared on no official roster and which the generals in Milli-com knew nothing about, intercepted the transmission and beamed it on to its ultimate destination, adding several more impenetrable layers of S-Three cipher encryption to further protect the contents of the message. A few hours from now, his patron in Milli-com would be reading the decoded message on his desktop screen.

"Secondary target's presence in Nordstadt confirmed. Acquisition and neutralisation of primary and secondary targets imminent. Estimate twenty-four to forty-eight hours for successful completion of mission. Require final confirmation of secure extraction operation from Nordstadt once mission has been completed."

Venner bedded down for the night after first assuring himself that the booby traps and security remotes he had set in place to guard all the approaches to his personal little eyrie were all functioning as they should be. Tomorrow, the hunt would begin in earnest, starting in the steelworks sector.

Outside, the sounds of gunfire and explosions would rumble on all through the night. Like every other living soul in Nordstadt, Venner didn't know that tomorrow's dawn would be the last one to ever rise over the city. The Hammerfall was now less than twenty-four hours away.

FOURTEEN

He didn't have a name, not really. The name he had been born with he had left behind long ago along with the face that went with it. He had lost both in the burned-out wreck of a crashed life-pod somewhere out there in no-man's-land, after his near fatal escape from the destruction of Buzzard Three. Since then, he had taken on other names and other faces and identities, many of them stolen from dead men. Beneath them all, however, was the fire-ravaged features of his real face, and the new name that went with it, the name that marked him as an outcast pariah no matter where he tried to hide on this miserable, god-forsaken planet.

The Traitor General. That was what they called him now and, in time, that was the only name that really mattered.

The Traitor General: the man responsible for the destruction of the Genetic Infantry Regiment, the man who planted the seeds of the trap that ultimately saw them wiped out almost to the last man in the infamous Quartz Zone Massacre.

The Traitor General: the faceless, nameless double-agent inside Milli-com who had been secretly feeding information to the Norts for years, all the time working behind a facade of loyalty to the Souther cause to ensure that victory ultimately went to the Nordland enemy.

The Traitor General, a name that was as much a well-known myth in the minds of most Souther soldiers on Nu Earth as that of the blue-skinned genetic freak that so relentlessly pursued him across the planet's many different warzones.

For maybe the thousandth time, the traitor cursed the events that brought him to this lowly fate. Once he had been a high-ranking officer in the Southlands military forces, a favoured son of Milli-com on the promotion fast-track and no doubt destined for great things. The fact that he was also a Nort double-agent gave him the assurance that no matter which side won the war, his future prosperity was still secure. And then the Rogue Trooper had appeared, tracking back through the sequence of events behind the Quartz Zone Massacre with a relentless and superhuman patience to find the man responsible for the deaths of his fellow genetic freaks. Buzzard-Three had been destroyed, and the traitor had been cast down from his lofty position, cast down into the living hell of the war on Nu Earth.

Cast down to hide and dwell in hellholes like this, thought the traitor, looking at his present surroundings.

It was dark in the underground shelter, the place lit only by a few flickering glow-lamps from the pack's supply of scavenged equipment. Figures moved in the semi-darkness, many of them crippled or deformed, dressed in the ragged, patched remains of chem-suits and armour stripped from the dead and wounded on the battlefield above. These chem-suits, patched and then repatched again, often crudely put together from pieces of Nort and Souther equipment alike, offered little real protection from the long-term effects of Nu Earth's toxic atmosphere, and many of the figures before the traitor showed the telltale symptoms of chem-poisoning: weeping sores on hands and faces, limbs twisted by the effects of rad-disease and viral mutation, eyes blinded by cataracts, breathing ragged and laboured from lungs hopelessly damaged by tox-inhalation.

He looked at the crippled, diseased forms of his followers, and laughed bitterly to himself. Perhaps he had found his rightful role after all; a disfigured outcast, leading a pack of similar freaks.

It hadn't been difficult to assume a position of natural leadership over them in the short time he had been in Nord-stadt. Most of them came from the pitiful remnants of the city's original civilian population. Deformed and diseased, their minds shell-shocked beyond repair by more than two decades of continuous warfare, reduced to a feral state of existence from scavenging for survival among the ruins of their former homes, they were easy to manipulate and dominate for a man of his abilities. It was the others amongst them who had predictably proved to be the real challenge; the mercenaries and deserters who had formed the leadership of the scavenger tribe.

The *previous* leadership, the traitor reminded himself, with a smile. The coup d'etat had been brief, but bloody. The tribe's leader and his inner core of followers had been set upon and hacked apart by his own followers in a few hours of violence that the tunnels in which they sheltered filled with the sounds of shrieks and screams. In a show of ruthless force designed to dispel any further dissent in the ranks, the survivors of the previous regime had been rounded up on his orders and crucified out in no-man's-land. The victims had been arranged in a circle, each one of them with a time-set plasma sphere grenade hung round their necks. The fuse settings had been staggered, so that each man watched the others around him explode, knowing that, in a few minutes or even seconds, his turn would be next.

The lesson had not been lost on the rest of the group. No, thought the traitor, he did not think there would be any dissent against the new regime anytime soon.

Most of the tribe had been sheltering down here in the tunnels while the battles and artillery bombardments raged above. It was obvious to the traitor that a major offensive was just beginning, possibly one that would deliver Nordstadt back into the hands of its original owners for good. The traitor's followers had collected enough information in their scavenging forays to the surface to make it abundantly clear that the Souther forces in Nordstadt were now seriously under-strength. It had been the traitor's plan to sit the worst of the battle out, emerging only near the end to join in the battle on the victor's side, callously and casually expending the lives of his rabble of followers in the process. Afterwards, he would reveal his presence to the city's new masters and seek some kind of position among them. Even after its final conquest, Nordstadt would still be a lawless and alien place that bore no resemblance to the city the Norts had originally built, and surely the Norts would welcome the aid of an ally who had an army of rubble scouts and scavengers at his command.

Now, however, the latest news that his followers had brought back from the surface had caused him to rethink that plan. The Rogue Trooper was here in Nordstadt.

Of course, it was no coincidence that his pursuer was here in Nordstadt so soon after his own arrival in the city. Somehow, in some way the traitor couldn't understand, the Genetic Infantryman must have learned of his presence here and come to Nordstadt to continue his relentless hunt.

At first, the traitor had screamed in rage and frustration at the news, knowing that, as always his enemy would somehow track him down in his new lair. Track him down and try to kill him, as he had tried to do in the past. The traitor might escape as he had done before, but it would still mean abandoning this new hiding place, wretched as it was, and returning to the even more wretched existence as a wandering fugitive.

He had forced himself to calm down, instructing his suit's med-system to administer an extra-large dosage of narco-fix into his veins. The synthi-morphine mixture floated through his bloodstream and the traitor's thoughts floated with it.

He considered his options. His bargaining power with Nordstadt's soon-to-be new owners was poor, he knew. No one ever trusted a traitor, not even those who had bene-fited most from his acts of treason. He knew enough about the Nordland mindset to realise that whatever valuable ser-vices he had done for them in the past would now count for very little. At best, when he emerged from hiding and announced himself to the victorious Nort forces, he could probably only expect to be given some humiliatingly low-ranking and servile position, a deliberately insulting gesture from his Nort masters to show him just how little use he was to them. At worst, it would be a las-round through the back of the skull, an efficient tidying-up of the last loose end from a now long-ago defunct intelligence operation.

What he needed, he realised, was a proper bargaining chip. Something the Norts must want but were unable to acquire for themselves.

He sat motionless on the scrapheap throne his followers had built for him, brooding. He sat so long that those gathered before him began to stir uneasily, some of them perhaps wondering with a thrill of secret delight if the narco-fix they had seen him administer to himself hadn't actually killed him off.

Eventually, the bravest of them shuffled nervously forward to check if he was still alive, and that was when the figure on the throne moved. Moved and raised his head to smile at them.

Those brave few drew back in fear. They had followed his commands for long enough now to know what such smiles meant. When the man who led them smiled, then death and pain for somebody followed soon afterwards.

"Listen to me carefully," he told them, in his rasping, burn-disfigured voice. "The blue-skinned man who wears no chem-suit, the one the voices on the radio speak about. The one the Southers call the Rogue Trooper and the Norts call the Genetik Infantryman. You know the man I speak of?"

Heads nodded vigorously. Figures shambled forward, eager to carry out the commands of their tribal leader. The traitor smiled again.

"Good. I want you to go out into the city and look for him. You will search for him and you will find him and when you find him, this is what I want you to do…"

FIFTEEN

As Rogue expected, the morning sun cast a heavy pall of low-lying chem-mist over the ruined city. During the night, much of the pollutant material in the air had frozen into a toxic chem-frost that clung to every available surface. Now, in the heat of the rising sun, it melted into a hovering layer of poison mist that offered just as much cover as the shell-shattered buildings and strewn fields of rubble.

"Been listening to the Souther Command daily weather bulletins, Rogue," reported Helm, their appointed squad comedian. "Outlook today, after these mists burn off, is supposed to be clear and sunny, although heavy acid rain downpours are expected later in the evening. The Milli-com weatherman says if you're going out today then to be sure to bring along some hard target headgear and any armoured plasti-skin you might have, since otherwise unexpected showers of random artillery shelling and not-so-random incidents of enemy sniper fire may put a serious crimp in your day-tripper excursion plans."

"In other words, just another ordinary day on Nu Earth," grunted Rogue, not in the mood for Helm's early morning wisecracking.

"Yeah. Synth out, Helm," said Gunnar irritably. "We're here to do a job. We find the traitor, we plug him, we hand ourselves in, we get sent back to Milli-com, we get re-gened and then maybe after that, if you're real lucky, we start paying attention to you and your lame-ass jokes."

"Amen to that," echoed Bagman. "Don't know about you two schmoes, but the first thing I'm gonna do is hit the bars big time and get myself a drink. And I mean a real drink.

Been biochipped so long, I can't even remember what a slug of the proper hard stuff tastes like. And then, after that, I'm gonna call in all those bets you three suckers have lost to me over the years, cash myself in and retire out of this chickenshit operation an honest-to-god millionaire, with all you three dopes' backpay in my pocket."

Rogue allowed his team their usual moment of pretend ill-tempered banter. Most of it was pure fantasy, of course. GIs were officially classified as military hardware created and owned by Milli-com, and not as ordinary enlisted soldiers, so all Bagman's talk about retirement and backpay was just knowing make-believe, as was his spiel about going to an enlisted man's bar and getting pissed. When you were a GI, built to withstand the most toxic substances created by man, it was kind of difficult to get drunk on a few shots of synthi-scotch. A GI could probably drink an entire battalion of ordinary soldiers under the table, one man after another, and still get up and walk away sober.

There was one thing that was true, though, and that was the part about getting back to Milli-com and getting Helm, Gunnar and Bagman re-gened. That was the whole point of what they were doing, Rogue knew. Kill the man responsible for the destruction of the GI Regiment, and then get the members of his biochip comrades returned to life. After the traitor was dead, Rogue would quite happily turn himself over to Souther military justice and face however many Milli-com interrogation officers as they wanted to bring in, telling every one of them that it was his decision to desert and go rogue, and that his biochip squad members were always just unwilling accomplices to his many breaches of military regulations. He would do whatever it took and face whatever punishment was coming to him, just as long as it gave his friends a second chance of life, their biochip memories and personalities implanted back into new re-gened GI bodies.

While the others bickered good-naturedly, Rogue crawled out from beneath the upturned slab of rockcrete that had been their home for the night and scanned the surrounding terrain. He knew the biochips' sensor systems would already have checked for signs of danger, but there was still no kind of sensor system invented yet that Rogue trusted better than his own combat experiences and GI augmented eyes.

He saw nothing, but instinctively ducked back into cover as soon as Helm gave an urgent beep of alarm. Rogue hugged rockcrete. A few seconds later, a flight of three low-flying atmocraft zoomed directly overhead, their bomb and missile racks laden with high-explosive death, the sound of their approach masked by their stealth engines and the rubble of artillery duels in the near distance.

"Nice going, domehead," grumbled Gunnar. "You see the markings on the underside of those things? Those were Souther crates you had us hiding from."

"Helm made a good call, Gunnar," interceded Rogue. "We didn't know what they were until they were right on top of us. Could have just as easily have been Norts. And besides, doesn't matter much that they were supposed friendlies. After all, how many times in this war have we found ourselves on the wrong end of a Souther gunsight, either by accident or because some creep at Milli-com wanted us out of the picture for good?"

"Okay, so where do we go from here, Rogue?" asked Bagman as Rogue climbed back out of the cover.

It was a question Rogue was wondering himself. Nordstadt was huge, covering more than two hundred square kilometres of ground. It would take weeks to cover it all on foot, and that was even without the added inconvenience of the major conflict being waged here at the moment, or the equally inconvenient fact that much of that ground was strictly off-limits to him, either in the hands of Norts who would shoot at him on sight, or Southers who would probably just try to arrest him as a wanted deserter.

Still, the traitor was here, alright. Rogue could feel it in his bones, his hunter's instincts telling him at some mysterious, deep-down level that his prey was not too far away. There was nothing on any of the intercepted radio traffic he'd listened into about the traitor or his whereabouts, a fact which didn't surprise Rogue at all. The traitor would stay away from both sides, making his presence as invisible as possible to both of them, as he always had done in the past. He would be lying low somewhere, keeping out of the way of the main battle, waiting for an opportunity to benefit from its outcome. It wouldn't be easy finding him, but that didn't worry Rogue. If need be, he was more than prepared to look under every rubble pile, search every burned-out building and crawl around in every sludge-filled shell crater to find the man who killed his comrades.

There was the crackling sound of las-fire in the near-distance. It came from the direction of the broken but still towering stumps of the steelworks' giant kiln chimneys. Rogue turned, listening to the sounds.

"Small-arms fire, probably no more than squad level or maybe even less. Maybe a three or four-man patrol coming up against something similar," judged Gunnar.

"Maybe. Or maybe not," decided Rogue, his GI instincts pulling him in the direction of the gunfire.

Venner tracked a path through the rubble, alert for any threats around him. He had downloaded the latest tactical reports via a secure S-Three backdoor into Souther Warzone Command's data files, and knew there was a Souther sniper operating in this area, in the district over by the loading yards. Even if he hadn't been warned of his presence, Venner would still have spotted the fool easily enough. This sector wasn't yet seeing even nearly the worst of the Nort attacks now happening elsewhere, thanks to the Rogue Trooper's efforts in blocking the Nort armoured advance yesterday, but Nort infantry units were still infiltrating forward through the ruins, giving the Souther marksman plenty of work.

Venner had heard the man's rifle sound four times in the last few minutes and could tell from the direction of the gunshots that he was barely bothering to move position after each kill. The sniper might be racking up the score of his kill tally, but he also might as well send up a photon flare to mark his position to the enemy. If the situation remained as it was, the Norts would either outflank and kill him, or if they were smarter, pin down his location and call in an artillery strike to take care of him.

Either way, the idiot's fate mattered little to Venner. If he'd had the time, he might have decided to set up a position of his own and give this novice a short, sharp lesson in what it meant to be a real master sniper.

Venner stopped moving, hugging the cover of a nearby wall as he heard the sound of atmocraft engines. He looked up and saw a flight of three low-flying gunships pass by, about half a kilometre or so away, heading east towards the Nort positions. They were Souther craft, but Venner still couldn't risk them spotting him. He was wearing a non-standard chem-suit without any identifying insignia or Souther military markings. To a gunner aboard one of those craft, he would just look like another target of opportunity, something to be freely blasted at on the way to their real mission objective.

He watched as they flew off, satisfying himself that there was no other sign of danger before moving off again. Despite all the excited radio chatter on the Souther airwaves, there had been no other confirmed sightings of the Rogue Trooper since yesterday. Venner was still convinced his target hadn't yet moved out of the area. He was boxed in here now with the Southers taking up strong defensive positions to the west and the Norts sitting in waiting positions to the east and north. Venner didn't doubt the Genetic Infantryman's ability to find a route through the Nort lines almost at any point he wanted, but such action would almost inevitably have resulted in sightings of him being sounded over the Nort comm-channels, and Venner hadn't picked up word of any such thing.

No, he was still here, his hunter's instincts told him. To the south was the river and one of the dockyard sectors. Venner didn't need to listen in to the radio chatter to know that there was heavy fighting going on there. The Souther forces were desperately battling to turn back the attacking Norts and deny the river crossing points to the Nort armoured divisions now massed on the other side of the river.

Venner suspected that this might be the direction his target would be heading. The lure of outnumbered and trapped Souther troops and the chance to make the same kind of difference as he had yesterday might just be too much for the man's genetic programming to resist.

Venner prepared to change course, calling up an updated image on his visor's digi-map facility to check the disposition of the Nort and Souther forces in that direction, looking for natural choke points on the route to the dockyards where he could set up position and lay in wait for the Rogue Trooper's passing.

He was stopped short by the sound of las-fire from nearby. He crouched down for a few moments until he was satisfied that none of it was being directed at him. A few moments later he was scaling up the jagged remains of a collapsed building, lying low on top of it and scanning the terrain with a sniper's practised eye. He saw figures in chem-suits scrabbling across the rubble a few hundred metres away. He raised his rifle's magno-scope to his eye and studied the scene in better detail.

What he saw made him smile. He abandoned any further thoughts about the battle at the dockyard sector and settled in to watch and wait. A hunter's instinct told him that, with luck, he might find exactly what he was looking for right here.

The Nort patrol squad scrabbled across the rubble field, calling out excitedly to each other as they pursued their prey. The targets were faster than them and able to scale rubble heaps and negotiate a route through the ruins with astonishing ease, but luckily they still weren't able to run faster than a las-round.

The patrol squad fired off potshots as they ran, forcing their targets to duck for cover among the rubble. Karl, a corporal in the Tenth Nu-Sevastopol Infantry, paused on top of the wreck of a Souther armoured car, taking careful aim with his AK-477 las-carbine. He'd already expended more than half a clip in taking potshots at the piece of rubble rat scum he had been chasing, and now considered it a matter of personal honour to bring the little shit down once and for all.

These rubble rat scavengers had been raiding his company's supplies for days now, stealing ration packs, med-boxes and anything else they could get their sub-human thieving hands on, and now he and his comrades finally had them in their sights.

Karl knew that the rubble rats were supposed to be the Nordland citizens, the remains of the original inhabitants of this miserable, god-forsaken heap of ruins, but their company political officer had assured them that they had willingly reduced themselves to the status of sub-human refuse, and so could no longer be considered part of the glorious Greater Nordland race. Extermination, the political officer had patiently explained, was the only fate they now deserved. The sacred soil of Nordstadt must be cleansed free of the contaminating presence of Southers and sub-human scum alike.

Such a licence to kill only added to the Nort troopers' bloodlust. The failure of yesterday's armoured advance into this sector had caused Nordland Command to order Karl's division to remain in position until the required break-throughs were made in neighbouring sectors. Karl and his comrades had been forced to sit back and watch as other divisions marched off into battle to grab their share of glory in the final taking of Nordstadt.

And so Karl pulled the trigger of his las-carbine with a free conscience, watching in satisfaction as his shot struck its target in the lower back, felling him and sending him tumbling down the slope of the rubble heap he had almost reached the top of.

"I got one!" Karl called excitedly, listening to the answered whoops of congratulations over his helmet comm-link.

The sub-human was still alive, thrashing feebly and help-lessly at the bottom of the rubble heap. Karl ran forward to finish him off, slinging his rifle over his shoulder and draw-ing his dagger from its sheath. He rolled the body of his victim over on to its front, severing the air-tubes of its

crude, scratch-built chem-suit with a single sweep of the
dagger blade. The sub-human's eyes rolled white in toxic
shock, the inside of its helmet visor splattering with blood
as it took its first gasping, lung-destroying breath of Nu
Earth air.

Karl abandoned the sub-human to its death throws, eager
to claim further kills while there were still more targets
available. There was the crack of a las-carbine, followed
moments later by another excited shout over his helmet
radio.

"I got one too, Karl. A clean kill. One shot, that's all it
took, not like yours."

Karl cursed. It was Feydya, the squad blowhard. If Karl
didn't at least match his marksmanship, he would never
hear the end of it.

He leaped on top of a rubble platform, taking aim at the
last remaining target. It was a child, judging by its size. Difficult to hit, smaller than the others, moving fast, dodging
in and out of the cover of the surrounding rubble.

Karl took aim, competing with the other members of his
squad for the thrill of the last kill. They opened fire almost
simultaneously, someone – not Karl – clipping the sub-
human with their shot. The sub-human fell with a squeal of
pain. Karl was too fast with his follow-up shot, missing the
target by a good two metres. Feydya cackled with glee and
lined up his own kill-shot. A burst of las-rounds rang out
and Feydya's head vaporised in a red spray.

Karl swung his aim round and saw a blue-skinned figure
without a chem-suit standing on a rubble heap fifty metres
away and calmly gunning down the members of his squad,
one man after another.

Venner saw the GI gun down the five-man Nort squad in a
matter of seconds. Tight controlled bursts, fired without
panic or malice into each of the enemy soldiers' heads and
chests, killing them all instantly. One managed to get a
shot off, but it went wide and the Nort was sprawled on
the ground dead before he ever had a chance to correct his
aim.

The Rogue Trooper stood for a moment, gun at the ready as he scanned for any more enemies. Satisfied there were none, he slung his rifle on his shoulder and advanced slowly towards the injured rubble rat child, holding his hands up to show the terrified child that he meant no harm.

Venner saw all this through the scope of his rifle, tracking his target's every move. He smiled in satisfaction, pleased that his hunch had played out correctly. The Genetic Trooper was biologically and psychologically conditioned to take Nort lives and save Souther ones, but again, some rogue element seemed to have entered into the behaviour of this particular GI. Study of his past exploits had quickly shown Venner that the target showed a tendency to needlessly risk his own life and jeopardise his mission in order to go to the aid of the injured and helpless, especially if they were non-combatants. It was a weakness in his character, one that was now going to cost him dear.

Venner took careful aim, capturing the figure of the GI dead centre in the crosshairs of his rifle's magno-scope.

Rogue flinched and turned suddenly, scanning the ruins to his left. He paused for a moment, his eyes narrowing in suspicion, his gaze looking for signs of anything out of the ordinary.

"Something wrong, Rogue?"

"Not sure, Helm. Could have sworn I just sensed something out there for a moment. You picking up anything?"

"Nothing on my sensors," confirmed Gunnar.

"Nada here," reported Helm.

"I got zip too," said Bagman.

"Must just be getting jumpy," said Rogue, placing Gunnar on the lip of a shattered wall. "Guard duty, Gunnar. Set scanners to max and watch my back."

"Gotcha, Rogue."

"Bagman, dispense suit patches and med-kit and let's get this kid fixed up."

Rogue worked quickly and efficiently, patching up the las-round tear in the boy's chem-suit and applying anti-burn salve to the skin beneath. The kid's chem-suit was a wreck even before the Nort round tore into it, with slow leaks in about a dozen different places, and the filter mask was a joke. Rogue could only guess at what kinds of poisons it had been failing to protect the kid from, and all he could do was give the kid whatever anti-tox tabs he had remaining in his med-kit.

Rogue didn't have much experience with children. The only ones he'd ever known were his clone-brothers in the GI Regiment, all of them growing up at the same time back on Milli-com. He guessed the one he had here now was about thirteen, and he guessed that the kid probably wouldn't survive into adulthood, not running around Nu Earth in a chem-suit like the one he was wearing.

The kid's face was marked with the signs of disease and chem-poisoning, and he looked half-starved. If he was thirteen, then Nordstadt and the horrors of its war was the only existence he had ever known. Rogue was born to wage war on Nu Earth, but even he couldn't imagine what it must have been like to grow up as a child in a place like this, and what it must have taken for the kid to survive this long.

He was feral, more animal than human. He had whimpered and snarled while Rogue fitted the suit patch and tended to his injury, even snapping his teeth savagely at Rogue's fingers when he had applied the stinging anti-burn salve to his wound. Now he crouched there, staring at Rogue in undisguised awe.

Never mind the blue skin, thought Rogue, what's got to be really freaking him out is the fact that I'm not wearing a chem-suit or using a breathing mask. He's spent his entire life in this hell-hole. He's never seen a human being walking about in the open without a chem-suit.

"Bagman, dispense a couple of ration packs."

Rogue offered them to the kid and they disappeared into the pouches and pockets of his rag-tag chem-suit just a few moments after the kid had eagerly grabbed them from Rogue's hand. Rubble rats; that was what the Nort and Souther troops here called survivors like him, and the name wasn't so insulting. Rats were good survivors and smart, as well. Suddenly a thought struck Rogue.

"Bagman, dispense hand-compu."

Rogue activated the device, calling up an image from the compu's memory files. He showed it to the kid, immediately registering the look of frightened recognition on the kid's face. The image on the hand-compu's screen was that of the scarred and burn-ravaged face of the Traitor General, as he had looked the last time Rogue had encountered him.

"You've seen this man, haven't you?"

The kid nodded vigorously, snarling at the face on the screen.

"Good kid. Bagman, dispense more ration packs."

These too disappeared into the hidden folds of the chem-suit as quickly as the first one had. Rogue looked at the kid, tapping the image on the compu-screen.

"Okay, now comes the million cred question. Can you show or tell me where he is? Him?"

More vigorous nods, the kid pointing urgently off towards the west. He rose to go, indicating just as urgently for Rogue to follow.

"Hope you got plenty more of those ration packs, Bag-man," said Rogue, standing up and gathering up his equipment. "If this kid can take us to the Traitor General, then he's going to get every last thing you got in there that's even halfway edible."

A safe distance away, Venner settled down and checked the display on his visor plate. He had got what he wanted; a lock on the unique electronic emissions from the GI's biochip equipment. Now he could track the target anywhere it went.

He'd done what he wanted to do, and now the mission was already as good as halfway over. All he had to do now was follow the Rogue Trooper and let him do all the foot-work in tracking down the primary target. After that, Venner would move in, kill them both, and complete his mission.

SIXTEEN

"A lovely lot of fireworks going off in Nordstadt today, Mister Bland. Lots of lovely pickings for the likes of us, I shouldn't wonder."

"Indubitably, Mister Brass. More's the pity that we won't be able to get our hands on any of it, not after the Norts finally take control of the blasted place."

They were flying high above the surface of Nu Earth, their route skirting the edges of the Nordstadt warzone, and allowing them a good look at the carnage taking place below.

Messrs Bland & Brass: "war suppliers to the galaxy", as it said on their business holo-cards. Vultures. Scavengers. War profiteers. Body looters. That was what others called them. They were professional freelance salvage operators, looting the battlefields of Nu Earth for abandoned Nort and Souther hardware which they would then recover, repair and usually sell back to its original owner, or failing that, the next highest bidder.

Body looters were universally despised by both sides of the war, but were also equally employed by both sides too. Body looters went out into the very worst warzone areas, where the Norts' and Southers' own salvage units were unable or unwilling to go, and had an unerring knack for tracking down and recovering the most valuable pieces of military technology. Many body looters sold not just salvage, but also information too, which they collected in their roaming travels across the battlefields.

Some of these body looters got greedy and tried to be clever, selling information to both sides simultaneously.

Some of them even becoming paid agents of either the Nort or Souther intelligence services, or sometimes even both at the same time. These body looters rarely lasted long, and their fates usually resulted in a brief but bloody back-alley assassination on one of the lawless neutral free-zones that sprung up around the main warzones, or in a longer and far more painful final resolution in the interrogation chambers of the Nort or Souther intelligence services.

Morrie Brass and Augustus Bland despised such shoddy amateurism and prided themselves on their uniformly professional approach to their work. They were strictly independent operators, favouring neither one side nor the other and happy to do business with anyone, be they Nort or Souther, human or alien, just as long as the money was there on the table at the end of the day.

Morrie Brass had been a Nort computer expert during his time in the service of the Greater Nordland military forces, while Augustus Bland had worked in the pay corps of the Souther army. They had met in one of the free-zones. Brass was there to find a buyer for the thousands of scraps of classified information he had been steadily stealing for years from the computer records of Nordland High Command, while Bland was there laying low and living off the proceeds of the hundreds of thousands of creds he had embezzled from the army pay corps. Their partnership, business and otherwise, had been mutually rewarding for both of them. Brass's computer skills had been put to good use erasing all trace of Bland's crimes from the Souther central records, while Bland's money had bought them both new faces and identities, and provided all the start-up finance they needed to set themselves up in the freelance battlefield salvage business.

The years they had spent together since then had been happy and extremely profitable ones. Nu Earth wasn't exactly to everyone's taste, but for a pair of smart and careful operators with a sharp eye for money-making opportunities and a necessarily keen sense of self-preservation, it was a highly lucrative place to do business. All you had to do, they had once agreed with each other during a short but extremely enjoyable break together on the pleasure-world of Nu-Martinique, was to understand everything about how many ways there were to be killed on Nu Earth, and be ready with ways to avoid all such unpleasantness.

Like now, for instance.

"One of those Souther Seraphims coming in at us, Mister Brass," reported Bland, looking at the readings on their scanner screen. "Heavens, just look at the speed and manoeuvrability of the thing! What I wouldn't give to have one of those things listed in our next price catalogue."

"Never mind the profit margins for once, Mister Bland," said Brass, irritably. "What about our own personal survival? In case you hadn't noticed, your precious Seraphim appears to have locked onto us with its targeting systems, and no doubt we can expect to be blown out of the air any moment now."

"Not to worry, Mister Brass," said Bland, leaning forward and flicking a switch on the console in front of him. "That's why I insisted we install this little device, remember?"

A few moments later, the scanner screen readings showed the Souther fighter breaking off from its pursuit and disengaging its targeting systems. Thanks to the alien cloaking device he had just switched on, their shuttle would now have a completely different transponder signal and target profile to hide its real identity. To any inquisitive Norts, it would appear to be a Kashan Legion command craft, carrying a high-ranking member of the Norts' most elite and notorious fighting unit. To the pilot of that Souther fighter, it would have looked as if he was mistakenly about to blow a Souther med-shuttle out of the air. Whatever each side saw on their target scanners, the device's abilities still more or less guaranteed Brass and Bland a safe journey through the hazardous skies of Nu Earth.

Bland tutted to himself in satisfaction, not able to resist a brief bit of point scoring with his partner. "Hmmm, and to think someone didn't want to buy the thing in the first place, because they said the price was too high."

"And I still think so. Twenty thousand creds and a whole consignment of undamaged chem-suits? I still think I could have bargained that alien ruffian down to half that price, if you hadn't insisted on handling the negotiations yourself," sniffed Brass.

"Well, be my guest this time then, Mister Brass," responded Bland. "Let's see if you can get as good a price out of our next customer as I did last time we did business with him."

Their destination, via a route that would now take them well away from any active warzones, was a Souther airbase. There was an extremely accommodating squadron commander there who was not only willing to purchase recovered Souther air-craft salvage from the two body looters, but was equally happy to sell them whatever they needed from his squadron's own supplies. There were many such obliging and corrupt souls amongst the personnel of both sides, and Brass and Bland were always delighted to do business with any of them. It was considerably safer than salvaging war materials from the bat-tlefields, and this way you got them in pristine condition, without having to go to the expense and inconvenience of repairing them before selling them onto another buyer.

Nevertheless, Brand couldn't resist a final, lingering look at the image of Nordstadt as it faded away into the distance. So much lovely, valuable scrap and salvage material down there, he thought to himself, just waiting for someone to come and find it all. What a pity they were never going to see any of it. Sometimes, Brass reminded himself, this war and all its events could be a serious inconvenience when it came to keeping up your profit margins.

"Break off, Rafe. It's one of ours, a Type IV med-shuttle. Registry ID and transponder codes check out, even if it has strayed kinda far off the safe conduct flight paths."

"Check on that, Gabe. Could have sworn a few moments ago it looked like one of the old Nort Magyar-pattern cargo crates."

A thought struck Rafe. "Gabe, open up a comm-channel to them and ask them if they want an escort up into safe orbit. The skies anywhere near Nordstadt aren't a good place for an unarmed med-shuttle to be wandering about on its own today."

"Cancel that order, Bluegirl," broke in the voice of her flight commander. "You go glory hunting in your own time. Right now, we've got a mission to carry out. Return to formation and resume original course. That's an order. Those med-boys want to go joyriding about up here, then that's their lookout."

Rafe cursed off-mic, but did as ordered, swinging her Seraphim around on a heading that would bring it back over the rapidly shrinking, Souther-held portion of Nordstadt.

"Roger that, Flight One. Bluegirl returning to formation."

The Seraphim cut through the upper layers of chem-cloud like a shark cruising for prey. Rafe looked down with her fighter's targeting sensors and saw plenty of prey on offer down there at ground level. Waves of Nort bomber and gunship atmocraft were making low-level sweeps over the city, pounding the Souther ground forces dug into the rubble down there. Secondary waves of hopper and atmocraft troop carriers followed in behind them, dropping Nort stormtrooper units right down into the midst of the Souther survivors of the bombing raids. The Souther anti-aircraft artillery units were taking a fair toll of the Norts – as she watched, Rafe saw several enemy atmocraft target icons blip out of existence – but it was still a turkey shoot going on down there and so far the battle was still going the Norts' way.

Meanwhile, she and dozens of other Souther fighters were carrying enough firepower to blow half those Nort atmocraft tin crates out of the sky. And what were they doing? Flying in a protective circle around the main Souther drop-zones in Nordstadt, holding open a corridor for some big, secret shuttle drop-op that Milli-com had ordered.

Something big was on, that was for sure. "Operation Hammerfall"; that was the name she and the other pilots had been told, although no other details had been forthcoming. Their orders were simply to maintain position and wait for the shuttle drop to commence, while all the time watching as mere interested observers as thousands of Souther troops on the ground were bombed and strafed out of existence.

The other Souther fighter pilots might have been happy with this state of affairs, but Rafe certainly wasn't.

"Gabe, check the feed intake levels on the starboard wing engine. I'm picking up a power drop on that one. Feels kinda sluggish, like maybe we're taking in too much ionised dust from these chem-clouds."

"You sure, toots? I don't detect anything... Oh wait, now I see what you mean. Yeah, definite signs of dust clogging in that starboard engine. As your navigator and onboard flight computer, I recommend we take immediate remedial action before it becomes a real problem."

Rafe grinned. Yeah, Gabe was definitely starting to learn a thing or two about the noble human arts of lying and talking bullshit.

"Bluegirl to Flight One. Got a dust-clog problem in my starboard engine. Taking it down out of these chem-clouds and closer to the ground to allow engine systems to effect auto-clearout."

The reply was both immediate and strident. "Request denied, Bluegirl. Return to main formation and reassume previous position. Say again, request denied. Get your ass back here now."

"Can't copy, Flight One. Chem-cloud interference is disrupting radio comms. Taking it down now, Flight One. I'll see you later."

Gabe cut off the comms-link and the flight leader's outraged response with a suitably noisy burst of static. Rafe then sent her fighter plunging down through the chem-clouds towards the nearest formation of enemy atmocraft.

The Nort atmocraft didn't even knew what hit them. Rafe came diving down out of the chem-clouds, picking off two fat troop carriers with Hellstreak missiles. Two platoons or more of Nort stormtroopers died instantly as their carriers blew apart in midair. The third troop carrier and its gunship escort desperately tried to peel away. Rafe gave them no chance and opened up with her nose cannons. The gunship exploded under the hail of cannon fire. The carrier, riddled from cockpit to stern, died a slower death, keeling over and falling out of the sky to crash and explode in the ruins below.

Rafe cut her speed to the minimum necessary to keep the roaring fighter aloft and flew lower, zooming down over the heads of the Nort troops on the ground in a lethal strafing attack. Her keen GI eyes picked out targets moments before they flashed by below.

Cannon fire scattered through lines of advancing Nort infantry, blowing apart a dozen or more of them and sending the others diving for cover.

She spotted a Nort artillery observation post on top of a bombed-out ruin and took out the whole building with another Hellstreak. It crashed to the ground, burying the Nort infantry squad sheltering there.

She spotted a Nort command vehicle and tracked it with twin lines of cannon fire, cutting it in half and detonating its fuel tanks.

A massive Loki-class siege platform, a mobile artillery unit built on the chassis of a Blackmare tank, ground a path through the ruins. The anti-aircraft gunners on it pointed at her in alarm and frantically brought their las-cannon turrets round to bear. Rafe launched another Hellstreak at it and then peeled away just before it struck. The explosion destroyed not just the Loki, but also touched off the stack of hundred kilo shells carried by a nearby ammunition limber vehicle. The Loki and its fleet of support vehicles and infantry escorts disappeared in an expanding cloud of flame and blast-hurled rubble that made those watching kilometres away assume the Southers were now using mini tac-nuke ordnance on them.

And then Rafe was gone, opening up with the after-burners and vanishing back up into the cover of the overhead chem-clouds seconds before anyone on the ground could get a lock on her with their weapons.

"Bluegirl to Flight One," she cheerfully reported into her radio. "Comms interference and that dust-clog problem now taken care of. Returning to formation, as ordered."

Flight One's reply was a stream of angry profanities, punctuated by several repeated promises of court martial investigations. Rafe didn't care. She knew the damage she had just inflicted on the Norts was really little more than a pinprick in comparison to the total size of the offensive now being mounted, but it was better than doing nothing, she judged. If what she had just done gave even one Souther soldier in Nordstadt a better fighting chance of survival, then she was happy to face whatever consequences awaited her back at base.

She thought about the battle going on in the city below and the tens of thousands of Souther troops now trapped there and fighting for their lives. She thought of one soldier in particular.

The Rogue Trooper. The man she had sent into the crucible with that radio message of hers. Now it didn't seem like such a bright idea, not when Nordstadt was in its death-throws and an excursion into the crucible looked more and more like a one-way death trip.

"Solid blue", she had promised him, not knowing then what she was sending him into. The comms reports from Nordstadt of the sightings of the Rogue Trooper hadn't surprised her at all. If anyone could have made it solo through into the crucible, it would be him. Something bothered her though, her GI intuition setting off alarm bells in her head about Operation Hammerfall and its implications. She didn't know what Milli-com was planning, but she felt sure it meant nothing good for the ordinary grunt on the ground.

"Need another favour from you, Gabe. You still got those bypass codes from when we hacked into Milli-com's secure comm-channels to send out that message on the old GI frequencies?"

"You even have to ask, conchita? What's up?"

"As soon as we get back to base, Gabe, I want you to start sneaking around the Milli-com data channels and find out whatever you can about this Hammerfall op."

A minute later, they rejoined the main shield formation that was circling in a wide holding pattern above the Souther drop-zones. A minute after that, the first wave of shuttles dropped down from orbit, heading into the besieged city.

The shuttles came in four waves, with eight or ten shuttles to a wave. Each wave was directed in to one of the four remaining main landing zones still in Souther hands.

Flights of Nort Grendel and Gorgon fighters prowled the skies, lurking at the far fringes of the Souther fighter screen's scanner range. At the first sight of the descending shuttles, they opened up their afterburners and darted in to attack.

They were destroyed in droves. Almost every remaining Souther anti-aircraft unit – the same guns that might have done something to stop the waves of Nort atmocraft attacks still pounding the Souther positions in the city's outlying districts – had been pulled back to defend the landing zones and put up a barrage of covering fire for the incoming shuttles. Those Nort fighters that weren't destroyed or beaten back by the fire from the ground were eagerly claimed by the squadrons of patrolling Seraphims. In the space of a few minutes' furious aerial dogfighting, twenty-eight Nort fighters were downed, nineteen of them falling to the guns and missiles of the Seraphims, against a loss of five Souther craft. Outgunned and outnumbered, the surviving Norts retreated to lick their wounds.

Not one of them made it through the Souther fighter barrier, and every shuttle made it into its landing point unscathed.

The Seraphim pilots and anti-aircraft gunners all assumed the shuttles were bringing in much-needed reinforcements for the ground troops in Nordstadt, perhaps the vanguard force for the mysterious but much-heralded Operation Hammerfall. Thirty-seven shuttles, each one carrying a maximum of sixty troops, couldn't be bringing in much more than two battalions of troops, but two battalions of troops was better than nothing, and everyone assumed this was just the start of something much bigger.

They were right at least in thinking that much. What they didn't know – since Milli-com had gone to great pains to conceal the fact – was that every one of those shuttles was virtually empty.

"You believe this shit?" Halmada growled to Matthews, his copilot. The man just shrugged, knowing better than to comment on Milli-com strategy when there was a full squad of Milli-fuzz military police riding in the shuttle's passenger compartment behind them.

The military police, several hundred of them in total, had boarded the shuttles just before departure from the orbital bases. They were heading for Nordstadt, but they didn't look like they were planning on staying there very long, not judging by the scant amount of equipment they were taking with them. Halmada and his copilot had exchanged looks but said nothing, sensing another Milli-com black bag operation at work.

"Still," grunted Halmada, "even Milli-fuzz has got to be better than that chilly son-of-a-bitch we took down the other day."

This elicited more of a response from Matthews. Both of them remembered the silent, grim-faced sniper operative who had travelled down with them the last time they had dropped down into Nordstadt. Both of them had looked at the other and had come to the same conclusion. Their passenger was S-Three, for sure, which meant it was in both their interests not to even wonder anything else about him. Halmada was glad when the man had disembarked without a word to them, and the temperature inside the shuttle seemed to rise a few more degrees in the absence of his cold, grey presence. Halmada didn't know who the man was or why he was being sent into Nordstadt, but he dearly hoped never to encounter him again.

The S-Three assassin was the only passenger they had carried that day. The rest of their manifest had been a few tonnes of ammunition and food supplies, barely enough to

fill half of their otherwise empty cargo hold. The shuttle
had been full on its return journey, however, the hold and
passenger compartment crammed full of wounded Souther
troops lucky enough to be evacuated out of the warzone.

, Halmada looked out through the cockpit windows as the
shuttle descended through the final layer of chem-cloud and
saw that Nordstadt was spread out below them. They were
above the landing zone now, with the terrain beneath them
secure and still in Souther hands, but from his aerial vantage point Halmada could clearly see the distant columns of
smoke, lines of burning buildings and concertos of artillery
explosions that marked the areas of front line combat.
These were now quite clearly far nearer to the landing
zones in the centre of the city than they had been previ-
ously, and it was horribly easy to see the advances the
Norts had made in the last few days.

Halmada prepped his craft for landing, convinced that,
unless Milli-com had something very special up its sleeves,
this would almost certainly be the last time he would be
touching down in Nordstadt. From what he had seen from
the air, the landing zones would be overrun by the Norts in
less than a day.

SEVENTEEN

"General, with respect, I really must remind you again of our original orders."

Ghazeleh Fyalla turned patiently to his executive officer, affecting an air of quiet puzzlement. "Maybe you should, Major Garr. What were they again?"

Garr shifted, obviously suspecting he was being mocked again by the general. In the seal-protected, temporary head-quarters dome, the other members of Ghazeleh's staff watched the exchange with amusement, some smiling in anticipation of its inevitable conclusion.

"Sir, our orders from Milli-com were to abandon our advance immediately, break off from all contact with the enemy and fall back to rejoin the main Souther front line at our original start-up position."

Ghazeleh smiled, nodding in agreement. "Ah yes, that was it, wasn't it? Well remembered, Major Garr. And now tell me, what are we doing at the moment, then?"

Garr swallowed nervously. "Sir, we're retreating, as ordered, but—"

Ghazeleh cut him off. "Retreating as ordered, yes. That's what we're doing exactly, isn't it? And is it our fault if we seem to be suffering an abnormally high number of mechanical failures among our vehicles, forcing us to stop frequently to make urgent repairs? And is it our fault if the Norts then keep on catching up with us, forcing us to stop again to engage them in battle to protect our rearguard? And is it our fault if at times other Nort units somehow keep on crossing the path of our route, forcing us to break off and engage them in battle in order to protect our flanks?"

Garr reddened, stammering for an answer. Many in the command dome openly smirked now.

Everyone knew that Ghazeleh had ordered all his tank company commanders to report every minor malfunction, whether it was flickering console light or a broken storage locker latch, as a major mechanical failure which necessitated the whole three division strong armoured column to stop to allow the item to be repaired. When no genuine malfunctions were forthcoming, unit commanders were encouraged to create some of their own, and Ghazeleh himself had "accidentally" shot out the headlights of his command vehicle with his service pistol, and then insisted that the retreat be halted for four hours, until the unfortunate damage was repaired. The fact that, in those four hours, the force's rearguard units engaged and destroyed almost a full company of Nort armour was neither here nor there.

Likewise, no one other than Colonel Garr saw fit to mention that the route they were retreating to bore little resemblance to the one they had originally advanced from. The advance had been a blazing, almost straight-line thrust through Nort-held territory, making a direct, rapid advance push towards Nordstadt. The retreat, in comparison, was a slow-moving, meandering affair, as Ghazeleh's army weaved its own oddball course back home. Encouraged by Ghazeleh, forward reconnaissance squads and meteorology and intelligence officers on board suddenly started finding various problematic obstacles along the direct route back to the Souther lines. In some places, dense banks of chem-mist blocked off the road back home. In other places, it was unexpected large concentrations of Nort forces – which on subsequent reconnaissance seemed to have disappeared as strangely as those banks of chem-mist – or the fact that the radiation and tox-levels of an area of terrain seemed to have unaccountably risen to dangerous levels since the time the column had first advanced through them. One imaginative meteorology officer had even predicted a violent meteorite storm in the column's path, and the detour Ghazeleh had taken to avoid this disastrous event had somehow accidentally led them straight towards a fortified Nort strongpoint, which of course had to be attacked and destroyed to secure a safe path through for the rest of his force.

Yes, General Blood and Guts Ghazeleh was complying with orders and retreating alright, his staff joked amongst themselves, but if this was retreating, then at least it was retreating in style. It was a manner of retreat unlikely to be found in any military history textbooks, causing almost as much damage to the enemy as their original advance had done.

Ghazeleh looked at the dome's holo-map display, once again silently cursing the orders he had been given, and the Milli-com fools who had issued them. Despite all the delays and detours he had managed to contrive, they had still travelled more than five hundred kilometres away from Nordstadt, and were now only about a hundred and sixty kilometres from the Souther front lines. The thought of all the damage he had inflicted on the enemy along the way did little to ease his simmering anger.

"Sir, a message from Milli-com. They're requesting an immediate update on our current position," reported one of his staff officers, almost apologetically.

Ghazeleh deactivated the holo-map with an angry flick and turned to bark orders to his waiting division commanders.

"Damn it, break camp and get ready to move out. Look on the bright side, boys. There's still a few Norts left standing between us and the front line. Let's see if we can't find some of them and remind them what this bastard war is supposed to be all about."

Hanna liked Surgeon Major Henri Artau. She had met too many senior medics who just seemed to view the wounded men and women under their care as a necessary inconvenience, objects to be sewn up and stitched back together and then shipped out as quickly as possible, either sent back to their units or med-evaced out of the warzone before the next batch of broken and bleeding bodies were delivered into their care. Artau was different from these other war weary medics whose humanity seemed to have been worn away by the endless stream of injured and dying bodies passing through their field surgery operating theatres. He was not like those full of bitter resentment at being drafted into military service and called away from their comfortable and lucrative civilian practices.

Artau wasn't like any of those. For one thing, he seemed to actually passionately care about the wounded soldiers that filled his field hospital to overflowing. And, for another thing, he had volunteered, not just for service on Nu Earth, but for here in Nordstadt itself.

"Ah, Sergeant Coss, how are you doing today? That leg and thick trooper skull of yours feeling better?"

"No complaints, doc," she answered, returning the grey-haired surgeon's smile. "Any idea when I can get out of here and give up this bed to someone who needs it more than I do?"

When she had arrived at the field hospital, the medics had quickly discovered that she wasn't just suffering from a broken leg and tox-exposure, but also had a hairline fracture to the skull. The explosion from that Nort Blackmare round had knocked her around worse than she thought. Still, the anti-pathogen drugs they had administered had flushed the chem-pollutants out of her system, and a few hours plugged into a rapi-heal machine had mostly repaired in hours what would normally have taken weeks to heal otherwise. The skull and leg fractures were gone although her leg still caused her some pain. She was eager to get out of there. The field hospital was deep inside one of the secure zones, but the relentless rumble of artillery in the distance and the ever-increasing flow of casualties into the wards told her that the Nort attack was still growing in ferocity. Some of her squad had survived yesterday's nightmare battle in the steelworks sector and she knew her place was with them back on the front line.

"Hmmm," mumbled Artau, making a notation on his handheld compu. "That head injury must be worse than I thought, sergeant. I could have sworn I just heard you volunteering to run back out there and get shot at again, right after we've barely finished fixing you up from the last time that happened to you."

Hanna opened her mouth to respond but was silenced by a look from the surgeon. "The accelerated rapi-heal treatment takes its toll on the body's natural resources, sergeant. You need to rest for a day or two longer and build your strength back up before we can let you out of here to get yourself blown up again."

"Surgeon Major Artau."

It was more a command than a question. Artau looked up, annoyed at this interruption of his daily walk of the wards. His annoyance increased considerably when he saw who it was that was doing the interrupting.

Two military police officers stood there, both of them wearing holstered sidearms. Artau didn't allow weapons inside his hospital. His annoyance increased even further.

"I've told you people already," he snapped, "I won't allow you to pester Sergeant Coss here while she's still a patient under my care. I'm sure she'll be happy to answer all the questions you've got to ask her about her alleged encounter with this mythical Rogue Trooper fellow, but not until after I'm fully satisfied she's recovered from her injuries and I've signed her official medical discharge order. If you have any problems with that, I suggest you take them up with my divisional commander."

"With respect, Surgeon Major, I haven't got a clue what you're talking about," said the more senior of the two Millifuzz men. "We're here for you. Our orders are to escort you to the landing zone for immediate shuttle evac out of the warzone."

"I see, lieutenant. Am I to consider myself under arrest, then? Can't say I'm surprised. Lord knows, I've complained enough over the years about this idiotic war and the way our beloved leaders are fighting it."

This time there was an edge of barely-restrained impatience in the military policeman's voice. "I wouldn't know anything about that either, sir. Our orders are merely to make sure you're on the next shuttle out of Nordstadt."

Artau purposefully turned his attention back to his handheld compu, scribbling case notes into its memory files.

"Well, as far as I'm aware, I don't have any leave furloughs coming up, and as you can see, lieutenant, we're all rather busy here at the moment, so I'm afraid I'm going to have to decline your generous offer of a free trip out of the warzone."

The two Milli-fuzz stiffened in anger. Hanna wasn't the only one to notice the other policeman's hand moving towards his holstered pistol. Other surgeons, medical orderlies and some of the more mobile of the hospital's patients were also now watching the encounter closely. If it came to an open confrontation between Artau and the Milli-fuzz, there was little doubt about which side everyone here would be jumping in on. The other policeman must have noticed this too. His hand strayed closer to his pistol holster.

"I'm afraid that won't be possible, sir," warned the first Milli-fuzz, indicating the compu device he was holding. "Our orders are very specific, straight from Milli-com, and you're not the only one who's been scheduled for immediate evac."

"Let me see that thing!"

Artau snatched the compu out of the policeman's hand, scanning the information displayed on its screen. What he saw there appalled him.

"My god! You've got just about every senior officer in the warzone listed here. If you strip away every division's command cadre, then how in hell are we supposed to be able to…"

His voice trailed away, realisation dawning in his eyes. "I don't believe it… Those maniacs in Milli-com, they're planning on pulling out of here and leaving all the poor bastards here to rot, aren't they?"

"I wouldn't know anything about that either, sir," said the Milli-fuzz lieutenant, forcefully. "All I know is that we're

leaving for the landing zone and we're taking you with us."
The man drew his shock-baton, activating it for extra effect
and looked meaningfully at Artau.

"I assure you, sir," the policeman told Artau, "one way or
another, you most definitely will be coming with us."

A medical orderly stepped forward, obviously looking to
grapple with the military police lieutenant. The other Milli-
fuzz, standing beside Hanna's bed, drew his pistol and took
aim at the orderly. Hanna lashed out with her uninjured
foot, kicking the gun out of the man's hand and sending
him sprawling. The gun dropped to the floor where someone else kicked it out of harm's way beneath one of the
nearby beds.

The Milli-fuzz lieutenant swung his shock-baton, felling
the orderly. The police issue weapon was designed with
several settings, shocking its victims with electro-blasts of
varying intensity. From the way the orderly shot backwards
for several metres across the room and smashed headfirst
into a wall with a sickening skull-cracking sound, Hanna
could tell that the Milli-fuzz man had definitely selected one
of the higher settings.

The lieutenant had his pistol out now, waving it threat-
eningly at the crowd around him. Artau was shouting,
telling everyone to stop fighting, but no one seemed to be
paying any attention to him.

"Stand back!" screamed the lieutenant, firing a warning
shot into the hospital dome's shielded roof, sending the
crowd of medical staff and patients scattering back in panic.
"I have orders from Milli-com to summarily execute anyone
attempting to interfere in our mission. We're leaving and
we're taking this man with us."

"Damn right we are, but not before I teach this bitch a
lesson about interfering in official Milli-com business."
The second Milli-fuzz man now clambered to his feet and
drew his own shock-baton, pointing it in fury towards
Hanna.

She knew there was little she could do to stop him since
she was lying on a bed with one leg still numb and unre-
sponsive.

He drew his arm back to strike. The sound of an explosion, loud and shocking, from directly outside stopped him in his tracks.

Both Milli-fuzz men gawped in disbelief. Clearly, they'd never been this close to live artillery fire before. Even through the walls of the hospital dome, Hanna could hear the whistling shriek of more incoming shellfire.

"Nort artillery. Everyone get down!" she screamed, ignoring the pain in her injured leg as she threw herself off the bed, instinctively grabbing her would-be executioner and pulling him down with her.

A few seconds later, the Nort artillery fire landed inside the field hospital compound. Two evac hoppers and a supply half-track were destroyed, along with their crews. The most recently arrived wounded and the orderlies attending to them were torn to pieces by shrapnel. A secondary meddome took three direct hits and collapsed inwards, killing everyone inside, patients and med-staff alike.

The battle for Nordstadt had finally reached the Souther forces' inner city secure zones.

EIGHTEEN

It was just past 16:00 hours when the first storm broke over the city; the winter sun set over Nordstadt for the last time.

A few minutes after that, the second storm broke also.

The first storm was the one predicted by both sides' meteorology experts. Lightning flashed in the chem-cloud skies, setting fire to parts of the heavens above the city as the heat from the electrical blasts ignited the highly combustible contents of some of those same clouds.

Steaming and corrosive acid rain fell all over the city. In those areas where the sky was aflame, it fell as droplets of liquid fire. Troops on both sides cowered in whatever cover was available, or donned special protective capes over their chem-suits. Shell-holes filled with acid water runoff and toxic sludge and became lethal death-traps. Trenches became bubbling, acid-filled ditches. Roadways were transformed into coursing rivers of acid water which flooded out bunkers and defensive positions, forcing their cursing, panicked occupants to seek shelter elsewhere. In some areas of the city, the acid bled down into the blighted soil in the ground, reacting with the toxins already there and causing a vile, poisonous green mist which even the best chem-suits couldn't offer any protection against to seep up into the air.

Interference from the storm and acid rain hampered radio communications and rendered scanner screens blind. Hundreds of troops on both sides died in the downpour. Many, many more than that were to die in what followed next.

The second storm was the crushing weight of the final Nort offensive. Thousands of Nort vehicles and hundreds of thousands of Nort troops moved forward through the rubble,

161

advancing under cover of the storm. The storm and the rains would last for only an hour or so, but the carnage of the final phase of the battle for Nordstadt would go on for many long, bloody hours more than that.

Another great wave of Nort atmocraft swept in low over the battlefields, attacking the rings of carefully prepared defences around the inner secure zones. The Souther air defences there were in position and ready for them. The skies above the secure zones were filled with tracer fire, explosions and the flaring lights of missile and rocket streaks. More than fifty Nort craft were lost in the first ten minutes of the attack of it and six times that number by the.

Whatever glory the Nort ground forces might win tonight, the pilots of the Nordland Air Force would long remember the final commencement of the Battle of Nordstadt as one of the blackest of days. Not even taking into account the losses sustained by the Grendel and Gorgon high-altitude fighter squadrons in the earlier abortive battle, entire squadrons would be lost in tonight's engagement, and many Nort pilots' messes would be bleak, empty places for months to come.

Despite the cost in men and machines, Nort High Command deemed the losses more than acceptable. High above the battlezone, spotter craft and low-orbit surveillance satellites hovered invisibly. They were monitoring everything; calculating levels of enemy firepower and the points of origin of that firepower. Every Nort craft destroyed helped them pinpoint the location of another enemy anti-aircraft battery, another surface-to-air missile squadron.

The target data was fed through to the artillery units behind the main Nort lines. The gun crews waited there impatiently, tonnes of shells or missiles stacked up beside each weapon. At last the remnants of the atmocraft attack wave received the merciful order to withdraw. They fled back to their home bases, many of them damaged and never making it that far. The lucky ones managed to bail out from their stricken craft in time. The unlucky ones found anonymous graves in whatever nameless area of rubble their craft crashed into.

As soon as the atmocraft were clear, the artillery battalions opened fire. They were spread out in lines many kilometres long, arrayed in batteries of fifty or more guns. When they all opened fire simultaneously, it sounded as if Nu Earth itself was cracking wide open.

The artillery barrage hit the Souther positions like the wrath of God. Zeroed in by satellites and spotter planes, the Nort shells struck home by the thousands with devastating accuracy.

More than a dozen Souther AA units were wiped out in the opening salvo, eradicated completely. The others tried to weather the storm, losing more men and guns with every passing second. Rockrete bunkers offered no shelter, their metre-thick roofs succumbing to the relentless hail of shellfire until they collapsed in on the heads of their screaming occupants. The Nort guns kept on firing, even after most of their targets had been reduced to little more than fields of churned mud littered with the scraps of men and the guns they had once manned.

Finally, the barrage ceased, and the gunners stood down from their positions, recalibrating their sights and pouring coolant fluid into overheated gun barrels in readiness for receiving their next firing solutions from the spotter planes. The guns stayed silent for a few minutes. They wouldn't stay silent for long.

In the brief respite, the Norts initiated the next phase of the assault. In staging areas behind the Nort lines, almost an entire division of Nort stormtroopers scrambled aboard ground assault hopper craft. They were airborne in minutes, the hoppers skimming across the rooftops of the smashed city, passing over the heads of the cheering throngs of advancing ground troops. The Souther air defences had been comprehensively smashed by the artillery barrage and these airborne units were able to cross over into Souther-held territory almost at will, taking only a handful of losses from whatever fire could be thrown up from the ground-based enemy infantry positions below.

They landed in waves inside the Souther defensive perimeter. Some had been designated to turn round and assault the Souther positions behind them, coordinating with advancing ground infantry to catch and crush the enemy troops there in a lethal crossfire. The majority pushed on towards the centre of the secure zones, following orders to storm and destroy the vital shuttle landing zones, cutting off all hope of escape or reinforcement for the remaining Souther forces in Nordstadt.

Behind them, the hoppers took off again, returning to the rear echelon staging areas to pick up the second wave of the airborne assault phase of the offensive. Within the hour, another two Nort stormtrooper divisions would be deployed into the interior of the Souther defensive perimeter.

The borders of the inner crucible wavered, but held against the face of the first phase of the Nort assault. This situation was one that wouldn't last much longer.

"Forward! For Nordland. For Nordstadt. For victory!"

Centurion-Kolonel Graff stood at the prow of his assault craft, daring the Souther snipers and machine-gunners on the near shore to try and pick him off.

He and his regiment, the Third Kashan Sturmvulkk, nicknamed the Bulletproofs after their legendary action in attacking and capturing the rebel stronghold of Vasrin during the Fourth Battle of Nu Sevastopol, were assaulting the Souther positions on the north shore of the main river through Nordstadt. It was Graff who had personally climbed to the top of the highest point on Vasrin's main citadel and planted the regimental standard above the burning city, and he had every intention of doing the same thing here. With all the bridges across the river now destroyed, the only way across was by waterborne assault. Waves of troop-laden ships and skimmer craft launched across the river and straight into the face of ferocious fire coming from the Souther defenders dug in on the far shore.

Two enormous waves of assault craft, comprising of two whole divisions and more than twenty thousand men, had tried to make the crossing already. The first hadn't even

made it past the halfway mark of the river's eight hundred
metre expanse. Their corpses floated in the water all around
the boats carrying Graff and his men. A few clung to the
burning wreckage of their assault vessels, crying uselessly
out for help to the Kashans as their boats sank into the toxic
waters of the river.

The second wave had fared a little better, some of the elements of that division even making it to the enemy shore.
Wading clumsily ashore, trying to climb the steep and
muddy river banks of the river, they had been easy pickings
for the enemy infantry lying in wait there. Their corpses and
the wreckage of their beached assault boats choked the
waters of the shoreline. The survivors, barely a battalion's
worth by this point, were pinned down at the water's edge,
unable or unwilling to advance any further and still taking
horrific casualties from the withering hail of fire from the
shore defenders. Scattered and disorganised, most likely
with the majority of their officers already dead, Graff knew
they would be of little use to him when his troops made it
ashore. Still, he was glad of their presence. Every las-round
and shell aimed at them was one less aimed at Graff and his
precious Kashans.

Graff kept his eyes fixed on the far shoreline, counting off
the metres and seconds to their arrival there.

Five hundred and forty metres.

Artillery rounds screamed over his head as the Nort and
Souther batteries on each shore traded punishing bouts of
shellfire. At least one Souther salvo was aimed at the
assault craft. Two boats to his right exploded and sank, taking all hands with them. Another suffered a near miss,
overturning in the wake of the shell's explosive splash and
spilling everyone aboard into the water. Graff could hear his
men's screams above the sounds of the explosions as the
weight of their equipment and chem-suits dragged them
down into the poisonous water.

Four hundred and fifty metres.

Another flight of Souther gunships flew up the length of
the river, strafing and bombing everything in their path and
leaving a trail of burning and sinking boats in their wake.

"Lazookas!" ordered Graff, and was rewarded a few moments later by the sight of a hail of lazooka and even las-carbine shots reaching up into the sky in search of their targets. Most missed the fast moving gunships, but one lucky or well-aimed lazooka shot struck true.

One of the gunships fell from the air, trailing flames. Its pilot was a brave and determined man, Graff realised, because he directed his dying craft straight down on top of the assault craft carrying the commander. Gunship and assault boat disappeared into the river together.

Three hundred and eighty metres.

More than halfway there now. By Graff's reckoning, the division had lost roughly a quarter of its strength already, but that still left about seven thousand men still alive, all of them Kashans. More than enough to get the job done, judged Graff, even if they lost another quarter or more before they reached the shore.

Three hundred and ten metres.

An artillery skimmer in front of Graff's boat was suddenly blown out of the water. Graff hadn't seen any of the shore-based fire hit it and guessed it must have struck a floating mine. His guess was confirmed when he saw one of the deadly plastic spheres floating in the water directly ahead of his own craft. A shot from his officer's pistol detonated it while it was still a safe distance away.

"Graff to all vessel commanders," he ordered over the regimental radio net. "Be advised, enemy mines in the water ahead. Get your best marksmen up into the prows of your craft to pick them off."

Two hundred and fifty metres.

The Souther gunships were back making a return sweep over the Kashan assault wave. Graff saw the craft carrying his second-in-command cut in half by a strafing blast of las-cannon fire. The man had been a good friend, a comrade since their days together in the Nordland Youth and Graff deeply regretted his death. The time for mourning would have to come later, however, after Nordstadt had finally been liberated.

One hundred and eighty metres.

They were well within range of the guns of the enemy infantry now. Graff was still standing in the open at the prow of the boat, testing his reputation as commander of the Bulletproofs to its very limits. A Souther sniper round whipped past, missing him but hitting and killing one of his men crouching down behind him.

One hundred metres.

The enemy fire intensified. Souther heavy weapon fire raked boats from prow to stern, killing everyone aboard. Individual Souther soldiers picked off their opposite numbers aboard the Nort assault boats with single shots from their las-carbines.

Fifty metres.

Heavy salvos of Nort artillery fire crashed into the Souther-held river bank, seeking to clear a way through the defences for the arrival of the third Nort attack wave. The shellfire collapsed tunnels, gutted bunkers and struck silent heavy weapon emplacements. The fact that it also killed dozens of the survivors of the second attack wave who were still trapped there on the shoreline was of little consequence. They had failed in the task given to them and now had to face the penalty for their failure.

Twelve metres.

Almost there. Graff's boat ran aground on the submerged wreckage that lined the edge of the shore. He drew his las-sword and leapt into the water, eager to claim the honour of being the first man from the first boat of this assault wave to reach the enemy shore.

He waded through the water, feeling its toxic contents starting to eat into the material of his chem-suit. "For Nordland! For Nordstadt! For victory!" he shouted again, urging his troops onwards, knowing how vital it was to get them out of the water and onto the riverbank before they succumbed to the enemy fire or the effects of the lethal pollutants in the water.

Las-rounds struck the surface of the water around him with a hot sizzle. An explosion behind him blew four men into the air, showering the rest of his platoon with body parts and vile river muck. They charged forward, taking casualties with every metre they went, stepping on and stumbling through the bodies of the dead and dying that floated all along the shoreline.

Zero metres.

They hit the muddy, carnage-churned slopes of the river-bank, feet and hands clawing for purchase, the men behind pushing those in front of them up the steepest parts of the incline, those that made it to the top turning and pulling their comrades up to join them, while others crouched in the blood-soaked mud and began to return fire on the Souther troops dug into the slopes above them.

Although diminished in numbers, they had survived the very worst of everything the Southers had had to throw at them. Now the enemy would learn exactly who it was they were dealing with.

"KASHAN! KASHAAAAAAAN!" screamed Graff, pointing his las-sword at the enemy and leading the charge up the hill. His men followed suit, taking up the cry, their suit communicators amplifying it many times over, until the whole river line seemed to echo with the savage war-cry of the Kashan Legion. Artillery-launched photon flares floated overhead, turning night into day, starkly illuminating all the gruesome details of the battle that followed.

A Souther infantryman reared up out of a foxhole in front of Graff, raising his las-carbine to fire. Graff gunned him down with his pistol. The Souther's foxhole partner was trying to scramble up out of the rear of the hole. Kashans leapt down into the foxhole, bayoneting him through the back.

A Souther machine gun nest sprayed shots into the Kashan line, cutting down ten or more men in an instant. A lazookaman crouched down, took aim and blew the weapon and its crew out of existence.

More las-fire came from a bunker to Graff's right. Two men from his platoon hurled grenades with pinpoint accuracy through the narrow opening of the firing slit. The dual explosions abruptly cut off any more fire from that direction.

Graff ran through a Souther infantry trench, accompanied by a squad of Kashans. Grenades and incendiary bombs

were thrown into the entrance of every bunker and dug-out
that lined the walls of the trench.

A Souther officer accompanied by a squad of his own
infantry appeared out of the gloom ahead of Graff. The
Souther paused as he caught sight of the Kashans and their
commander and then drew his own las-sword in an unmistakable gesture of challenge. Graff raised his las-pistol and
shot the vainglorious fool through the face-visor of his
chem-suit.

The Souther troops accompanying the officer, armed with
bayonet-fixed rifles and sharp-edged trenching tools,
screamed in rage and threw themselves forward at the
Kashans. Graff shot one of them, gutted another with a
thrust of his las-sword and then decapitated a third with his
return blow. The others he left for his men to deal with.
Many of their Kashan brethren had died during the river
crossing and his men were eager for revenge.

The Kashans surged onwards. Bunkers and dug-outs were
cleared out with grenades, bayonets and searing blasts of
las-fire. Some Southers remained in position and died
where they fought. Others tried to flee and were shot down
and bayoneted to death. The Kashan attack was relentless
now. Graff could feel victory almost in their grasp.

The regimental standard bearer running beside him stumbled and fell to the ground when he was shot through the
chest. Graff reached down and grabbed the haft of the standard, rescuing the precious relic before it was defiled by
contact with the bloody, mud-covered ground. The standard
accompanied the Third Kashan Sturmvulkk on all their
campaigns and had proudly flown over the site of many
famous victories. It was the same standard he had planted
atop the ruins of Vasrin and now it would soon be flying
over Nordstadt too.

Graff shot the Souther that had killed his standard bearer
and then dropped his pistol and charged in amongst a group
of two other Southers, wielding the standard like a quarter-
staff. A flurry of blows from it sent one of them sprawling
to the ground. A shout from one of his men warned him of
the attack from the other remaining Souther. Graff parried

aside the Souther's lunging swing with a trenching tool, breaking the man's right arm in the process. The Souther staggered back and Graff reversed his grip on the haft of the standard, smashing the spear-like point of it straight through the man's face-visor, killing him instantly.

"That one, I want him alive," Graff directed his men, indicating the form of the semi-conscious, last remaining Souther. "Take hold of him and follow me."

The Kashans followed their commander, dragging the weakly struggling Souther with them up the last few metres to the final crest of the slope of the riverbank. There, they pinned the man down to the ground, knowing what was in their commander's mind. They held the terrified Souther down, holding him by his arms and legs as Graff stood over him, holding the standard pole tightly in both hands. He raised it above his head and brought it down, impaling it through the Souther's chest and into the ground beneath.

It had become a tradition among the Kashans, starting with the epic victory on Flavian III, eighteen years ago, when Grand Centurion Militant Horth, the Kashans' founder, had marked his Legion's epic victory on that planet by thrusting his standard into the heart of the commanding general of the defeated Souther garrison.

One of his men played a victory salute on a set of warpipes as Graff raised his flare gun and fired the preset sequence of photon flares up into the sky. Red-green-red. His men were hunting down Souther stragglers on their section of the riverbank and in the territory behind it, but the mission was over and the objective had been attained. He looked east and west, seeing other colour-coded flare sequences rise up into the sky all along the shoreline, as the other regiments in the attack wave reported similar success in their own target objectives.

The river was theirs, and now the next stage of the Battle of Nordstadt could begin.

With both sides of the river in their hands, the Norts quickly went to work. Heavy lifter hoppers carried massive sections of pontoon bridging over to the newly secured riverbank, while troop carrier hoppers dropped off teams of military engineers. Formed into fifty-man workcrews, the engineers and Kashans started assembling the pontoon sections, dropping each one into place as another hopper delivered the next piece.

Three bridges were being constructed simultaneously on both sides of the river, the ends of each one growing out to meet its twin on the other bank. While the Kashans and engineers sweated and strained to assemble and haul each section into place, impatient officers and NCOs shouting curses and orders at them, Nort gunships prowled overhead, protecting the precious bridges and the vulnerable beachhead on the far bank from enemy aerial attack. Those Kashans not engaged in the bridge building work spread out to form a defensive perimeter, protecting the beachhead from any ground-based counter-attack, even assuming the increasingly beleaguered and disorganised Souther forces could mount such an operation.

Forty minutes after Centurion-Kolonel Graff raised his regiment's standard over the Souther positions, the last rivet was fired into place on the first bridge to be completed, and the columns of Nort armour lined up on the northern bank began to cross the river. They were Nort light and medium tanks, weighing as much as the pontoon bridges would bear, accompanied by even more columns of troop-carrying APCs. Over the next hour, four entire Nort armoured divisions would cross the river, with another nine reserve divisions moving through the Nort-held sections of the city's northern half to join them.

The target of all this armoured might was the enemy's southernmost secure zone, their principal safe haven in Nordstadt, containing the Southers' largest shuttle landing base, as well as their command headquarters. If this zone fell, then the rest of Nordstadt would surely fall soon afterwards.

Facing these thirteen Nort armoured divisions, and the third and fourth reinforcement waves that would come after them, was a mixed Souther force of four under-strength divisions, composed mainly of different units hastily thrown together from the shattered remains of other, larger units already destroyed in the last few days' fighting.

All over Nordstadt, the story was the same. The Norts attacking in overwhelming force, often suffering appalling losses to spirited enemy opposition, but nevertheless pushing relentlessly through to achieve their objectives.

In the steelworks sector, four whole infantry divisions, three Nort and one Souther, were consumed in a few terrible hours of intense, close-quarters fighting. If Sergeant Hanna Coss made it back there now to find the remnants of her squad, she would have to look for them among the piles of dead, where Norts and Southers lay tangled together and almost indistinguishable from each other in the charnel houses of the burned-out remains of the giant steelworks.

In the main financial district sector, a Souther battalion commander, cut off and faced with the crushing weight of the Nort forces now closing in all around him, adopted a desperate scorched earth tactic. Those of his men who could respond to his urgent fallback order did so, pulling out with orders to find any way they could back to the nearest secure zone. The others died where they stood, buried along with their commander and their Nort opponents beneath millions of tonnes of rubble as the commander gave the order for the long-ago positioned demolition charges to be blown. The shattered glass and steel towers of the financial district came tumbling down in one single moment of catastrophe, falling in on the heads of both sides. The Southers lost almost a full battalion, the Norts more than a division.

Even before the dust had started to clear from the scene of the cataclysm, the Nort forces following behind the main assault were pushing forward in search of alternative routes through or around the mass burial site.

All over Nordstadt, the story was the same. The Norts advancing in force. The Southers retreating in disarray or crushed by the weight of the enemy offensive. The final fate of Nordstadt now seemed inevitable. It was, but not in any way any of the combatants could imagine.

Hammerfall was now less than ten hours away.

PART THREE
HAMMERFALL

NINETEEN

"We need more chem-suits! I don't care whether they need patching up or not. If they're good enough to last a couple of hours, then get them on these injured men. Find what weapons you can and issue them to the best of the walking wounded. If we're going out of here on foot, we might need to use them before we get to the secure zone!"

"Sir, what about the critical cases? How are we going to evacuate them out of here?"

Artau looked at the rows of badly injured men lined up in the beds in front of him. Many of them were still hooked up to narco-drips and life enhancer equipment. Disconnecting them would almost certainly mean a death sentence for these men. Even trying to move some of the lesser critical cases – the burn and chest injury cases – would also probably result in death. Artau knew that what he was attempting; the evacuation of an entire field hospital at only a moment's notice. It was an almost impossible task, but the circumstances left him with little other choice. He had to think now of the well-being of all his patients and staff, even if the decisions that policy entailed meant the deaths of so many of the more hopeless cases.

He turned to the group of meds and orderlies gathered around him, waiting on their commanding officer's orders.

"Myles, check the stores again. I'm sure we've still got a few of the old Type Two bubble stretchers in there. If they're even halfway serviceable, get them unpacked and get some of these critical cases into them for immediate evac. Toshiro, assemble a team of your best people and run triage over the critical cases. If you think any of them have even a better than evens chance of surviving the evac, then I want them along for the ride. Garnier, start assembling stretcher carrier parties. Use the least injured of the walking wounded if you have to. Anyone who can't walk out of here on their own two feet gets carried out. That's an order. Karlsen–"

His next words were interrupted by the sound of a fresh salvo of explosions from outside, sounding closer than ever. Medics and patients alike ducked instinctively. Artau waited for the panic to subside. He had assumed the earlier rounds that had hit them and wiped out about a quarter of his field hospital had struck by accident, falling short of their intended target, probably the AA battery situated a few kilometres away in the marble ruins of the museum quarter. The field hospital hadn't come under fire since then, but Nort artillery rounds continued to scream overhead, and the sounds of explosions from the collapsing front line seemed to creep closer with every passing minute. Artau estimated they probably had an hour or less until those sounds arrived at their front door.

He scanned the frightened faces around him, spotting the one he was looking for, that of Lieutenant Karlsen, the unit's communications officer.

"Karlsen, any word yet of any hopper or truck transport to help get our wounded out of here?"

Karlsen grimaced. "Sorry, sir. Whatever Nordstadt Command's transport priorities are, we don't seem to be too high up the list. So far, I haven't even got a reply back from them."

Artau wasn't surprised. He'd listened in to the near-hysterical radio chatter now filling the Souther comm-channels in a futile attempt to use the authority of his rank to get some kind of priority status for his transport request. The Souther airwaves were full of panicked news of the battles now raging all round the borders of the crucible. Frontline units everywhere were radioing in reports of heavy Nort attack.

Many were requesting permission to fall back and regroup in the face of the overwhelming odds against them.

Others were reporting that they had already retreated, or had been pushed back, and were urgently requesting new orders. Others still were reporting that they had been surrounded and cut off and were calling in to make one final report on their imminent extinction. By far the most common talk on the dozens of radio channels, besides the ever-mounting toll of reported casualty figures, was the urgent request for reinforcements, or artillery or air support coming in from the front line units. What was most frightening about these was the fact that there was little to no response to any of them coming back from Nordstadt Command. Artau thought of the number of names of high-ranking command personnel he had seen on that list on the Milli-fuzz compu-device, and wondered if there was even any command staff left in the crucible. Maybe they were all gone already, safely evacuated away and leaving everyone else here to die, trapped and leaderless.

The Milli-fuzz men were gone too, disappearing in the immediate aftermath of the artillery strike on the field hospital. Artau wasn't surprised, but cursed the military policemen for their cowardice. Authority like theirs, backed up by everyone's instinctive fear of the Milli-fuzz, was exactly something he could have used now, to help get this evacuation underway.

"Orderly Seath?"

The pale-faced, frightened-looking medical orderly snapped to attention at the sound of her commanding officer's voice. "Sir?"

"Look around and see if you can't find me some kind of sidearm. Any kind of pistol will do and as many ammo clips as can be spared."

"A sidearm, sir?" asked Seath, doubtfully. Everyone knew how much the surgeon hated weapons of any kind, and no one had ever seen him wearing a pistol and holster, even when regulations required him to do so.

"Yes. A sidearm, sergeant. I'll be staying here to look after the patients who are too badly injured to be moved. Since the fighting seems to be heading in this direction, it's perhaps best that I'm prepared for whatever might happen. At least until transport can be found to come back here and pick up the rest of the wounded. In the meantime, while I remain here, Major Jacks will be leading the evac column back to the secure zone."

Seath and the other medics stared at him, aghast. All of them knew, just as Artau did, that there wouldn't be any extra transport coming back and what they were hearing was a man calmly pronouncing his own death sentence. The Nort advance was coming this way, apparently led by units of the infamous Kashan Legion and the Kashans weren't well known for their humane treatment of enemy wounded.

"Sir, with all respect, I think you should reconsider–" began Seath, before Artau cut her off.

"You've all got your orders, and I've got a duty to do as well. I worked for days to keep some of these men alive. I'm not going to give up on them now."

"Permission requested to stay behind with you, sir?"

Artau turned in surprise, seeing the figure of Hanna Coss standing there. She was wearing a patched-up chem-suit and had scrounged up an infantryman's las-carbine from somewhere.

Artau smiled. "Sergeant Coss, I don't remember giving you your medical discharge orders yet."

She returned the show of grim humour. "I told you I wanted to get back to the front, sir. Since that couldn't happen, this seems convenient. At least now the front line has to come to me, instead of the other way around."

"Permission denied, sergeant," Artau told her. "You're still under my medical supervision and that means you're also still under my orders. You'll do more good elsewhere than here, so–"

He was interrupted by the sound of explosions from outside. Coming from nearby. Too nearby for it to be sounds from the front line, no matter how few kilometres away the fighting there might he now.

It was followed seconds later by the hissing chatter of las-fire, and an answering chorus of screams from the people outside the hospital dome.

Hanna then heard another sound, a distinctive dry, coughing sound that every soldier on Nu Earth knew and feared. Something struck the outside wall of the med-dome with a sickening boom and harmlessly ricocheted off its shielded surface.

A misaimed hit. Hanna knew they wouldn't be so lucky with the next shot.

"Seal-bursters!" she shouted in warning, pulling down the visor of her chem-helmet. "Get your visors down and respirators on!"

More seal-burster shots struck the exterior of the dome. This time, as Hanna had feared, the other Nort snipers' marksmanship was lethally on target.

The med-dome was catastrophically breached in at least four places. Environmental hazard alarms instantly went off, their screaming alerts sounding over the screams of the people inside the dome as the poison air from outside rushed in.

More las-fire sounded from outside. More screams, more sounds of death. The main airlock of the dome blew inwards. Chem-clouds swirled in, adding to the rapidly changing poison atmosphere inside. Hanna saw figures bearing guns and wearing chem-suits inside the chem-mist. She recognised the silhouette shapes of their suits.

Kashans. She didn't know where they had come from or how they had already got this far behind the front line, but it was brutally clear what their task here was. Las-fire shot out through the spreading chem-mist, cutting down men and women already choking to death on the vapour from outside the breached dome. The wounded were shot or bayoneted where they lay, lined up for the slaughter in row after row of beds. Grenades were hurled into the room through one of the holes opened up by a seal-burster hit, the detonations further adding to the chaos and carnage inside.

A female orderly in front of Hanna, one of the few who'd reacted in time to her shouted warning and managed to secure her chem-visor in place, pitched over backwards, shot through the chest by a las-round. More rounds sprayed through the air, whipping through the air around Hanna. One struck Artau and he too fell to the ground. Hanna crouched down beside him, seeing that he had taken a glancing hit to the side of his chem-helmet. The armoured material of the helmet was scorched and dented, with a but otherwise intact. The real problem was the air-tube that had been sliced into by the same shot. The surgeon was thrashing about in panic as he felt, or at least imagined, the poison stuff of Nu Earth's atmosphere leaking into his suit. Hanna grabbed his hands, pinning them to his sides, and stared at the terrified face beneath the suit's chem-visor.

"Don't panic," she told him, her two years of hard-won combat experience more than making up for his decades of medical knowledge. "Your tube's cut, but its not that serious. I'll patch it up as we get out of here. Until then, I've disconnected your respirator so you'll have to use your suit's emergency air supply. It's only good for a few minutes so take shallow breaths."

A few minutes, she thought to herself. They'd either be dead or out of here long before then.

More las-rounds cut through the air above where she was crouching. The Kashans were advancing methodically through the large ward room, killing everything in their path. The nearest one was only a few beds away and would spot them any second. Desperately, she looked around her for a weapon. Her eyes instinctively went to Artau's belt, looking for the customary officer's sidearm that should have been there, but there was nothing. Nothing, except...

"Stak!"

She heard the Nort's shout as he spotted her and Artau. He came at them with his bayonet fixed, clearly intending to finish them both off. She grabbed the med-tool from Artau's belt, activating it with a flick of her thumb. She'd seen the things used before, but had never actually held one. She'd never seen one used as a weapon before, either, except maybe in spy drama propaganda vid-flicks, where dashing and resourceful Souther intelligence operatives routinely despatched legions of Nort fifth columnists and agent provocateurs with any kind of weapon that came to hand.

She thumbed the power setting up to maximum power and beyond, hoping for the best. The las-scalpel buzzed into life in her hand, its bright cutting blade extending to the length of about thirty centimetres. What was intended to be a finely balanced and delicate tool for making surgical incisions into human flesh and bone had now been transformed into a lethal weapon. She slashed out with it, evading the Kashan's bayonet lunge. The las-scalpel's beam blade cut through the Nort's air-tubes and then effortlessly into the meat of his neck. The Kashan died just a second or two before the burned-out power cell of the las-scalpel did. His body fell one way, his head fell another.

She grabbed the las-carbine out of the hands of the headless corpse, turning it on the other Kashans. It was on full auto. Hanna, unfamiliar with the design of the thing and not having time to remedy that situation, just kept her finger on the trigger, directing a furious stream of fire into the body of the nearest enemy. He jerked backwards, struck by round after round. The Nort las-carbine, more powerful but with a stronger recoil than the Souther equivalent, kicked in her hands, throwing off her aim off, forcing her to choose quantity of firepower over quality of marksmanship. Fire enough shots, she reasoned, and you would eventually probably hit what you were aiming for in the first place.

She was right. Half a cycle into the Nort carbine's ammo clip, a las-round struck and touched off the pack of plasma grenades strapped to the corpse's belt. The explosion caught three more of the Kashans who were at that moment rushing forward to deal with the tenacious Souther sergeant.

By the time the smoke cleared and the surviving Kashans pushed forward to avenge the deaths of their comrades, their prey was long gone.

Hanna pushed the stumbling figure of Artau ahead of her, pushing harder every time it looked like he was thinking about stopping to help any of the choking, dying figures on the floors of the wards or in the corridor outside it. Without chem-suit protection, there was nothing that could be done for any of these poor bastards when the seal-bursters struck.

Then they were through the building's rear airlock, ducking behind the wreckage of a burning med-vehicle to avoid a squad of Kashans milling around in the compound outside. As soon as the coast was clear, Hanna pushed the surgeon on, making for the cover of the surrounding rubble. The older man was hyperventilating now, drawing heavily on his suit's limited air supply. Hanna hoped it would last long enough for them to get a safe distance away from the remains of the field hospital and the enemy troops now crawling all over it.

She hoped she would last long enough too. Before she put on the chem-suit, she had injected half a stick of stim-tabs into her injured leg. The remaining pain had gone away almost instantly, giving her the strength to do everything she had done in the last few minutes, but she had no idea how long the effects would last.

Only once the sounds of las-fire from behind them, as the Kashans finished off any remaining survivors in the field hospital, faded into the distance did Hanna relent and allow them to stop and rest in the cover of a broken pedestal that had once borne the long-destroyed statue of some Nordland martial hero.

"Sit down and take it easy. Your air gauge is almost in the red so start taking shallow breaths," she commanded the senior officer. If either of them noticed that their positions of doctor and patient, of commander and commanded, had been suddenly reversed, neither of them chose to comment on it.

She reached into the large flap on the front of her chem-suit, pulling out the sealant patch kit that was always kept there by all Souther troops. She opened it up and expertly went to work, splicing in a new length of air-tubing to replace the damaged section, which she then closed up with patches and fast-bonding sealant spray. She checked the damage to Artau's helmet, saw that it was negligible, and then gave him the thumbs-up, signalling that it was safe for him to start using his respirator rig again.

The old man gratefully gulped in a lungful of respirator-filtered and purified air. "The... the field hospital," he croaked, still gasping for breath. "There were still people back there..."

"Forget them," Hanna told him matter-of-factly. "They're all dead by now. They were dead as soon as those seal-busters hit. You can't do anything for them anymore."

She reached down, offering her hand, and then pulling him to his feet. She looked around, scanning the horizon of nighttime Nordstadt. The whole horizon, fully three hundred and sixty degrees all around them, was lit up with the flashes of explosions and gunfire. The whole breadth of the borders of the crucible was evident from where they stood, its lines marked out in light and fire. The extent of those borders was now frighteningly small.

"C'mon," she said, gesturing back in the direction of the destroyed field hospital. "We can't do any good back there, so let's go find someplace where we still can."

All over Nordstadt, the story was the same. Front line Souther forces were smashed by the weight of the Nort advance. Retreating or routed Souther forces were harried by artillery fire or strafed and bombed from the air as Nort power was allowed free rein in the skies over the city. Dropped in by waves of hoppers, Kashan stormtroopers and Nort commando squads ran riot behind the front line, ambushing columns of retreating Southers, attacking divisional HQs and rear echelon supply bases, sowing panic and confusion everywhere they struck.

The northernmost secure zone was the first to fall. Nort light armour, following a path opened up by the trademark brutalities of the Kashans, stormed through the last line of defences, breaking through into the field of landing bays just as the last evac shuttles there were touching off. One of the shuttles barely made it off the ground and was shot out of the air before its pilot could hit the afterburners. The others rocketed skywards, climbing hundreds of metres in seconds, racing to reach the safety of the high-altitude fighter screen that still circled invisibly above the city, waiting impatiently to escort the shuttles to the orbital bases. Aboard the shuttles were those lucky few whom Milli-com had deemed worthy of rescue. Left behind them in the burning ruins of Nordstadt were the still tens of thousands of ordinary soldiers whose lives had been deemed as surplus to requirements by the dictates of Operation Hammerfall.

Yes, all over Nordstadt the story was the same. Meanwhile, in the dark tunnels below the city, one lone Souther soldier was still trapped in his own private crucible.

TWENTY

"Rogue? Wake up, Rogue. C'mon, trooper, don't give up on us now…"

Rogue heard the biochip voice calling to him through the darkness, but did his best to ignore it. The voice was somewhere outside the darkness and Rogue knew there was nothing but pain and despair waiting for him out there.

Better to stay here in the darkness. Better to stay in oblivion and unconsciousness, where the pain couldn't quite reach him.

In the end, the choice wasn't his to make. He felt something wet and cold splash across him, running in trickles down his face and body, shocking him back into consciousness. He instinctively licked a few drops of it from his lips, his GI senses automatically analysing its contents. It was water. The typical Nu Earth version of it, anyway, fouled with various biochemical pollutants and with some trace elements of viral and radioactive contamination. Lethal, or at least extremely hazardous to humans, harmless to him.

So the water wasn't going to kill him, but there were plenty of other things that could and probably would. He stared at the most dangerous of them now. The figure of the Traitor General, standing just a few feet away from him, although he might as well have been on the dark side of Nu Earth's blue moon for all that Rogue could do against him at the moment. The shambling, crippled and malformed figures of the tribe of rubble rats stood around their leader or lurked in the shadows around the sides of the underground chamber. Alerted by Helm's voice, one small group inspected Rogue's biochip gear in eager curiosity, making noises of quiet excitement as they held Rogue's GI rifle, helmet and backpack in their hands, studying the device's unfamiliar design.

Rogue barely spared any of them a second glance. It was the figure sitting hunched at the traitor's feet that caught his attention. The figure of the grinning child hungrily tearing with his teeth into the contents of the ration pack that Rogue had given him. It was the kid whose life Rogue had saved, the feral rubble rat child who had deliberately and happily led him straight into the traitor's trap.

Rogue remembered the circumstances that had brought him here. He had scrambled over the rubble in pursuit of the kid, even his GI speed and stamina pushed to keep up with his guide. He found ways through the ruins that Rogue would never have stumbled upon. He squirmed his way through barrier heaps of collapsed masonry that Rogue had to climb over or bypass and go round.

He instinctively took careful detours round areas of open ground that looked innocuous enough to Rogue's eyes, but which a later scanner check showed to be laden with hidden mines or booby traps. Several times, he had suddenly halted, taking cover and signalling for Rogue to do likewise. Rogue had done as directed, even though he had picked nothing up. Neither had the electronic senses of his biochip equipment. A few moments later each time, though, a Nort or Souther atmocraft flight had passed overhead, their weapons systems hot and searching for any targets of opportunity hiding in the rubble below.

The kid was good, Rogue had to grudgingly admit. His own childhood was almost beyond human comprehension: born out of the Milli-com clone-vats, trained and taught from infancy to be a living weapon of war. These were Rogue's experiences of what had passed for a childhood, but even he couldn't imagine what it must have been like to have been born into a place like Nordstadt.

They had travelled for more than an hour across the rubble landscape before they came to the place the kid had been looking for. At first, it just looked like another deep shell crater, the leftover remnants of some stray bunker-buster shell strike from long ago. A dense, permanent cloud of chem-mist had filled most of the crater, rising from the acidic pool of toxic sludge that had collected at the bottom of it. The stuff was impenetrable to both normal human sight and most battlefield scanning devices, but Rogue's GI eyes could pierce the veil, seeing the vague shadow shape a few metres within the edge of the lurking chem-mist. There was a tunnel entrance hidden down there.

"We're going underground, Rogue?" Bagman had said. "Could be anything waiting for us down there, you know."

"I'm with Bagman," Helm had added. "Maybe we should think about this first."

"You guys got any better leads on finding the traitor, I'm all ears," Rogue had growled. "I wasn't re-gened yesterday. We go in there, we go in alert and with scanners tuned to the max."

They had followed the kid down into the crater, entering the hidden tunnel entrance and passing through a crude but serviceable bubble-seal airlock just beyond.

They were in a tunnel, some kind of old Nordstadt municipal service-way, judging by the lifeless and burned-out power conduits running along its crumbling rockrete walls. The kid had removed his respirator mask as soon as they had passed through the airlock. Rogue had sniffed at the air, analysing it with his GI bio-senses. It was stale and foul-tasting, tainted with various minor contaminants that would almost certainly be hazardous to anyone spending a lot of time down here, but it was still the nearest thing to normal, breathable air they had found yet in Nordstadt.

The kid had given an excited yelp and ran off at speed along the corridor, carrying and lighting a spluttering and nearly spent phosphor torch and beckoning for Rogue to follow.

"Home sweet home, I guess," Rogue had muttered as he warily trudged after him.

They had soon lost sight of the kid, following only the faint afterglow of his torch, the sound of his footfalls and the shouts that carried back to them.

"Blueman, this way! This way!" had come the shout at the junction they had encountered a minute or two later. The original passageway was gone, blocked by tonnes of collapsed rubble. Two other branching tunnels had been crudely created there, laboriously hacked out with whatever materials were available, their uneven and sagging roofs propped up by makeshift supports scavenged from battlefield debris. The kid's voice had come from the tunnel to the left, although there was no visible sign of the voice's owner. Even Rogue's eyes, backed up by his biochips' electronic senses, were unable to penetrate the inky darkness of the tunnel.

"Rogue…" Helm had warned.

"I know," Rogue had responded. "Come this far, too late to back out now. Gunnar?"

"Locked and loaded and ready for trouble," his rifle had confirmed.

He had gone into the tunnel, climbing over the small mound of rubble that partially blocked its entrance. There was no light at all now. Bagman's sensor receptors projected twin beams of IR light, invisibly illuminating the way ahead, allowing Rogue's extra-human vision to pick out valuable details of his surroundings.

They had only gone about thirty metres down the tunnel's length when the ambush came.

They had been waiting for him all along, Rogue realised now. Lying there motionless, to defeat his equipment's scanner senses. Not talking, barely even breathing, to defeat the biochips' sensitive audio receptors. Their bodies smeared with cold mud and filth, so that Rogue's IR vision passed invisibly over them.

They had been waiting for him and when he passed the place where they had been waiting, they attacked. They came out the walls at him, they dropped down from the roof upon him, they came up at him from out of the rubble beneath his feet. Screeching and yelling. Naked and primitive. Hacking and clubbing at him with whatever weapons they had.

They had been everywhere, all over him. Something had smashed out one of Bagman's IR beams, and after that

Rogue had fought near-blind. There had been too many of them in the narrow tunnel, and not enough space or light to use Gunnar, so Rogue had matched their savagery with savagery of his own. Something came out of the ground in front of him and Rogue had stamped down upon it, feeling bones break beneath his foot. Something had tried to wrench his rifle from his grasp, and Rogue had smashed the butt into its face, rewarded moments later by the dull sound of a lifeless body hitting the ground.

Something had leapt on his back, stabbing at him with a jagged shard of metal and Rogue had hurled himself backwards against the tunnel wall, using all his strength to crush his unseen attacker. He had felt more bones breaking, and had heard a high-pitched squeal of pain. He had just killed or maimed a woman or child.

The shock of that realisation had been enough to momentarily stop him in his tracks and that moment of hesitation was all his attackers had needed. More hands had pulled Helm away from his head. Another pair of hands had brought a broken lump of rockrete down upon his unprotected skull in a blow that would surely have killed a normal man.

Rogue had fallen into the filth of the tunnel floor, darkness closing in around him. He had been unconscious as hands had reached down do strip away his remaining pieces of equipment. Other hands had taken hold of him and dragged him off to their waiting master.

Rogue raised his head and looked into the face of his enemy. A smile, crueller than any of the other scars and livid burn marks there, cut across that face.

"Awake again? Shall we see how long you can stay conscious this time, Genetic Infantryman?"

Rogue weakly struggled against his chains. He was suspended by his wrists by chains fixed to the low ceiling of the underground chamber. Other chains secured his feet to heavy stone blocks on the floor. Too weak to stand, his weight sagged down, the manacles holding him up cut into the flesh of his wrists. Against his will, his gaze went to the

weapon in the traitor's hand. It was a shock-baton, but of a
kind far different to the ones wielded by the Souther Milli-
fuzz. This was a Nort weapon, the same kind issued to
guards and overseers in the Norts' POW camps and notorious gulag work installations and prison factories. The shock
points on it were pointed barbs running down the spine of
the weapon's haft, designed not merely to stun their victim
with blasts of electricity, but also to rip and tear their flesh.

Rogue's back, torso, shoulders and arms were criss-
crossed with the evidence of the weapon's most recent use.
The filthy water that had been thrown over him to revive
him dripped down his body, stinging into the cuts and
burns that the traitor had left upon him. This was the third
time he had passed out and been brought back round again,
and he no longer knew how long the torture had been going
on for. His wounds would heal, his superhuman GI stamina
and constitution would see to that, as they always did, but
Rogue doubted he would ever be allowed to live that long.

The face of his enemy hovered in front of him. The man
he had criss-crossed the surface of Nu Earth to find and kill
was standing in front of him, less than a metre away, and
Rogue was helpless to do anything about it.

"We both know you're going to kill me, so why don't you
get your sick fun over with and just finish the job?"

The traitor laughed. "Trust me, my friend, nothing would
give me greater pleasure than killing the last of the Genetic
Infantrymen and finishing the job I started in the Quartz
Zone. You took away everything I had. My rank, my
anonymity, my position in Souther High Command. My
face, even. Now, though, thanks to you, some of these
things will be given back to me and that is why I must keep
you alive."

The chamber shook with the faint rumble of explosions
from the surface above their heads. Rogue didn't know how
long he had been unconscious, but the explosions were definitely getting louder and nearer.

The traitor seemed to read his thoughts. "Yes, Nordstadt
will have new masters soon. Imagine how delighted they
will be not only to have their precious city back, but also

when they receive you as an extra gift to celebrate their victory!"

"Dream on, psycho. The only reward a scumbag like you is going to get from your old Nort buddies is–"

Gunnar's retort was cut off as one of the traitor's tribe of savages switched off his biochip's voice-synth speaker with an angry flick. Disarmed and in the hands of the traitor's followers, Gunnar and the others were helpless bystanders to Rogue's predicament.

"We have time yet before I emerge to begin negotiations with Nordstadt's new owners. How shall we spend it, I wonder?" smiled the traitor, reactivating the shock-baton. The weapon hummed into life in his hand, set on a new and more damaging power level.

"Yes. Your face, I think. You took away my face, so it seems only fair I return the favour. I'm sure your new captors won't mind receiving goods that are only a little spoiled, and there will still be enough of you left for the Nordland gene scientists to work with when they begin their dissection work on you."

The traitor brought the energy-crackling weapon up to begin the next and more damaging round of Rogue's torture. A commotion at one of the tunnel entrances interrupted him. He turned in annoyance as one of his followers entered and shuffled nervously towards him. The hunched, malformed figure grunted a few urgent words in a debased version of the Nort language.

The traitor deactivated the shock-baton with an air of obvious regret and handed it to one of Rogue's guards. "Watch him," he commanded. "Anything happens to him, and you'll all pay the price."

He looked at Rogue, who glared back at him in silent defiance. "It looks like we're both in luck tonight, my friend. The Nort advance is going better than I expected, and the fall of Nordstadt is probably only a few hours away now. There are things I have to do to safeguard this place and to get ready for my negotiations. But don't worry, we'll have plenty of time to continue this later, before I hand you over to my former employers."

He left, taking most of his followers with him, but leaving behind enough of them to ensure his prisoner remained
closely guarded. Rogue slumped forward on his chains
again, a black wave of despair washing over him.

He wasn't sure if he imagined it, but he thought he heard
Helm's voice whispering to him from somewhere nearby.

"Hang in there, Rogue. Something's gonna happen to get
us out of here, I know it. Stay solid blue, Rogue, and just
keep on hanging in there. Don't quit on us now…"

TWENTY-ONE

"Run that by me again, Gabe, and this time don't skimp on the stuff about how those psychos at Milli-com are actually planning to nuke Nordstadt and everyone there who's still supposed to be on our side."

They were back at their squadron base. Rafe had been confined to quarters on the orders of an outraged flight commander as soon as they landed, pending a disciplinary investigation for disobeying orders. Rafe wanted to get back in the air again, but any change in her current restricted status wouldn't make any difference to that wish. The entire squadron was grounded. Milli-com was planning something big, everyone said, and had imposed a five hundred kilometre no-fly zone around Nordstadt for every Souther pilot and aircraft. "Operation Hammerfall" was the whispered name on everyone's lips, although no one had a clue what the hell it was.

Gabe knew, though. Armed with the access codes he had picked up during their last illegal expedition into the Souther high command's intelligence and communications network, he had picked up enough to find out what Hammerfall was all about. Going into Milli-com's central system would have tripped dozens of security alerts and brought him crashing up against the impenetrable barrier of Milli-com's inner core cyber-hack defences and Gabe wasn't programmed to be that stupid or reckless. Instead, he had lurked amongst the hundreds of auxiliary systems and satellite networks, picking up a small clue or nugget of information from many of these different, scattered locations. The information he had amassed might have taken a human team of Milli-com's own data analysts and intelligence strategists days to sift through and extrapolate some kind of meaning out of it all. Gabe had accomplished the same task in a matter of minutes, unlocking the secret of Operation Hammerfall.

And now Rafe knew it too. She had no doubt that what she and Gabe had uncovered would be enough to get Gabe's personality matrix and memory files wiped and her condemned to whatever it is Milli-com and the gene-genies did with GIs who had proven to be more trouble than they were worth. No, she had no doubt about what would happen to them if Milli-com knew what they had discovered, just as she had no doubt what it was she had to do now.

She reached into her footlocker, rummaging through the sparse collection of personal effects stored there. GIs, without families or a life before military service, didn't tend to amass much in the way of personal belongings. She soon found what she was looking for, checking and loading it in one well-practised move. She had had to surrender her regular sidearm as a formality when she had been confined to quarters, but like any other combat pilot, she always made sure of being in possession of a strictly non-regulation backup piece.

"We going somewhere, babe?"

"Yeah. Nordstadt," she answered, moving towards the door. Gabe's drone shell obediently hovered after her.

"We sent Rogue into there," she told him. "He's still there, so we've got to go find him and get him out before they nuke the place right off the face of Nu Earth."

"And how we going to do that, toots?"

She opened the door, checking that the coast was clear. Luckily, despite her confinement to quarters, even her asshole of a flight commander hadn't managed to swing having an armed guard put on her door.

"Simple, Gabe. We're going to steal a shuttle. They want to put me in front of a court martial, then I figure it might as well be for something worthwhile."

. . .

Stealing a shuttle wasn't as simple as it sounded. With the squadron grounded, the fighter and shuttle hangers were all in lockdown, the ground crews taking advantage of the unexpected halting of all flight ops to run full maintenance checks on all the squadron's aircraft. Even if Rafe could find a shuttle to steal, there was no guarantee she would be able to even take off in it, not with its flight systems stripped or one of its engines disassembled and lying in pieces on the hanger floor around it.

Rafe's progress through the base drew a few looks and raised eyebrows – Bluegirl, isn't she supposed to be confined to quarters, they probably wondered? – but thankfully there were no challenges from anyone in authority.

"Out of luck, hon. No shuttles, no rescue mission."

Rafe's eyes scanned the tarmac of the runway, tracking the trace of a memory of something she had seen as she had brought her Seraphim into land less than an hour ago.

She found what she was looking for, parked in a secluded corner of the base perimeter, well away from the ordinary, day-to-day business of the squadron. She even recognised the two figures walking towards it.

"Saddle up, Gabe," she smiled. "We've found our ride."

"A good bit of business, Mister Brass?"

"Agreeably profitable, Mister Bland. Agreeably profitable."

They were crossing the runway, heading back to where their shuttle was sitting. Two pairs of their picker robots trailed after them, carrying several bulky containers of brand new Souther aircraft spare parts and computer boards between them.

"Yes, not bad at all, Mister Brass. A few more trips like this and we won't have to look for one of those lovely Seraphim fighters to salvage and sell on. We'll have enough spare parts to build one of our own!"

"An excellent plan, Mister Bland. We'll have clients queuing up to purchase such an item. We'll just neglect to tell them until after the deal's done that this particular bargain only comes in kit form."

They laughed, both of them thinking of the nest-egg they were building together. The proceeds from their entrepreneurial activities were all salted away in various secret bank accounts lodged on worlds far away from the war. One day, when either the war was over and there was no more material left to salvage, or when even their combined avarice was satisfied by the vast sums of money they had accumulated together, they would retire and live off the rewards of their labour on some remote and luxurious retreat.

Mister Bland favoured one of the pleasure worlds in the Vargas Cluster where, for a price, anonymity was assured and almost every whim and desire could be catered for. Mister Brass, however, considered the Vargas Cluster pleasure worlds and their inhabitants to be rather too vulgar for his tastes and preferred something a little more private and sedate. When not engaged in the important business of making money, one of the salvage merchants' main pleasures was arguing between themselves about what to do with the money itself.

They arrived at their shuttle and quickly went through their usual routine. Bland disarmed the shuttle's expensive security systems and went into the cockpit to begin the launch procedure and programme in the flight plan to their next port of call. His partner supervised the loading of the merchandise through the main cargo hatch to the rear. Their craft was deceptively antique looking, but a considerable amount of their profits had been ploughed back into it, to give it various hidden features that made it quite unique, even on Nu Earth.

Bland hummed a tune to himself – one of his favourite arias from one of his favourite operas, a far cry from those terribly bombastic Nort musical affairs that his partner tended to favour – while he flicked switches and entered flight programme codes.

"Ready to go up here, Mister Brass. Everything secured and sealed back there?"

No answer. He frowned. Morrie tended to fuss too much over the safe securing of the merchandise, Bland thought, but it usually didn't take him this long to get them ready to go.

"Mister Brass?" he asked again into his chem-suit's comm-unit.

He saw a light blinking on the console in front of him, signalling that the rear cargo hatch was now closing. A few moments later, the cockpit door behind him hissed open. "About time, Mister Brass. Time is money, as you always tell me, and–"

He stopped right there, seeing the figure accompanying his partner into the cockpit. A tall, blue-skinned figure was holding a gun to the back of Brass's head.

"Nice shuttle. Mind if I hitch a ride with you boys?" asked Rafe.

The salvage dealers' shuttle took off a few moments later. No one on the base paid it any attention. The squadron commander's private dealings with those two vultures were his own affair, and if they knew what was good for them, everyone did their best to ignore the scavengers' frequent and completely unofficial visits to the base.

No one watched it go. No one paid any attention to its course. No one noticed that it was heading straight into the no-fly zone around Nordstadt.

"What kind of comms and encryption packages this thing got?" asked Rafe, inspecting the shuttle's control systems, careful not to take her eyes off the two body looters sitting in the cockpit seats in front of her. Gabe hovered nearby, also watching them closely. Gabe's drone-shell was equipped with a short-ranged but surprisingly powerful mini-blaster weapon and he had already made the necessary power and targeting calculations. One shot and the body looters would be smeared all over the inside of their cockpit window.

"The best money can buy, naturally," answered Brass. "You name it, my dear, and we can call it up or hack into it with the equipment we have here. You wouldn't believe how many bargains Mister Bland and I have chanced upon just by keeping our ears open, so to speak."

The two salvage dealers exchanged glances while Brass spoke. They had been together so long, were so in tune with each other's minds, that with a few glances and a twitch of a raised eyebrow or a pursing of the lips, it was almost as if they could exchange thoughts.

A GI female, Mister Brass!

And one of those fascinating auto-flight drones we've heard so much about, Mister Bland. The Wachowski-Linder Industries GABRIEL-302 model, if I'm not much mistaken.

Their minds worked simultaneously, each of them doing a quick appraisal of the relative market value of the goods under discussion. Both came up with a pleasingly high figure, an agreement they reached with another glance.

Rafe and Gabe didn't notice any of this.

"Gabe, can you hook into this comms-rig and broadcast another signal on the old GI Regiment frequencies? We need to get another message out to our friend in Nordstadt, to warn him what's about to happen and let him know we're coming to pick him up.

"With the equipment they've got here? Definitely not going to be a problem, Rafe."

More glances between the two salvage merchants. More looks of silent agreement.

You hear that, Mister Brass? "Our friend in Nordstadt?" The Rogue Trooper, you think?

My thoughts exactly, Mister Bland. This little hijack escapade gets more and more interesting all the time. And more and more potentially profitable for our own humble little operation.

My thoughts exactly, Mister Brass.

"Help yourself to whatever meagre resources we have, my dear," Bland told Rafe. "My partner and I are always happy to lend a helping hand to the brave men and women of the Confederacy, isn't that right, Mister Brass?"

"Indeed, Mister Bland."

Another shared glance. Another silent agreement.

Let's play this one by ear, Mister Brass, and see where it takes us, shall we?

Indeed, Mister Bland.

. . .

Rogue leaned his head back, stretching his neck back as far as the chains holding him in place would allow and opened his mouth, catching some of the droplets of water that dripped down from the ceiling. The stuff tasted foul, full of Nu Earth contaminants. Rogue's system would have no problem neutralising them, however, and right now, his body needed all the sustenance it could get.

One of his guards broke off from what he was doing, raising his head to watch him suspiciously, but did nothing to stop him. He and the other guards were busy ransacking the equipment carried by Bagman and much of it lay scattered on the floor around them as they squabbled and rolled dice to contest ownership over the choicest items. They must have switched off the Bagman biochip's voice modulator as well, since there were no sounds from Bagman as the scavengers eagerly emptied him out.

There was no sign of Gunnar and Rogue suspected the traitor or one of his lieutenants had already lay claim to that particular prize. Helm lay discarded on the ground a few metres away, not too far from Rogue's feet. Clearly, none of the scavengers were interested in what looked like just another helmet. Rogue guessed this situation would change once the Norts arrived on the scene. His biochip equipment would be almost as big a prize as he was, and Rogue guessed that Helm, Gunnar and Bagman would probably end up as war trophies decorating a Kashan Legion officers' mess or the private office or dining room of some Nort general.

Too low for human ears to hear, a faint static hiss emerged from Helm's voice speaker. Hidden within that hiss was Helm's synthesised voice, speaking at the biochip equivalent of a hushed whisper.

"Rogue? Can you hear me, Rogue?"

Rogue shifted slightly, emitting a sound that his guards would have interpreted as a random grunt of pain.

"Glad to hear you're still with us, buddy," whispered Helm. "Listen carefully, Rogue. I'm picking up a message on the same old GI frequency as before. It's Guardian Angel, again. She's coming to get us. I'm going to use every bit of signal juice I've got left to beam back our location coordinates so she can zero in on us. Hang in there just a while longer, Rogue, help's on its way. You copy?"

Rogue stirred again, drawing another suspicious glance from one of his guards. The glance was longer this time.

Rogue played possum, hanging limp and lifeless in the chains. Help might be on its way, but that didn't mean he was going to stay here helpless while someone else stuck their hand into the fire to pull him out of trouble.

A plan formed in his mind. He swilled those last few precious droplets of water around his mouth, taking all the energy he could draw from them, then swallowed them and concentrated as he kick-started a bio-process unique to GI physiology. All he needed now was for someone to step within a metre or two of him, and then he would show them what being a Genetic Infantryman was all about.

"Copy on that signal we just sent out, Rafe. We're getting a response back. It's faint as hell. Trying to get a proper location lock on to it…"

Gabe's personality matrix programming was getting better all the time, thought Rafe. His voice was filled with an over-excited tone. She was more wary.

"Authentication?"

"It's solid blue, babe. Sounds like Soldier Blue's in trouble and in need of help, fast."

"Good work, Gabe. Once you get them, feed the location coordinates into this crate's nav systems. Hey, this crate of yours got boosters?"

The last question was directed to Brass and Bland. Brass nodded in response.

Rafe casually pointed the pistol in his direction. "Then let's see them in action. There's a friend of mine there who needs our help."

TWENTY-TWO

Venner spotted the two hidden watchers guarding the crater mouth easily enough. They were hidden in a small tumble of ruins overlooking the entrance. Both of them were armed with las-carbines, although Venner doubted the marksmanship of either would be much threat. There had been several others with them, but they had departed an hour or so earlier, following the Rogue Trooper into the crater.

Venner had followed his target at a distance, hanging well back and out of sight, but able to keep track of the Genetic Infantryman's progress through his lock on the biochip equipment he carried. The triple-pulse signal had faded out, but not dropped away entirely. Venner had cautiously circled the area, suspecting his target had literally gone to ground. It didn't take him long to realise that the crater almost certainly contained a hidden underground entrance, or to spot that same entrance's hidden surface watchers. Now it was time to make his move.

He crouched low in the ruins, taking care to choose a firing position that wouldn't leave him silhouetted against the flashes and explosions of the battle now taking place on the near-horizon all around them. At least one of his targets was not so careful, crouching and believing himself to be invisible in the gathering darkness, not realising his upper body silhouette and occasional shifting movements were perfectly visible against the flickering battle light behind him. Even without that, Venner would still have found them. His helmet's ambient light IR vision and spectrogram systems picked them out with ease, their crude and poorly-maintained chem-suits and respirator rigs bleeding heat signature traces and telltale oxygen-exchange elements out into the air around them.

Venner took aim, waiting for the next rumble of explosions to mask the sound of his shot. He didn't have to wait long. A series of flickering blasts lit up the horizon. Venner expertly counted down the seconds until the sound of those explosions reached them and then fired just as the dull roar of the artillery strike rolled over them.

The first target dropped out of sight, its silhouette shape suddenly altered as the sniper bullet blew away most of its skull. Dumbly aware that something significant had just happened, the second guard began turning. Venner shifted aim and fired again, killing him before the last echo of the explosion had died away, and before the man had even finished turning around.

Venner slipped out of his hiding place and climbed down into the crater, looking for the tunnel entrance he now knew was there.

His progress through the underground network of passageways he found was both swift and deadly.

He bypassed the airlock and its primitive alarm device with ease. He travelled at speed along the lightless tunnels, using his suit's sensor systems to find his way. The lock-on signal was much stronger down here, now that he was at the same underground level as the biochips, and he had little difficulty tracking them back to their current location.

He had to kill on two different occasions during his progress through the place. The first time was when he heard the sound of human footsteps running along the tunnel towards him. There was nowhere to hide and nowhere to retreat back to, so he struck as the creature turned the bend. A quick chop to the throat, to silence its surprised squawk of alarm, and then a brutal wrenching of the neck bones and the task was done. He went to work quickly after that, breaking more bones, folding the corpse up and jamming its resized remains into a narrow alcove in the tunnel wall where it would remain undiscovered long enough for Venner to do what he came here to do.

The second time was when he came across two more of the inhabitants of this place blocking the way ahead in the tunnel he was travelling along. They were standing isolated in a pocket of light created by the phosphor torch one of them was carrying, both engaged in some mundane and mostly futile maintenance task on one of the tunnel's sagging roof supports. The assassin advanced confidently and silently forward until he was standing just beyond the edge of the pool of light. It was a simple pair of shots, contemptuously easy, and he barely even bothered aiming, choosing to fire his rifle from a hip-held position. One of the scavengers sensed something, looking up and took off running just before Venner squeezed the trigger.

Venner cursed and switched his aim to the other one, dropping it with one shot. The other one fled up the tunnel, screaming in panic. Venner dropped to a kneeling position and fired, sending a second silencer shell through the back of its head.

He remained there for several minutes, waiting to see if the sounds had alerted any others. Either the noise hadn't carried, he surmised, or the sounds of panicked screams were the norm down here in this dismal place. Whatever the truth of the matter, no one seemed to be coming to investigate the disturbance.

Venner continued along the tunnel, still following the lock-on signal from the biochip emissions. He was close now, he saw. Just a few hundred metres short of at least two of the pieces of GI equipment, if the readings he was getting from his suit systems were at all accurate.

Not long now. Just a little further, just a little more time, and the end of his mission would be in sight.

Unheard by the guards, Helm's voice started to whisper to him again. "Someone coming, Rogue. The tunnel at seven o'clock, behind your left shoulder. Whoever it is, its not one of the traitor's people. I'm picking up traces of electronic emissions from a whole bunch of fancy stuff they've got with them. They're scanning this place we're in right now. Could be Guardian Angel, maybe."

Rogue listened, still feigning semi-consciousness for the benefit of the watching guards. If it was that female GI pilot, then she was outnumbered. She was a GI, and she was undoubtedly armed, but Rogue still figured she might need some help. A distraction, maybe, to allow her to make whatever move she had planned.

Deliberately, Rogue pretended to stir to life, opening his eyes and shouting over to his guards in rough Nort.

"Hey, you guys found the secret compartment in my backpack yet? The one with all my best tech in it?" They looked up at him, eyes glaring in suspicion and surprise. A moment later, several of those same pairs of eyes flickered towards the discarded shape of Bagman, and that was when Rogue knew he had them.

"Guess you haven't then, seeing as how we're all still here and in one piece." One of the scavengers reached out to pick up Bagman and then hastily snatched his hand back at what Rogue said next. "It's booby-trapped, with a couple of sticks of C-10, just to give it a little extra protection."

They glared at him, angry now. He kept on talking. "I'll tell you how to disarm it, though, if you let me go. You won't believe the stuff I've got hidden in there. The Norts that are coming here soon would probably be extremely grateful to whoever gave them all this extra GI tech that no one knows anything about. It's all yours, if you let me go. What do you say?"

The scavengers muttered quickly amongst themselves. Then, just as Rogue had hoped, one of them climbed to his feet and advanced on Rogue, the shock-baton held in his hand. The scavengers had thought of a much better way to get the information out of him about Bagman's non-existent secret compartment.

Which was all fine by Rogue, since it put at least one of his enemies exactly where he wanted him to be.

The scavenger activated the weapon, looking to start with a little light body work to help loosen Rogue's turn. He drew his arm back to swing the baton into Rogue's ribs, and that was when Rogue drew up all the material he had been storing in the back of his throat and spat it out full into the man's face.

A GI's body had several extra organs, in comparison to a normal human being. These were mostly to allow them to survive the lethal climate of Nu Earth, to breathe its air and to drink its water. Nu Earth's toxins, poisons and viruses were filtered away by these organs, rendered harmless by a GI's natural immunity system, broken down and then expelled in the normal human way. One of these organs was in Rogue's throat, and its job was to store various samples of of these pollutants, so that Rogue's GI biochemistry could analyse them and, if necessary, manufacture the relevant enzymes and anti-bodies to give him extra immunity to them.

This was the organ Rogue was emptying out now, spitting a stream of acidic tox-sludge straight into the guard's unprotected face. The man screamed, his hands going to his face as the stuff Rogue spat went to work on him, eating into his eyes and skin. At the same time, Rogue hauled hard on his manacles, pulling down with all his weight, grunting in pain as he deliberately dislocated the thumb of his right hand, allowing that hand to bloodily scrape free of the manacle holding it. Dangling by one hand, he reached out to grab the screaming, blinded guard, pulling him towards him, partly to use him as a human shield and partly to get at the pistol belt the man was wearing.

It wasn't easy drawing and firing a pistol with a dislocated thumb, but somehow Rogue managed it. He hit two of the guards, only one of them fatally. The others were on their feet now and firing back at him in panic. Las-rounds hit the body of the guard Rogue was using as a shield, abruptly cutting off his agonised screams.

Just as Rogue prayed, more gunfire sounded from the tunnel entrance behind him. Rifle fire, it sounded like. A series of calm, perfectly-spaced, perfectly-taken shots, each of them unerringly finding their target and sending a scavenger guard falling to the ground.

In a few brief seconds, the battle was over. Rogue dropped the body he had been holding and, still dangling by his one manacled hand, twisted his body round to face the figure standing there in the tunnel mouth. Whatever he was expecting, this wasn't it.

It was a man, wearing a state of the art black chem-suit free of any kind of identifying insignia. His face, covered by a blank helmet visor, added to his anonymity. He carried a slug-thrower rifle and Rogue could tell his profession and his expertise just by the look of his weapon and the way he held it. His rescuer was a sniper, and a skilled one, if Rogue was any good judge of a fellow expert killer.

There was a chill stillness about the man, an air of lethal intent that made Rogue tighten his grip on the pistol in his hand. One part of Rogue's mind made the necessary computations about his chances of raising and firing the pistol before the sniper could respond. Rogue knew how good his own speed and aim were, but the answer he got to the equation his mind had just run through wasn't much to his liking.

The two killers stared at each other, both holding guns in their hands. Rogue broke the silence.

"Guardian Angel send you? Where is she?"

"She sent me on ahead. She thought you might need some help. Looks like she was right," answered Venner, studying his target's face for any sign that the GI knew he was bluffing.

Whoever or whatever Guardian Angel was, Venner's quick thinking reply seemed to satisfy the GI.

"I need to get out of these chains. There's a las-cutter somewhere over there," said Rogue, indicating the sprawled corpses of the scavengers and the litter of Bagman's equipment lying around them.

"Got one here," said Venner, reaching for an item on his suit belt. A few moments work and Rogue was free of the manacles on his ankles and other hand.

Rogue massaged his hand, popping his dislocated thumb back into place with only the merest grunt of pain. Tough son of a bitch, thought Venner, with more than a hint of grudging admiration. It would almost be a pity to pull the trigger on him, once he'd done what he came here to do.

He watched as the GI retrieved his biochip helmet and backpack, reactivating their speech facility before gathering up and repacking his backpack's equipment. Venner kept a careful watch on the other tunnel mouths opening out into the chamber. The noise of the gun battle had not gone unnoticed by the others down here and it wouldn't be long before they had company.

"So how'd you find me so quick?" asked Rogue, gathering up the last of his equipment.

Venner showed him the tracker system attached to his rifle. "It's keyed to detect biochip energy signatures. The range is pretty limited, but as you can see, it gets the job done."

Rogue studied the device, his eyes narrowing as he recognised its design. "You're S-Three?"

"Guilty as charged," said Venner, putting as much friendly levity into his voice as he could muster. "Hey, we're not all soulless spooks and Milli-com ass kissers. There's still a few of us left who want to win this war and aren't afraid to put our heads on the block to try and make that happen."

"Good to know," said Rogue, retrieving the best of the lascarbines from the hands of one of the dead scavengers. "We're not ready to leave yet, Not while we're still a man short. Gunnar's still down here somewhere. The traitor, or one of his goons has got him."

"The Traitor General, he's here too?" said Venner, careful to inject a note of surprised disbelief into his voice.

"You bet he is, and we're not leaving until we find Gunnar and do what we came here to do."

"Copy that," replied Venner, smiling behind his mask. This was going to be easier than he thought. He could pull the trigger on the GI and accomplish the secondary part of his mission right now, but there were a lot of unknown variables down here and two guns were always better than one. Besides, he thought, other than himself, the Rogue Trooper was probably the most expert killer on Nu Earth and he welcomed the chance to study the Genetic Infantryman in action. It was always good to study another professional's moves, and Venner was interested to see if the GI really was as good as his reputation suggested.

"This way," he told Rogue, heading up the same tunnel that the traitor had taken. "I'm still picking up the biochip energy emissions from your missing comrade. As you say, we're not leaving just yet."

"Rogue…" warned Helm quietly, as they followed the sniper up the tunnel.

"Copy what you're thinking, Helm," whispered Rogue. "You too, Bagman. Keep a good eye on our helpful new buddy from S-Three, guys. No way I'm going to turn my back on this freak without knowing someone's watching my six."

The traitor heard the sounds of gunfire echoing along the tunnels. He instantly knew what it meant; somehow, the Rogue Trooper had escaped. The old, familiar fear of once again being hunted by the blue-skinned genetic freak took hold of him. His suit's med-systems recognised the surge of panic and administered a surge of narc-stims into his bloodstream. The traitor relaxed somewhat as the narc-shot did its task, allowing his mind to consider the options available to him.

Even though none of the entrance alarms had been tripped, it was always possible that some advancing unit of Nort pathfinder scouts had found their way into his lair. It was equally possible that some of his own followers had turned on each other in one of their petty squabbles. Such events had apparently been fairly common before he assumed leadership of the group, some of the scavengers routinely murdering each other in disputes over ownership of a ration pack or chem-suit repair kit, but they had dropped away to almost nil when the scavenger band fell under his command, when he made it quite clear to his followers what the penalty for such unauthorised killings would be. Still, the battle still raging up on the surface had created a mood of unease in the minds of his followers, and it was always possible that some of them had fallen back on their old ways.

He barked orders, sending a large group of those here with him in the main chamber to investigate the source of the disturbance. His mood altered by the flow of narc-stims, he sat back in his throne chair to await the outcome.

He didn't have to wait long. A minute or two later, there were more sounds of gunfire, coming from just a few hundred metres up the tunnel taken by his followers. He listened closely to the sounds identifying each one. Most of it was a chorus of hissing, stuttering las-fire as produced by the scavenged, poorly-maintained las-weapons carried by almost all his followers. There was no evidence of the distinctive chatter of the GI's rifle, but of course, there wouldn't be. That particular weapon was here with him, the traitor intending to use it as proof of his capture of the Genetic Infantryman when he went out tomorrow to conduct the difficult task of beginning his parlay with Nordstadt's new masters.

He heard the sound of screams, the death-cries of his followers as they fell before the firepower of whatever force they had encountered but he heard another sound there too. The dry crack of a slug-thrower rifle, a weapon virtually unknown on Nu Earth. It fired with the steady, calm, rhythmic pulse of the beat of a human heart, each shot almost invariably ending in the cut-off scream of one of his followers.

A new thrill of fear passed through the traitor as he heard the pulsing crack of that weapon's shots. He knew of only one man who used such a weapon, or who could fire it with such almost inhumanly-calm and deadly assurance. Of course, it was almost impossible that that man could be here in Nordstadt now, but if he was, then the traitor could think of only one reason why: to kill him.

He stood up, shouting orders to his frightened followers.

Rogue charged down the tunnel, sending tight bursts of las-fire into the milling, panicked mass of enemies before him. Single shots from his new partner's sniper rifle punched through the air from behind him, picking off more targets from amongst the scavenger mob. Leaderless, uncoordinated, more of them dying with every passing second, the survivors of the pack broke and ran, fleeing before the two killers' dual advance.

Rogue and Venner broke through into the large chamber beyond. There were more scavengers there and Venner automatically brought his rifle up to his shoulder and started picking them off. Rogue ran forward into them, emptying the rest of the las-carbine and gunned down four more. Then he reversed the weapon in one smooth motion, and used it as a club. He swung it around him, the butt impacting against flesh and bone, breaking skulls and knocking bodies to the ground. Rogue still felt a shred of pity for these things, trying to pull his blows against the smaller, weaker ones, seeking to drive them away rather than kill them. The sniper showed no such similar compunction. More shots rang out, more bodies fell to the ground. The remnants of the second wave of scavengers finally fled, shrieking towards the other tunnel mouths round the chamber.

Rogue let them go. Venner didn't, dropping three more of them as they ran. The sniper's bloodlust was up. Rogue knew the type; addicted to death, they killed just for the sheer pleasure of taking human life. Rogue took note of the fact, his trust in the S-Three man moving a few notches further down the scale. Whatever the sniper's stated reason for being here, Rogue doubted that comradely concern for a fellow soldier in trouble had much to do with it, and his sense of wary caution toward his new ally increased.

"Picking up a lock on Gunnar's position, Rogue. Twenty-one metres in front of you at two o'clock."

Rogue looked, following Bagman's directions. He found himself looking straight at the Traitor General. The next second he was searching among the dead bodies on the ground, looking for a new weapon with which to kill his enemy.

The traitor watched in consternation as his followers were gunned down before him. Once again, the genetic freak had been responsible for the destruction of another of his bolt-holes. The sight of the Genetic Infantryman was alarming enough, but the figure following on behind Rogue filled the traitor with a fresh rush of fear.

He recognised him straight away, even in his featureless black chem-suit. Venner, the S-Three assassin. Marckand's man, the pet killer of the traitor's old Nort collaborator comrade within the Souther military. Marckand must be cleaning house, the traitor realised, getting rid of the last pieces of living evidence of his own treasonous past.

The traitor screamed more orders, urging the rest of his bodyguards forward, shooting one of them in the back with the GI's own weapon to encourage the others. The GI raised and fired the weapon he had found. Incredibly, the shot missed.

Venner raised his rifle too, drawing a bead on his target. The traitor grabbed one of his bodyguards and began pulling him in front of himself. A shot sounded and something punched a fist-sized hole through the bodyguard's back before he reached the traitor. The traitor ducked behind his throne just as the sniper's weapon sounded again. A chunk of scrap metal was blown off from the throne's back.

The traitor crouched in cover. Gunfire and screams came from the other side of the throne. The traitor considered his options and his luck so far. The two best marksmen on Nu Earth had, between them, fired three shots at him and missed all three times. He doubted his good fortune would hold out a fourth time. He looked down at the GI weapon in his hands. He had reloaded it, but wisely disabled its biochip functions, switching it to manual use. He smiled. How ironic if the GI's own weapon should be the thing that killed him in the end.

Rogue cursed as he saw his shot go wide of its target. Either the weapon's sights were badly calibrated, or the arrangement of las-focussing lenses in the barrel were out of alignment. The sniper fired at the same target twice. He missed both times. Once again the traitor's luck was holding out.

Medium-ranged shots might be a problem, but there was nothing much wrong with the weapon's short-range accuracy. Rogue sprayed tight, controlled bursts of las-fire into

the traitor's bodyguards. None of these shots missed their
targets.

Venner's gun had fallen silent. Rogue risked a quick
glance behind him, nervous about what the sniper might be
up to. While Rogue held off the remaining bodyguard,
drawing all their fire on to himself, Venner was circling
round the sides of the chamber. Rogue realised what he was
up to. So did Helm and Bagman.

"Looks like sniperboy's going after the traitor, Rogue."

"So much for that story about him being here to help us.
Anyone else get the feeling he's been kinda holding out on
us about something?"

"Copy that, Bagman. The traitor's ours. If S-Three want a
piece of him too, then they'll have to wait in line."

Rogue broke off, hearing a distinctive coughing roar from
behind the traitor's hiding place, as his GI eyes caught the
brief flash of something upwards from there. Helm and
Bagman's vid and audio sensors caught it too, instantly
recognising what it was.

"Sammy! Hit the dirt, Rogue!"

Sammies. The nickname for the miniature surface-to-air
guided missiles that Gunnar's auxiliary grenade launcher
barrel was equipped to fire. Capable of tracking and down-
ing a low-flying hopper or atmocraft, they gave a Genetic
Infantryman in the field a devastating additional source of
firepower against enemy aircraft.

But there weren't any low-flying enemy aircraft in the
underground chamber. Instead, there was just the chamber's
vaulted roof, some six or seven metres above all their
heads.

Rogue dived for cover, making for the greater safety of the
sides of the chamber. The Sammy struck the centre of the
roof, detonating and destroying the central supports there.
They gave way almost instantly, the roof splitting open with
a thunderous roar. Tonnes of rubble and massive metal
beam roof supports crashed downwards, burying most of
the chamber and crushing everyone caught beneath. The
avalanche continued as soil and rock from the ground
above poured down. The air was filled with a choking black

dust and something else too. The poisonous tang of Nu Earth's atmosphere. The cave-in had caused a crater-like breach up on the surface and now the atmosphere of the city above was rushing in to fill the tunnels and chambers of the underground complex.

Rogue hauled himself out of the space he had found and crawled over the mounds of rubble that now filled the place. His lungs could deal with the choking blanket of dust that hung in the air, just as they could handle the poison Nu Earth air, and his eyes and the sensors of his biochip equipment could pierce the blinding dust veil just as well as if it were any other kind of chem-cloud.

He scrambled across the rubble, his senses checking for signs of life or movement. There were none. The cave-in had cleared the place as clinically as any precision artillery strike.

Following his memory of the geography of the chamber before the roof collapse, he found the place where the traitor had been hiding. It was still mostly intact. Rogue wasn't surprised. He knew just how calculating the man he had spent years hunting across the face of Nu Earth was. If the traitor was going to collapse a roof in on the heads of himself, his enemies and his own followers, then the only part of that equation that mattered was the coldly-calculated chances of his own survival.

There was no sign of the traitor or Gunnar either, of course. Rogue wasn't surprised. He had been hunting his prey long enough to know that the man always had an escape route planned from any situation.

"Helm?"

"Still got a lock on Gunnar's biochip signal, Rogue. The traitor's on the move, heading back towards the surface. He's about a minute and three hundred metres ahead of us."

Rogue wasn't too worried. On the surface of Nu Earth, moving at GI speed in the environment he was born to fight in, he could run down an ordinary human in a chem-suit. There was just one problem, and the biochips knew it.

"Lost that las-carbine in the cave-in, Rogue. You don't have any weapons."

"Sure I do, Bagman. I've got a vibro-knife and whatever you've got left in the way of micro-mines and grenades. Better than that, I've got you guys and good, old-fashioned GI smarts."

Guided by Helm, he set off in pursuit of his prey.

Venner emerged from the rubble a minute later. Hugging the walls of the chamber, he had avoided the worst effects of the cave-in. Masked by the unique material of his chemsuit, his life signs had gone undetected by the senses of the Genetic Infantryman and his equipment. His left leg had been struck by a chunk of falling rubble and dragged painfully behind him. He suspected it was probably broken, but a quick jab of narco-stim from his suit's chem-kit allowed him to ignore the pain and keep his thoughts clear for the challenge ahead.

He checked the tracker device, noting with satisfaction that all three biochip signals were still coming through loud and clear. The single-source target was the traitor, while the double-source signal pursuing it was that of the Rogue Trooper. They were both up on the surface, hunting each other through the ruins of Nordstadt.

Guided by the dual signals, he set off in pursuit of his prey.

Everything was going to hell in Nordstadt. Colonel Daniels, monitoring the situation from the safety of Milli-com, couldn't be happier. He preferred not to listen to the chatter of the incoming radio traffic from the Souther forces still trapped – Daniels refused to think in terms of words like "abandoned" – in Nordstadt. The panicked tone in those voices as they reported in the latest Nort advances, the curses they used as they begged or demanded that someone in Milli-com do something to help them, offended Daniels's sense of military propriety. His neat strategist's mind much preferred receiving the intelligence in a far more sanitised form, either as hard data dispassionately scrolling across his monitor screen or as visual information projected up onto the strategy bridge's main screen.

The screen was enormous, ten metres on each side, capable of zooming in on any Nordstadt locale and singling out sections of individual streets and buildings. Had they wanted, they could switch the screen to a tactical setting and watch individual firefights in progress, the visual data relayed back to them in almost real-time by the numerous surveillance sats in geo-synch orbit above the city.

The display was on its standard strategy setting at present, showing a map of the entire city, split up into its different sectors. A checkerboard array of black, red and blue icons swarmed across the map, each representing a different Nort division so far identified by the Milli-com intelligence staffers. Blue for infantry, red for armour, black for elite units such as those belonging to the Kashan Legion. Unidentified enemy units still to enter the battle were gathered in clusters of glowing white icons around the fringes of the map, almost all of them advancing slowly but steadily towards its centre.

The Souther icons were highlighted in a matching mixture of green, orange and yellow. Pitifully outnumbered, they were being herded back into the ever-shrinking number of Souther-held sectors in the centre of the city. The Nort icons pressed in upon them from all sides. As Daniels watched, he saw another green-coloured icon flicker away and die, its position on the map replaced by two of the four enemy unit icons surrounding it.

"Forty-Seventh Tarrik Infantry Division overrun," the weary-sounding voice of a junior officer dutifully reported. "No communication received from them in the last ten minutes, following last-reported contact with advancing enemy forces. Unit is assumed to have been reduced to non-combat effective status."

Wiped out, you mean, whispered a rebellious part of Daniels's mind. Abandoned and left to die, isn't that what we're really talking about here?

Daniels did his best to quell such troubling thoughts. They had planned Hammerfall down to the last detail. Everything they had done, no matter how cold-blooded it might seem to others, was for the greater good. The big picture, that was all that mattered, and now was no time to allow these kind of faint-hearted doubts to come creeping into your mind.

"What's our status now, Daniels?" barked a voice from behind him.

Daniels turned, snapping to attention even before he saw the figure standing expectantly there. Grand Marshal Cohen. What was he doing here, Daniels wondered? The pompous old fool wasn't supposed to be due on the bridge until the Hammerfall countdown reached Zero Hour Minus One.

"Everything proceeding as scheduled, sir," he reported keenly. "We're at Zero Hour Minus Three Point Two Six, and I'm delighted to say the Norts are cooperating splendidly. They're advancing slightly faster than we expected through most sectors and in numbers even higher than we had hoped. Our latest intelligence estimates there are now almost one point two million Nort troops approaching or already within Hammerfall's field of effect."

Cohen clapped his hands in approval. If Hammerfall worked as well as it was intended to, he could expect another gold marshal's star on his collar to match the three already there, elevating him to a new rank position somewhere just barely below a seat at the right hand of God.

"Excellent news, Daniels. What about the evacuation of all essential personnel?"

"Completed, sir. The speed of the Nort advance caught us out in one or two places. The Charlie secure zone landing site fell an hour ago, and we haven't heard anything from Able in the last forty minutes, so we're assuming it's been compromised too, but initial reports suggest we've got at least eighty per cent of all listed essential personnel out of the city in time. I'm reliably informed that Field Marshal Vittus and his staff are already safely aboard one of the orbital stations."

Cohen clapped his hands in approval again. "More splendid news, Daniels. He's a good man, Vittus. He and I were at military academy together. I'm sure he'll understand the regrettable necessity of all this, once I sit down with him and explain it all."

"I'm sure he will, sir."

The grand marshal glanced round and a chair was brought forward for him. He settled himself into it, studying with relish the images projected onto the main screen.

"A great moment, isn't it, Daniels? Something to tell your grandchildren about, that you were there when we won the Battle of Nordstadt and turned the tide of the war on Nu Earth. And I won't be forgetting you and the others, Daniels. You'll get your share of the glory too, I promise you that."

"Thank you, sir. I just want to do my duty to you and to the Confederacy."

"Quite so, Daniels. Quite so."

Cohen eased himself back in his chair, beaming in self-satisfaction. The mission clock stood at Zero Hour Minus Three Point Two Three. The last act of the Battle of Nordstadt was about to begin.

TWENTY-THREE

Dropping down into Nordstadt was like dropping down into hell itself, thought Rafe. "The crucible" they called it, and that's what it looked like right now. An infernal cauldron where men and machines were melted down to nothing. Looking down on it from the night sky, it looked like the mouth of an erupting volcano. A ring of flame, alive with light and activity.

The salvage dealers' vessel's stealth capabilities had got them through the outer defences – there was a fleet of Nort Gorgon pilots out there somewhere who were probably still sweating at the thought of almost mistakenly shooting down what they had only at the last moment realised from its transponder signals was a shuttle carrying the Deputy Direktor of the Greater Nordland Political Kommissariat – but as they came closer to the ground, they would come within visual range of the forces there, and all the fancy alien stealth technology in the galaxy wouldn't convince a Nort anti-aircraft battery commander that he wasn't looking at anything other than an unrecognised and probably therefore hostile civilian shuttlecraft.

"Follow in the coordinates Gabe's fed through to your helm controls," Rafe told the body looters. "We'll land, pick up our people and be off the ground again before the Norts even know we're there."

Brass pursed his lips. Bland tutted in disapproval.

"I'm afraid that won't be possible, my dear. My partner and I have been considering the matter, and while we're delighted to help, we're also businessmen with a responsibility to maintaining our profit margins. The risk Mister

Bland and I are incurring here is quite considerable, not just to our lives, but to our craft and the great deal of valuable merchandise it's carrying. It only seems fair that we should be compensated in some way."

"Quite so," broke in Brass. "This drone of yours, for instance, would fetch a good price on the open market. Perhaps you'd be willing to enter into negotiations on this matter? We'll give you a fair price, minus of course, the cost of helping you with this little endeavour."

"Sure, why not?" said Rafe in a reasonable-sounding voice, just before she aimed her las-pistol downwards and shot Brass once through the foot. "Here's my opening offer."

She had put the pistol's firing capacity on a low power setting. The shot barely scratched the salvage dealer, burning away the material of his boot and maybe vaporising one of his smaller toes. On full setting, it would have blown his foot off and burnt a melt-hole into the metal floor beneath. If Brass realised how fortunate he was, he didn't show it. He howled in pain, falling out of his seat and clutching at his smouldering foot.

"Maurie!" cried Bland in alarm, vacating his own seat to tend to his injured partner. His attempts to treat the wound only brought more outraged howls of pain from Brass.

"Watch 'em, Gabe," instructed Rafe, taking control of the craft. "I'll bring it down myself."

"Something bothering you, toots?" asked Gabe casually, keeping the two salvage merchants covered with his drone-shell's inbuilt blaster weapon.

"You mean other than the fact we're flying into one big clusterfrag that's going to be nuked off the face of the earth in an hour or two, and that they're probably going to recycle my ass all the way back to the gene-vats for the number of regs I've already broken today? Yeah, Gabe, something else is definitely bothering me."

"You're thinking about all the other Souther troops still trapped down here, right, hon?"

"Read my mind, Gabe. We're going down there to pick up Rogue, but who's gonna pull those other boys' asses out of the fire?"

"You know, Rafe," observed Gabe innocently, "with those command codes I lifted and with the fancy comms-rig they've got on this crate, it wouldn't be very difficult to patch into the whole Souther radio network and beam out any kind of urgent message anyone wanted. Of course, my programming won't allow me to do that. Not unless someone orders me to."

"Gabe?"

"Hon?"

"Get to it. Send out a signal and tell anyone who's listening what's about to happen to Nordstadt. That's an order, by the way."

"If you say so, toots."

What happened next was the event Souther military historians would come to call the Miracle of Nordstadt.

A mysterious, apparently anonymous signal was beamed out across just about every known Souther comms-channel on Nu Earth, claiming that Nordstadt and the tens of thousands of Souther troops still trapped there were about to be destroyed by nuclear bombardment on the express orders of Milli-com.

In the Souther military command stations orbiting Nu Earth, comms staff worked feverishly to isolate the rogue signal and cut it off from the rest of the network, but as soon as they closed down one part of the net, the signal jumped frequencies to infect another part of it. Short of doing the unthinkable and imposing a blanket shut down of the entire Souther communications system on Nu Earth and handing an enormous strategic advantage to the Norts, the techs were powerless to stop it. There was also the possibility that some of them, secretly appalled by the enormity of what the rogue signal was telling them, didn't try too hard to stop its spread.

Bounced from satellite to satellite, boosted through hundreds of different relays and automated comms stations, Gabe's signal spread like wildfire across the Souther forces, appearing as flash traffic text on thousands of compu-screens, emerging from thousands of radio speakers as a spoken message, looped to endlessly repeat itself.

"This is a Souther friendly calling on open frequency to any Souther forces listening. In less than three hours, tens of thousands of Souther troops trapped in Nordstadt will be killed on the deliberate orders of Milli-com. If you don't believe this message, if you think it's a Nort trick, then listen carefully to what I'm going to tell you about Operation Hammerfall, and decide for yourself what you want to do about it…"

All over Nu Earth. Thousands of compu-screens. Thousands more radio speakers. Hammerfall's secret agenda was well and truly out in the open.

The Miracle of Nordstadt was about to begin.

Halmada was awakened by an urgent hammering on his bunkroom door. He didn't know how many hours he had been asleep, but however long it was, it still wasn't nearly enough. Exhaustion still filled him from the last few weeks of the almost non-stop shuttle runs down into Nordstadt, as well as from today's last hectic and drama-filled evac op. That exhaustion was also mixed with relief.

The reason for that relief was still clutched in his hand. A print-out of a private comms-signal from home. A letter from his wife, telling him that she had received word from the Souther forces in the Karthage system. Their youngest son Philippe had been reported missing in action, presumed dead, but now word had come through that he was aboard a hospital ship, wounded but still alive, and already on his way home. Halmada had fallen asleep with tears in his eyes, proud that his son had done his duty, but mostly just happy that his son's war was over and that he was coming home alive.

Halmada awoke to hammering on the door, and a voice calling his name. He wearily hauled himself out of his bunk and went to the door. It was his copilot, Matthews. Halmada blearily registered the fact that his friend was suited up in his flight gear and that the corridor outside was full of activity, shuttle crews rushing about and getting into flight suits of their own.

"What's up, Tom?" asked Halmada, still half-asleep. "I thought we'd all been grounded until this Hammerfall op was over?"

"Haven't you heard, chief? It's all over the comm-nets. There's something real big happening in Nordstadt!"

Matthews thrust a ripped-off piece of compu print-out into his hands. Halmada looked at it. What he saw there woke him up real fast.

Two minutes later, he had his own flight suit on and was running with the others towards the shuttle decks. They could hear the sound of shuttle engines already firing up ahead of them.

A squad of Milli-fuzz blocked their way. The most senior of them brandished an activated shock-baton and called out to them in warning.

"Go back to your quarters. The shuttle deck is off-limits to all personnel at present. Any attempt to disobey this order will be grounds for a court martial."

Halmada thought of his son Philippe on his way back home and then thought of all those other young Souther soldiers in Nordstadt who weren't going to get that same chance.

His punch caught the Milli-fuzz man square on the chin, laying him out cold on the deck. The other Milli-fuzz drew their sidearms and aimed them at the shuttle pilots. Halmada faced down the next most senior of them, a young, scared-looking corporal, probably no older than Halmada's son Philippe.

"Way I see it, son, you've got two choices. You can obey your orders and pull that trigger, or you can do the right thing and stand aside and let us do our job."

He stepped forward, locking eyes with the young Milli-fuzz man. "C'mon, son, what's it gonna be? Every second we stand here talking means another poor son of a bitch down there in Nordstadt isn't going to be making it back home."

A minute later, he was in the cockpit of his shuttle and prepping it for final takeoff. The Miracle of Nordstadt was underway.

. . .

All over Nu Earth, from ground bases and orbital stations, people responded to Gabe's signal. Hundreds of shuttle crews flew out on anything that the ground crews had managed to make ready for them in time. Cargo lighters, troop carriers, reconnaissance flyers, officers' yachts, civilian sloops, outdated and mothballed vessels, even a few luxury command craft reserved only for the use of senior command staff of the rank of general or above. If it could fly, and someone could get behind its controls and take off in it, then it was soon in the air and on its way to Nordstadt.

They descended on the city from all directions, pushing power systems to the max to get there in time, coordinating among themselves and forming up into loose convoy waves for some measure of mutual protection. Facing them were the unknown terrors of the crucible.

The Southers had completely lost air control over the city. Their ground-based anti-air defences had been utterly destroyed. No Souther gunship or fighter craft flew patrolling missions there. The Nort air forces had free rein, ruling the skies above Nordstadt, striking at will against any Souther targets still moving on the ground. Nort high-altitude fighters prowled the night airspace, lying in wait for the shuttle waves which they now knew to be heading their way. Souther radar operators picked up their presence on their screens. Souther radio operators relayed their comrades' warnings to the shuttle crews. The pilots now knew what was waiting for them, but still kept on going. The Miracle of Nordstadt had lasted this long, so maybe it would last longer still.

It did. Like their pilot brothers in the shuttlecraft squadrons, the pilots of the Souther fighter squadrons had heard Gabe's message. Like the shuttle pilots, they weren't slow to respond. There were shouts of excitement in radar stations and comms-rooms all over Nu Earth as the operators there picked up the radio signals and radar signatures of wave after wave of Souther fighters now following the shuttles in to Nordstadt.

The fighter pilots opened up with their afterburners, sending hailing signals to the shuttle crews as they sped past them, diving down towards the enemy craft now appearing all over their target screens. Battle was joined, and the first blazing wrecks of Nort Grendel and Gorgon fighters fell tumbling from the skies.

With the first wave of fighters engaging the Norts and the next wave flying on their wings as escorts, the way ahead down to Nordstadt was open for the shuttles.

Gabe's signal was still being heard all over Nu Earth. It wasn't just the pilots who were listening.

"I'm sorry, general, but I can't concur with your decision. We have no way of knowing if this signal is really authentic."

General Ghazeleh resisted the urge to reach for his sidearm and pistol-whip his executive officer to the ground. "Gut instinct tells me it's authentic, Colonel Garr. That and twenty years of soldiering on this bastard planet, and having to listen to one bastard lie after another from those lying bastards at Milli-com. No, my orders stand. We're still the nearest friendly forces to Nordstadt. We stop here, roll out the welcome mat and let everyone who's listening know there's a safe landing zone waiting here for them. If the reports coming in about this shuttle evac are true, then there's going to be a lot of pilots looking for a safe place to put their crates down on the ground when they get out of that bastard city."

Gabe's signal was still being heard all over Nu Earth. It wasn't just the Southers who were listening.

"Damn it, Daniels! What's happening down there?"

"I-I'm not sure, sir," stammered Daniels. "The Norts seem to be pulling some of their reserve forces back out of the city's suburb zones. I suppose they could be reacting to that rogue signal that we're hearing reports of from our Nu Earth listening posts."

Cohen's reaction was instantaneous and predictable. "You suppose, Daniels? You're supposed to be chief planning officer on this operation. There's obviously been a security leak of some sort on Hammerfall, and now there's going to be a thorough investigation when this is all over, I promise you that."

Daniels looked helplessly at the display screen. Every few minutes that passed saw another Nort infantry or armoured division icon disappear off the edges of the screen, signifying another ten thousand or more enemy troops retreating back out of Hammerfall's area of effect. As Daniels watched, Hammerall's projected enemy casualty count, the vital figure that its success or failure depended on, continued to fall with every passing moment.

Cohen's next statement was also equally predictable. "I won't sit here and see Hammerfall fail. You hear me, Daniels? We launch the damn missiles now and salvage what we can from this balls-up."

Daniels hesitated before answering, possibly seeing the rest of his career flashing before his eyes. "I-I'm afraid that won't be possible, grand marshal. The Hammerfall platform position is fixed in space. They can't launch until Zero Hour when the planet's rotation brings the target zone back around into range of the missiles."

Cohen stood stock still for a moment, digesting this information. Then he stood up, turned on his heels and stalked off back towards the elevator bank. With every step he took, Daniels could actually feel another part of his own career shrivelling up and dying.

"I'll be in my quarters, Daniels. Keep me appraised of the situation. Let me know when Hammerfall's been completed."

TWENTY-FOUR

Hanna and Artau picked a path through the ruins. Her chem-suit wasn't equipped with anything in the way of IR night vision capability, and she didn't dare use a flashlight in case its beam gave away their position to any hidden watchers. The only thing they could depend on to find their way and avoid any hidden shell craters, tox-pits or booby traps were the intermittent flashes of the battle raging a couple of kilometres in front of them. Hanna had a vague plan to keep heading towards the fighting. What they were going to do when they got there, since Hanna was fairly sure that they were now technically behind the Nort front line, and how they were going to make contact with whatever was left of the other Souther forces still fighting in Nordstadt, was something she had not yet figured out.

The main battle seemed to have swept through or completely bypassed the area they found themselves in. They saw a few freshly artillery-pulverised buildings and came across the still-burning wreckage of a crashed flyer, but there was little other immediate evidence here of the battle still raging elsewhere in the city. Twice now they'd had to crouch down in cover as they heard gunfire from close by, waiting for several minutes to see if it came any closer. Both times, it had faded away into the distance again. Hanna imagined squads of Norts prowling through the ruins, making sport of hunting down small, scattered groups of survivors just like her and Artau. She had heard what often happened to female Souther soldiers in the Nort prisoner of war camps, and had secretly decided that if the worst came to the worst, there was no way she was going to allow herself to be taken alive.

Gunfire sounded again, this time coming from a lot closer. Too close for comfort, in fact. Hanna grabbed the surgeon and pulled him down into an ancient shell hole, signalling for him to be quiet. A few seconds later, the same gunfire sounded again, coming from what seemed to be the same direction and range, about three hundred metres somewhere to their right, she estimated.

A third burst from the same gun. Artau looked at her, puzzled. He might have hated guns of any kind, and his field hospital might have been situated kilometres behind the front line, but he still knew something about the individual sounds of a gun firing.

"That's not a regular Souther las-carbine," he whispered to her. "Must be Norts."

Hanna shook her head. She'd heard the distinctive sound of that gun firing before, and very recently. "No," she answered. "Not Norts. That's a GI rifle."

Silently, she led Artau into the darkness, heading for the sound of the gunfire.

Venner heard the sound too, as he stalked the battlefield in pursuit of his dual targets. It sounded wild and panicked, so he assumed the traitor still had the GI's rifle and was using it against its original owner. The sniper checked his sensor readings, seeing that the traitor, marked by the single biochip signal, was stationary at a point three hundred and eighty metres away, hiding amongst the broken pillars and rockrete slabs of a collapsed elevated roadway. The twin biochip signals that indicated the Genetic Infantryman's location were moving towards the traitor's position, the GI using the rubble for cover and the traitor watching and waiting for his approach, firing off bursts of shots every time he thought he caught sight of his opponent through his weapon's night vision sight.

Venner smiled, delighted to see that both his targets were deliberately bringing themselves into the same killzone. He scanned the surrounding terrain, looking for a suitable concealed vantage point from which to make his shot. Idly, he wondered what the chances would be of the two targets getting close enough to each other to allow him to take them both out simultaneously. Now that would really be something, he decided. The mark of a true master sniper, and one with more than a touch of irony about it. The Rogue Trooper and the Traitor General, killed together, by the same single shot.

Rogue moved forward, making optimum use of the surrounding darkness and hard cover, homing in on the traitor's position. Even if Helm and Bagman weren't able to lock onto Gunnar's biochip signal, he would still know where the traitor was hiding, from the direction and muzzle flash of the bursts of shots being fired at him.

He ducked as another hail of las-fire spat into the rubble around him. He was close enough now to throw a plasma sphere straight into the traitor's position, or for Bagman to obliterate the place with a scattering round of micro-mines, but Gunnar was there too, and Rogue couldn't risk doing anything that might damage or destroy the fourth member of his squad. No, his best chance, he decided, was to go low and circle round behind the traitor, getting in close enough to take him by surprise from a direction different from the one he would be looking in.

"Can you hear me, Rogue Trooper?"

It was the traitor's voice, coming from one of Helm's open comms-channels. He must have patched into it through Gunnar's comms-signal. "Yes, I think you can. I know you are out there somewhere, crawling through the darkness towards me. Is your new ally out there too, I wonder? Did he say he would watch your back while you came after me? I expect he probably did. Let me tell you something about this ally, Genetic Infantryman. His name is Venner, and he is a very special kind of assassin, working for an S-Three officer called Marckand. He is here to kill me, Rogue Trooper, and I wouldn't be surprised if he has orders to kill you too..."

The traitor's voice whispered on, but Rogue had already tuned out, knowing that the traitor was probably just trying to distract him and throw off his concentration. "Helm, you recording all this?"

"Every word, Rogue, for what it's worth."

"Good, then you can give me the edited highlights after I cut his head off and put it on the end of a stick to take back to Milli-com with us."

Rogue kept crawling forward, his attention fixed on the traitor's position. Helm counted down the range that Gunnar's biochip signal was now coming in from. "Twelve metres, Rogue... nine metres... seven... Hell, we're almost on top of him. Can't you see him yet?"

Rogue paused, scanning the shadows with his enhanced vision. There, in amongst the jagged sections of rockrete, he saw him. A chem-suit silhouette crouching low in cover, facing the direction he thought Rogue would be coming from and holding the familiar shape of Gunnar in his hands. Rogue tensed his leg muscles and sprang, clearing the intervening rubble barrier and covering half the distance between them in one move.

He hadn't even landed before he realised the potentially fatal mistake he'd just allowed himself to make.

Venner saw the sudden flash of movement in the killzone and raised his rifle to fire. The biochip signals were so close together now that he couldn't tell which target was which. The challenge of trying to hit both targets with one shot was still a tempting one, but he decided on caution over showmanship. Two shots, two kills, and he would be free to make his way to the extraction zone, where the shuttle Marckand had sent would be waiting for him. In fact, he could already hear the sound of shuttle engines somewhere in the sky above him. He hoped it was his craft. The sooner he got out of Nordstadt, the better.

"Getting a final fix on the Rogue Trooper's position, Rafe. He's in those ruins right below."

"Copy, Gabe. Taking us down now."

Rafe checked the ground radar readings, looking for a safe landing area amongst the ruins. Other than the lock-on signal beamed back by the biochip called Helm, they had been running on radio silence throughout their final approach to avoid being detected by Nort air defence systems. She just hoped they were still going to make it onto the ground in time to help Rogue.

It wasn't the traitor. It was the body of a dead Nort soldier, propped up in the rubble, the decoy made all the more complete by the fact that Gunnar had been carefully placed in the corpse's hands. The traitor must have known about the biochip's locator signal, using it to lure Rogue forward. Which meant he must still be somewhere close, waiting to spring the trap.

Rogue saw and realised all this before his feet even hit the ground. After that, he was too busy concentrating on making it alive through the next few seconds to worry about anything else.

The first shot, aimed too hurriedly as he jumped through the air, missed him as he hit the ground and rolled for cover. The next shot, just a second later, was closer, hitting the ground near his head. Rogue felt the burning heat of it even through the protection of his GI skin. Rogue continued the roll, knowing the traitor's third shot would almost certainly be on target. His enemy's first two shots had given Rogue a fix on his location, however. GI reflexes and instincts did the rest.

He came out of the roll, hurling his vibro-knife in the traitor's direction. Thrown blind, it still managed to hit its target, sinking hilt-deep into the shoulder of the traitor's gun hand. The traitor managed to get a shot off just before the gun fell from his nerveless fingers.

The shot hit Rogue in the side, breaking three of his ribs and burning and blowing away a portion of flesh. He staggered back under the impact, leaving himself open to the traitor's follow-up attack. The traitor didn't try to recover his lost pistol. Instead, snarling in rage, he simply launched himself at his enemy.

The traitor's strength was phenomenal. Both men were wounded, but even with the shock and pain of the las-shot wound in his side, Rogue should still have been able to overcome any ordinary human in hand-to-hand combat. That wasn't the case here, however. One look at his opponent's glazed and bloodshot eyes told Rogue where the traitor's inhuman strength was coming from. He was hyped out on narco-stims. Rogue would probably have to break half the bones in the traitor's body before the man would start to feel anything.

If that was what it was going to take, then that was what Rogue was going to do. The traitor's hands clawed at his face, going for Rogue's eyes. Rogue grabbed one of those hands and violently wrenched it round, breaking the wrist. Then he head-butted his opponent, trying to smash the glassteel face-plate of his chem-suit with the rim of his GI helmet. The traitor's visor cracked, though it didn't break, but the blow was still enough to send him staggering back. Rogue reached out, trying to grab and tear out the air pipes on the traitor's chem-suit, but his enemy saw the move coming and managed to block it in time. Rogue's successful ruse allowed him to lash out with the heel of his boot, fracturing the traitor's left kneecap.

The traitor felt that one even through the narco-stim haze. He threw himself forward at Rogue again, his face beneath the cracked chem-visor a mask of rage and hate. With one leg crippled, the traitor's attack was stumbling and clumsy. Rogue caught him and threw him into the nearby rubble, hoping the impact would cause some damage to his opponent's chem-suit.

No such luck. The traitor rose to his feet again, wielding a jagged shard of rockcrete like a dagger. Rogue wearily prepared to meet the attack, the pain and damage from the gunshot wound in his side really starting to kick in now.

Venner looked through his target scope, seeing both targets in sight together at last. They were both injured; both easy kills. He picked his first target, training his sights on the Rogue Trooper, and pulled the trigger.

Bagman's sensors detected the targeter beam of the rifle as it invisibly touched the back of Rogue's head. "Rogue! Get down!" he shouted in warning, just as the sound of the sniper shot echoed off the rockrete surfaces around them.

Venner cursed, seeing his target move just as he pulled the trigger. He thought he had at least still managed to wing the Genetic Infantryman, if not succeed in killing him outright. That left one target down and the other one still up. Venner shifted aim, switching targets to the figure of the traitor, who was already starting to turn to run as soon as he heard the sniper shot. Venner smiled. He would kill the traitor and then return his aim to pick off the wounded Rogue Trooper.

"Rogue! Get down!"

Hanna heard the shout from the ruins over to her left, just a moment before she heard the sound of the sniper shot coming from nearby. She recognised the voice as belonging to one of the Rogue Trooper's pieces of talking equipment and knew instantly what that voice and the answering rifle shot meant; the Rogue Trooper was trapped in those ruins, pinned down by a sniper hiding somewhere near her own position.

Hanna dropped to her knees bringing her rifle up to bear, using what light she had to scan for the hidden marksman. She saw nothing but a jumble of shadows and rubble as vital moments ticked away while the sniper lined up his next shot. There was a flash on the horizon behind her from the battle going on there and, fleetingly, the scene in front of her was starkly if briefly illuminated. She saw something, or thought she saw something, lying amongst the shadows she had scanned over just a few moments ago. She tracked back on it, going more on memory of what she had thought she had seen rather than what she might have actually glimpsed. It could have been the shape of a man crouched in the ruins, or it could have been a briefly-glimpsed piece of rock or just a misleading pattern of shadows.

She didn't have time to dwell on the possibilities and fired the las-carbine, sending a stream of shots out into the darkness.

●　●　●

Venner drew his crosshairs dead centre on the back of the fleeing figure of the traitor. Two shots, he decided, right through the target's back, severing his spine, destroying his lungs and heart, blowing apart his ribcage as they punched out through the front of him. The traitor would be dead before his body hit the ground. His finger started to squeeze the trigger, just as he saw a flare of light somewhere nearby and to his right.

The trigger was never pulled. Hanna's burst of las-fire caught him full in the arms and head, blowing apart his rifle, sending his headless corpse sliding down the rubble pile he had been sheltering behind.

Rogue crouched, bleeding heavily from the deep score the bullet had gouged through his shoulder as he twisted around to avoid the sniper's shot. He lay there, bleeding, breathing heavily, waiting for the sniper's next shot. It never came. Instead, a few moments later, he heard a hissing burst of las-fire from somewhere off to his right where he estimated the sniper's position to be.

More moments passed. The traitor was gone, disappearing at the first sniper shot. Every passing moment took him further away, Rogue knew, further into the darkness and the cover of the ruins. Further away from any chance of immediate retribution.

Helm's inbuilt comm-link crackled into life. "Heads up, GI unit. You got friendlies in the area. Just bagged ourselves some kind of fancy Nort sniper looking to make a name for himself by killing the R–"

"No names over this frequency, Souther girl," said Rogue. "Come on in. I'll cover you."

Rogue dragged himself over to where Gunnar lay, picking him up, checking he was undamaged and then reactivating his biochip functions. Gunnar's circuits and speech synthesiser hummed back into life.

"Rogue! The traitor, he–"

"Forget about it, Gunnar. He got away from us."

Rogue stared out into the darkness, his night vision seeing no sign of the man they had come here to find and kill.

"No luck this time. But there'll be other times, and one of those times he won't be so lucky."

A minute later, the shuttle came down to pick them up.

TWENTY-FIVE

"Landing's got us noticed by the locals, Rafe. We've got two Nort hopper gunships heading this way."

"Copy, Gabe. We're out of here as soon as our people are aboard."

The shuttle stood on a patch of open ground, its engines and landing thrusters still rumbling, ready to take off again at a second's notice. Rafe leapt down from the open side hatch, running forward to help the three figures stumbling through the ruins towards the shuttle.

"Good to meet you at last, Blueboy," she told Rogue, grabbing one of his arms and helping the female infantry sergeant who was supporting the weight of the wounded GI.

"Likewise, Air Force. Good to know that solid blue still counts for something, even here."

They ran back towards the shuttle. Rafe turned, hearing the telltale whine of the engines of the approaching Nort hoppers. She saw their searchbeams sweeping across the rubble field and knew she wasn't going to make it back to the shuttle in time, not with a wounded GI and two slower-moving humans in chem-suits in tow.

Rogue heard them too. "Bagman, dispense a Sammy. I'll cover the rest of you while you get to the shuttle."

"The shape you're in? Not a chance," answered Rafe, noticing for the first time the med-flashes on the other figure's chem-suit. "The doc and me will carry you. The sarge here can do the honours."

Rafe handed Gunnar to Hanna. "Think you can handle this thing?"

Hanna took the weapon, testing its weight, studying its workings. "Guess I can figure it out."

"No worries, sarge. I'll give you all the help you need," Gunnar told her.

Hanna loaded the Sammy following Gunnar's instructions. She'd never fired a weapon like this before, but then again, she'd never handled a weapon that talked to her either.

The hoppers were in sight, coming in low-level across the rubblescape at them, spitting out lines of las-fire. She raised the rifle and took aim, ignoring the dual tracks of lascannon fire chewing up the ground in front of her as they raced in on her position. They would reach her in a few more seconds, blowing her to shreds, before moving on to target and destroy the shuttle.

"Range three hundred metres and closing," Gunnar told her. "Okay, I'm zeroed in... You're doing fine, sarge. Just keep me locked in and pull the trigger when I say."

The las-fire tracks raced closer. Hanna fought down the urge to throw the gun away and hurl herself out of their path. At last, after moments that seemed to last minutes, the biochip gave her the order she was waiting for.

"Fire!"

The Sammy struck the cockpit of one of the hoppers, blowing it out of the sky. The other hopper peeled away in panic, breaking off its attack run. Hanna heard the rising scream of the shuttle engine from behind her. She turned and ran, leaping aboard the shuttle just as it lifted off the ground.

There were more surprises for her once she was aboard. Artau was bent over the prone figure of the Rogue Trooper, applying med-patches to his wounds as the craft lurched upwards in emergency take-off. The female GI was in the cockpit, piloting the shuttle. Some kind of autobot drone hovered nearby, talking to her. Hanna thought her helmet's audio-syms must have taken a knock when she jumped aboard because she could have sworn she heard the drone using the word "sweetcheeks" to the GI pilot.

Two other slightly comical-looking figures were there too. A tall, thin, fussy looking man, and his shorter, fatter companion. They oddly both wore bowler hats on top of their matching, expensive and civilian-issue chem-suits. They both seemed to be staring in a strangely avaricious way at the Rogue Trooper and his equipment.

"Friends of yours?" she asked, giving the GI his rifle back.

"Not exactly," growled Rogue, staring back at the two salvage dealers with undisguised hostility. "Let's just say we've crossed paths before and leave it at that."

"Hang on back there," warned Rafe from up in the cockpit. "We're not out of the hotzone yet." She looked at Brass and Bland.

"This crate of yours got any offensive capability?"

"Certainly not," answered Bland, sniffly. "We're unarmed non-combatants; strictly neutral bystanders in this war."

"Great. Then you'd better get on the radio and tell that to the Nort gunship still on our tail."

Rafe desperately jinked the controls, dodging the shuttle through the hail of las-fire from the pursuing Nort gunship hopper. Her only hope was to keep on climbing, outrunning the vengeful Nort craft to reach a higher altitude where its limited anti-grav systems couldn't operate.

A craft-shaking impact from the rear section of the shuttle's underbelly put paid to that idea. Rafe saw the power levels on her console read-outs drop away instantaneously.

"Main power system hit," reported Gabe, plugged into the craft's compu-controls. "Switching to auxiliary back-up. We just developed a serious juice problem, hon."

The shuttle dropped back down towards the city. Rafe fought to keep the shock descent from becoming a full-on crash into the Nordstadt rubble.

"Mayday, mayday. This is Bluegirl looking for some friendly listeners. Bluegirl evac shuttle's got a hostile on her tail and she's in need of some friendly assistance."

"Friendly ears listening, Bluegirl. This is Happy Trails. I'm two thousand metres above you and incoming on your six. Friendly assistance is on its way."

Something streaked down out of the chem-clouds above. There was a blur of fire and the Nort hopper disappeared off Rafe's radar screen. The equally blurred shape of a Seraphim fighter shot across the view from the shuttle's cockpit, rolling once to wave its wings in acknowledgement before arcing back upwards into the chem-clouds.

"Thanks for that, Happy Trails. Bluegirl's got a berth over at the 77nd Air Attack. If she's still got a job there tomorrow, then you've got an open tab waiting for you there in the pilots' mess."

Rafe brought the shuttle up level and, at a reduced altitude, piloted it southwards on a heading out of Nordstadt at as much speed as she could nurse out of its damaged power systems.

"Still got a juice problem, Gabe. I can probably get a couple of hundred kays out of this crate before I have to put it down on the ground. What safe landing zones can you find within that range?"

Gabe patched through using the sophisticated comms systems carried by the salvage dealers' craft, into the Souther satellites above the planet, searching through the latest comms traffic and observation data. It didn't take him long to find what Rafe was looking for.

"Got something here, Rafe. Three Souther armoured divisions due south of us, just within juice distance. They're rolling out the welcome mat to us and anyone else evacing out of Nordstadt."

"Sounds good enough, Gabe. We got ourselves a landing zone."

The last Souther evac shuttle took off from Nordstadt some two hours after Rogue and the others had left the city. Nordstadt was wiped off the face of Nu Earth about twenty minutes after that, just before dawn.

Hammerfall activated exactly on time, twelve minutes before then, all twenty of the Hammerfall platform's missiles launching towards their target, which was now swinging round into range on Nu Earth's sunward side. The missiles, with drives more akin to those found on deep-space craft than any normal rocketry engine, sped towards Nu Earth, crossing the tens of thousands of intervening kilometres in minutes. Alerted by Gabe's earlier all-frequencies warning, a host of Nort killer-sats and the gun batteries of heavy weapons orbital platforms were waiting for them.

Hammerfall's planners had allowed for the possibility that the Norts' space defences might destroy some of the missiles before they reached Nu Earth. The hundreds of simulations the Milli-com strategists had run suggested that four was the most likely number of losses they would probably suffer. Pre-warned about Nordstadt's fate, the Norts managed to destroy eleven of the missiles before they entered Nu Earth's atmosphere. In the event, nine warheads would still be enough to totally destroy Nordstadt, even if the field of effect extending to cover the Nort forces surrounding the outer fringes of the city was just about half of what was expected. Daniels's precious Nort casualty statistics, upon which the whole success of Hammerfall depended, fell, and then fell again.

The missiles detonated in a mixture of medium-altitude airbursts and direct ground impacts in various different locations around the city. Nordstadt disappeared in nine simultaneous flashes of blinding light that banished the fading pre-dawn gloom from the battlefields of Nu Earth for hundreds of kilometres in all directions.

Hundreds of thousands of lives, Nort and Souther alike, disappeared in an instant. Tens of thousands more Nort troops, on the outer fringes of the city and retreating in panic away from Nordstadt, were consumed by the firestorm that swept out from the heart of the nine combined nuclear blasts. The blasts and the firestorms reached up into the skies, knocking down dozens of atmocraft, shuttles and fighters that had lingered over the city for too long.

The shockwave of Nordstadt's destruction was felt all over the planet. It appeared as a flash on the horizon thousands of kilometres away, causing troops on both sides to look up in fear and wonder at it. Communications were disrupted for a few minutes almost planet-wide, as massive amounts of electromagnetic radiation pulsed outwards from the centre of the blast, creating invisible energy storms all across the planet's ether.

Just about everyone on Nu Earth felt, saw or somehow detected some sign of Nordstadt's destruction and all of them knew exactly what it meant. Hammerfall's planners had long ago prepared their cover story: that the destruction of Nordstadt was the work of the Norts, who with their assault stopped dead by the city's heroic Souther defenders, had fallen back on this most final and brutal of scorched earth tactics. Now these carefully prepared propaganda lies would never be believed by their own troops, not since Gabe's warning had been heard all over Nu Earth. Now, with their plan revealed, Hammerfall's architects would not even have the benefit of Daniels's precious Nort kill tally to defend their actions with. An estimated less than three hundred thousand enemy troops had been caught and destroyed within the crucible. It was undeniably a grievous loss to the Nort forces on Nu Earth, but it still fell far short of the million plus casualties that had been confidently predicted. Souther losses were calculated at some ninety-four thousand. The last-minute, unofficial evac operation had brought almost nine thousand troops out of the crucible in the few confused and danger-fraught hours before Nordstadt's destruction, an act that was hastily declared to be a triumphant act of heroism by Milli-com's propaganda experts.

In private conference, however, Milli-com's masters pronounced quite a different verdict on Operation Hammerfall and its aftermath. Grand Marshal Cohen was allowed to resign in disgrace, citing unexpected health problems for his decision to leave the Souther military and retire to his extensive estates on Nu Sussex. From there he was able to dwell on the alleged achievements of an otherwise glittering military career.

His underlings were not allowed the same privilege. For them, there was only career-ending ignominy and a large number of demotions, courts martials and official courts of enquiry.

Most Souther military historians didn't trouble themselves to record the fate of these lesser players in the Nordstadt disaster. However, a careful checking of Milli-com records would have revealed the fact that, less than a year after the destruction of Nordstadt, a Captain Daniels, recently demoted and transferred out of Milli-com, was listed as killed in action in the latest outbreak of front line fighting in the Karthage campaign.

All this was still to come, however. For the present moment, there were other matters yet to be settled.

TWENTY-SIX

"You can't leave yet," shouted Artau, angrily. "For God's sake, man. You're wounded. Your injuries need time to heal."

"I'm Genetic Infantry, doc," Rogue told him, standing up and gathering his equipment. "They built us to be low med-maintenance and fast to heal, and there's plenty of others here who need you a lot more than I do."

Rogue was right. It was chaos in the landing zone. Every few minutes, another flight of shuttles came in to land, each of them disgorging another group of shell-shocked survivors from the crucible, many of them carrying some kind of wound, others hungry and exhausted and just needing a hot meal and a place to sleep and recover from the ordeal they'd just barely survived. Every med available in all three of General Ghazeleh's divisions had been brought in to help, but the number of casualties passing through the encampment was still overwhelming. The general's tank forces were drawn into a wide protective circle, old-fashioned wagon train style, forming a solid barrier of steel around the makeshift landing zone. Flights of Souther fighters made continual low-level passes overhead, protecting the encampment from aerial attack and flying escort for the next wave of incoming shuttles and their human cargos of more Nordstadt survivors.

Rogue shrugged off the surgeon-officer's objections and made his way to the med-dome's airlock, meeting Ghazeleh and a group of his most senior officers on the way. One of them pointed in sudden agitation at Rogue.

"There he is, general. He's a notorious deserter and renegade. I demand he be placed under arrest straight away."

Ghazeleh stared at the Rogue, seeming to look right through him and seeing nothing but empty space. "Are you sure, Colonel Garr? If there was any blue-skinned super-soldier in here, I'm sure I would be able to spot him."

Garr turned almost crimson with rage. "General Ghazeleh, you know as well as I do that Milli-com has issued specific orders that this deserter be arrested on sight. As a senior officer in the Souther army, it's your duty to carry out Milli-com's commands."

Ghazeleh turned in apparent puzzlement to one of his other staffers. "Captain Vickers, do you see any deserters here?"

"Not at all, sir," answered the officer, with a grin. "Perhaps the stress of battle is affecting the colonel's eyesight. A soldier with blue skin, who doesn't need a chem-suit? I must admit, it does sound all rather fantastical."

"Agreed, captain," said Ghazeleh, turning back to his executive officer. "Colonel Garr, you're relieved of your duties and confined to your quarters, pending a psychiatric report on your current state of mind."

A pair of large, burly sergeants stepped forward and dragged Garr out of the med-dome. Ghazeleh turned back to Rogue, looking in approval at him.

"Good work, trooper, and good to know you're still with us. If I had a few more like you under my command, we'd probably have won this bastard war years ago. I suggest you get out of here, though, before the Milli-fuzz get here, and the rest of us have to start suffering the same hallucinations as poor Colonel Garr."

"Understood, sir. Before I go, here's something you might find useful." Rogue handed Ghazeleh a data-disc. "It's a recording of something the Traitor General told me, about an S-Three officer called Marckand. I thought you'd know the right people to get it to."

"I'm sure I'll be able to come up with some reason about how it came into my care, without making up stories about blue-skinned figments of my imagination."

. . .

Rogue was outside, walking away towards the edge of the
encampment and the chem-mists beyond, when he heard
the shout from behind him.

"Rogue!"

He turned, seeing Rafe hurrying towards him. They stood
together, sharing a moment of awkward silence. Rafe was
the first to break it. "You could stay here, you know. General Ghazeleh's supposed to be a good man. He could
protect you from Milli-com."

Rogue shook his head. "Got a friendly warning that Milli-
com will be here any minute. The general's a good man,
and we need more like him. That's why I can't give Milli-
com the excuse they might be looking for to replace him.
Besides, I've still got a mission to finish."

"The traitor's dead, Rogue. He died back in Nordstadt."

Rogue wasn't so sure. He looked at the barely-diminished
radioactive glow on the northern horizon, which was now
all that remained of Nordstadt. "We got out, didn't we?
Maybe he did too. Been hunting him for too long to know
better than to take anything for granted when it comes to
that scumbag. Until I find out different, we stay rogue and
keep on looking for him."

Rafe offered him her hand. Rogue hesitated for a moment
and then took it. "Not many of us left, Rogue. Us GIs, we've
got to stick together, got to stay solid blue. You ever need
any help again, you know who to call."

"I'll bear it in mind, Air Force. Count on it."

He turned and walked away. She watched him go, following him with her eyes until the chem-mists had finally
swallowed up the last vestige of him.

TWENTY-SEVEN

Marckand was still in his office when they came for him. The hidden warning devices in the corridor outside had told him of their approach; a full squad of Milli-fuzz, armed with pistols and las-carbines, and wearing full body armour.

They hammered angrily on the door, their security over-rides unable to bypass the private encryption codes Marckand had installed into its electronic lock. The door was armoured and they would have to send for explosive charges or las-cutting equipment to force an entry through it. Marckand made good use of the intervening time, systematically wiping every file and all the incriminating evidence those files contained from his desk compu. When he had finished, he drew his sidearm and fired half a dozen las-rounds into the thing, reducing it to molten wreckage.

The room was filled with the smell of burning as the men outside started cutting through the door. Marckand knew he was almost out of time and there was still one plentiful source of evidence against him left in the room.

He sat back in his chair, put the muzzle of the pistol into his mouth and pulled the trigger, leaving nothing for his accusers to pick over.

TWENTY-EIGHT

The Kashans rode in silence, the shuttle they were travelling in riding out the last few fading shockwaves from the explosion far behind them, as Nordstadt disappeared in a column of nuclear fire.

Their injured and dying lay on the floor at their feet, a Kashan medic going from one to another, tending to each of them as best he could. One of the last of them to be loaded aboard, as the Kashans turned their guns on the panicked members of other, lesser Nordland regiments who had tried to climb aboard their evac craft, was a Kashan major. The man was in a bad way, his face gruesomely burned, his chem-suit slick with blood from his wounds but, like a true Kashan, he had never uttered one sound of pain.

The medic bent over him, scanning the details from the man's electronic dog-tags. "Have courage, Major Pasha," he whispered to the semi-conscious man. "You will recover from your wounds, and then you will have another chance of revenge against our enemies."

Beneath the mask of another man's blood that he had smeared across his face, the traitor smiled. *Major Pasha of the Kashan Legion.* It would do as a new identity, at least until he found a better one.

ABOUT THE AUTHOR

Gordon Rennie lives in a state of befuddled cynicism in Edinburgh, Scotland, where he writes comics, novels, computer game scripts and anything else anyone's willing to pay him money for. In between waiting patiently to become the main writer on the 2000 AD Judge Dredd script, he spends his time getting into Internet flame wars and pretending to be a lifelong supporter of Hibernian FC. He's recently started smoking again, and so hopes his wife isn't going to be reading this. His first contributiuon to Black Flame was *Judge Dredd: Dredd vs Death*.

DREDD VS DEATH

1-84416-061-0
£5.99/$6.99

WWW.BLACKFLAME.COM
TOUGH FICTION FOR A TOUGH PLANET

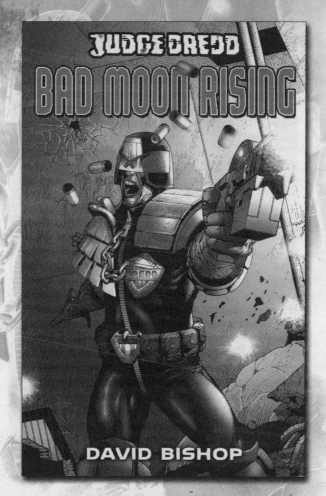

BAD MOON RISING

1-84416-107-2
£5.99/$6.99

WWW.BLACKFLAME.COM
TOUGH FICTION FOR A TOUGH PLANET

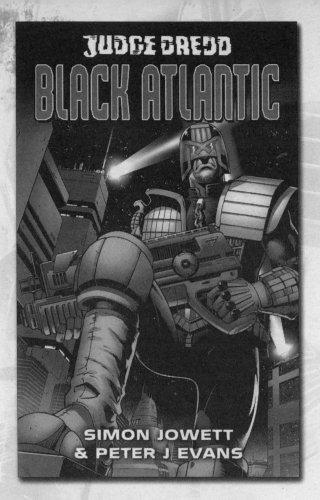

BLACK ATLANTIC

1-84416-108-0
£5.99/$6.99

WWW.BLACKFLAME.COM
TOUGH FICTION FOR A TOUGH PLANET

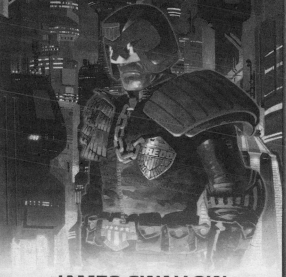

JUDGE DREDD

ECLIPSE

NO ONE ESCAPES JUSTICE, NOT EVEN ON THE MOON!

JAMES SWALLOW

ECLIPSE

1-84416-122-6
£5.99/$6.99

STRONTIUM DOG
BAD TIMING

1-84416-110-2
£5.99/$6.99

ABC WARRIORS
THE MEDUSA WAR

PAT MILLS AND ALAN MITCHELL

ABC WARRIORS
THE MEDUSA WAR

1-84416-109-9
£5.99/$6.99

THE UNQUIET GRAVE

Durham Red

Mutant, vampire, total babe - careful boys, she bites!

PETER J EVANS

DURHAM RED
THE UNQUIET GRAVE

1-84416-159-5
£5.99/$6.99